I BELONG WITH YOU

Book 2 in the Fircrest Series

SHANNON GUYMON

I Belong With You
Book 2 in the Fircrest Series
By Shannon Guymon

This book is dedicated to my children. This one's for you.

❀ Created with Vellum

Chapter One

THE PRAYER

Kit Kendall watched her sister Layla try on a bridal veil and smiled brightly even though her heart ached a little. She was still surprised that Layla was going to be the first of them to marry. Yes, she was the oldest, but she was also the one who had a deep aversion to men. Kit turned and glanced at Jane and couldn't help grinning though. They were here to help Layla pick out a dress, and there Jane was, trying one on herself. Jane was the dreamer and the romantic. She'd been planning her wedding since she was three.

Kit studied her little sister and hoped that Jane got her dream someday. Anyone looking at her would think *Jane* was the one getting married with her long, thick, rich brown hair flowing down her back and her face glowing. Of course Jane would pick a dress that was over the top feminine and flamboyant. The word meringue kept popping into her mind. The dress had layers and layers of lace and satin so poufy people would have to lean over to hug her. It was absolutely perfect for Jane. The only problem was, Jane wasn't the bride. Jane wasn't even dating anyone.

Kit shook her head and smiled as she walked over to a rack of dresses and lifted the one that had caught her eye as soon as they'd walked in the door an hour ago. It was form fitting until about mid-thigh and then flared out in an excess of material. She glanced at her sisters nervously, not wanting to be seen dreaming. But how could she not when the dress was not just calling to her – it was shouting. She casually walked over to a set of three mirrors and glanced quickly at Layla and Jane. Jane was still humming to herself and seeing her future wedding to her handsome prince in her mind. Layla was discussing styles and fabrics with the clerk. That left her with a few moments to herself. She quickly held the dress up to her front and stared into the mirror.

Kit gazed at her reflection and smiled sadly. Her long wavy, glamorous, red hair was dramatic against the stark white of the dress. Her hazel eyes looked serious but there was a touch of hope there too. Her wide, perfectly sculpted mouth curved up in a mocking smile. She tried to blink away the daydream, but it refused to leave. She was proud of being a realist. She might look romantic and played the part well, but her sisters knew the truth. She was the least romantic of the three sisters. So why was this dress, this symbol of dreams coming true and finding that one person in the world to love, why was it pulling at her? Why was she getting sucked in by a white dress and a lot of lace?

Kit moved to put the dress back, but paused as she saw Layla doing the exact thing she was doing. Standing in front of a mirror and smiling. The big difference was, Layla had found her dream. It hadn't been easy. Not with Michael's ex-wife Ashley throwing roadblock after roadblock at them. But Layla and Michael had done it. They'd found each other and decided not to let go. Layla. Her hard as nails, take on the world and every bad guy in it, ex-social worker sister, had fallen hard for a single dad and his sweet little girl, Stella.

Ironically, even though Layla distrusted and disliked men, it had never stopped her from dreaming for everyone else. Kit on the other hand, had a hard time seeing castles or handsome princes anywhere. She smiled and flirted with every man she met, but knew in her heart they were just another heartbreak waiting to happen. Every man that had come into her life during her 24 years on earth had been a huge disappointment. It was a pattern that had started early and had repeated itself frequently. Fun and excitement, followed by betrayal and disappointment.

Her father, Landon Kendall, had walked out on them when she'd been a young girl. He'd chosen a life of addiction over a life of love and family. Her first boyfriend, Austin, had sworn he'd loved her one day and then asked her best friend to prom the next week. She'd cried herself sick over him and had sworn to never trust a man again. And she'd been good to her word. Kit kept her relationships with men superficial, shallow and short.

Her latest disaster, Jake, had been just another slap in the face. Although she hadn't been stupid enough to open her heart to him, she had expected him to keep his word about the showing he'd promised her. He had told her over and over again, what an amazing artist she was, how she moved him with her passion and her talent. How, with his guidance, she'd be a star in the art world. And she'd believed him. She'd even considered marrying him. She felt a wash of shame when she remembered that. It had been more of a career decision than a love decision and she thanked God every day that things had fallen apart before she'd gotten in over her head. He'd changed his mind and thrown her over for a trashy, little sculptor who thought feathers and crushed soda bottles were the essence of life. The sad thing was, she hadn't even been surprised.

Her memories of past failures and past relationships faded though as she continued to stare at her image in the mirror. The woman in the mirror looked self-assured. She looked confident, beautiful and at peace. *That couldn't be her, could it?* During the past few months, she and her sisters had come together to take over their grandmother's bakery. They'd had so many chances to sell, but they'd agreed they all wanted to stick together and make it work. And now, Layla was an accomplished dessert maker, Jane's unique and flavorful cupcakes were becoming everyone's favorite, guilty pleasure, and she was famous for her sourdough bread. She'd always dreamed of becoming famous for her paintings, so being famous because of bread was a little surreal.

Kit frowned and turned side to side, trying to picture what the exquisite dress would look like on. She bit her lip and closed her eyes and allowed herself a little wish. She'd given them up so long ago, she'd almost forgotten how, but holding the dress in her arms and seeing her saddest sister, happy again, was making her a little irrational. She was too old for silly wishes. She'd been through too much and her heart was too cold, but today, right now, this very minute, she was going to do it. She was going to wish for something she'd sworn off and relegated to Disney movies and the naive. She was going to wish for a happy ending.

She was going to wish for love.

How incredible and amazing would it be if *she* were the bride standing here picking out the perfect dress? What would it feel like to be cherished and loved by a man who was willing to swear in front of friends and family and God to forsake all others, and love her *and only her? And then actually do it?*

She glanced at Layla and felt her heart warm, knowing that her sister had found that. Michael Bender was so in love with Layla that when she walked in the room, it was impossible for him to notice anyone else. She'd never seen a man so in love before. *Lust?* Yes. She'd seen plenty of that. But love? Real, true love that deepened and was kind and giving? Maybe never. This might actually be the first time she'd witnessed it.

Oh, how she wanted that too.

She'd never actually been all the way in love before. She'd been charmed, she'd been attracted, she'd even been a little obsessed that one time in college. But love? That was different. That was in a category all by itself. And she'd never even come close. But then, neither had Layla and look at her now.

Layla laughed at something the clerk said and then disappeared into the changing room with a new dress to try on. Layla Kendall was a woman surrounded, submerged and drowning in love. And if a miracle like that could happen to Layla, then couldn't it happen for her too?

Kit looked back at her reflection and noticed her face was softer now, her eyes were wide and the hope that she liked to shove to the back and hide in a corner was moving its way to the front, making her eyes bright and shining and her lips turn up in a real smile. Maybe life would surprise her? *Please God*, let there be a man out there somewhere, who would love her the way Michael loved Layla. Kit closed her eyes and sighed. She'd gone from a wish to a prayer. Maybe that was the first step in turning a wish into reality?

"*Wow*. That would look amazing on you."

Kit jerked out of her daydream and looked over her shoulder at Jane who was swishing toward her in her over the top Cinderella wedding dress.

"It's like someone designed it with you specifically in mind," Jane said, reaching out to touch the fabric with a finger.

Kit shrugged and tried to laugh. "I was just thinking how cute it would look in an icy blue or pale pink for a bridesmaids dress," she said lightly, as she blushed bright red at being caught.

Jane stared at her doubtfully. "Yeah, *right*. Go try it on."

Kit bit her lip and shook her head. "No way. This is Layla's day. It's one thing to daydream and another to be trying on dresses," she said dryly, as Jane's lips turned down in a pout.

Jane raised an eyebrow and put her hands on her hips. "We're here to have fun. Layla doesn't mind if I play dress-up. Come on, Kit. Don't be an idiot. Go try it on," she urged, pushing her firmly toward a changing room.

Kit frowned and felt like kicking her little sister, but there was so much lace in her way, she'd never feel a thing. "Jane, you little brat. *Stop it!*"

Jane grinned and put both hands on her sister's back, propelling her toward an open door. Kit was pushed inside and winced as the door was slammed into place.

"I'm not letting you out, until you try it on," Jane called, through the door.

Kit glared at the door and sighed. Jane, the youngest of the Kendall sisters was definitely the baby of the family. She loved getting her way. Kit turned and glanced at the small room she was in and noticed a bowl of wedding mints, sitting on a beautiful, ornate table. The lighting was soft and the romantic music playing in the background was all meant for one purpose. Setting the stage for a fairy tale.

Fine, she could play dress up. But not because she really wanted to try the dress on. It was really only to get Jane off her back. She hung the dress on the peg and slipped her clothes off quickly. Within five minutes she was zipping up the dress and stepping toward the mirror. Her head tilted as her mouth fell open slightly in surprise. Her throat tightened and she swallowed back a sigh of pure feminine yearning.

This was her dress.

Kit let a shaky breath out and turned and opened the door. She walked out and came face to face with Layla. Layla looked at Kit in surprise at first, but then her face split into a wide happy grin.

"Kit, you are buying that dress. *Today*," she said, with a shake of her head.

Jane nodded her head and sighed happily. "Kitty, it was made for you."

Kit winced at the use of her childhood nickname and smiled sheepishly at her sisters. "Don't be ridiculous, you guys. I was just playing around. *Of course*, I'm not going to buy a wedding dress. That would be crazy," she said softly, catching a look at herself in the mirror.

The clerk walked up and smiled calculatingly. "Many women buy their wedding dresses years before they even get engaged. If you find the perfect dress now and let it go, it might not be there later when you need it."

Jane's eyes went big and she stared down at her own dress.

She caressed the lace and bit her lip. "I *have* to have this dress," she whispered to herself.

Kit blushed and ran her hands through her hair. "I couldn't possibly buy a wedding dress! I mean, I love it. It's the most gorgeous dress I've ever seen in my life. And if I ever did fall in love and decide to get married, this is the only dress I'd want to get married in, but it's too silly. Right, Layla?" she said, turning to her sister desperately, wanting to hear cold, hard logic.

"Kitten, if you don't buy that dress today, I'm going to buy it for you. You can't leave this shop without that dress," Layla said, her eyes lighting up as she walked over to Kit. "Look in the mirror, Kit. You're so beautiful. You look like a woman ready to fall in love," she said softly.

Kit blushed brighter and looked down at her hands. "What if I don't, Layla? What if it never happens for me? I mean, I still can't believe it happened to you."

Layla hugged her tightly and pushed a strand of red hair out of her eyes. "Sweetie, I promise love will find you. I don't know how and I don't know when and I don't even know who. But Kit, you were born to fall in love and fall hard."

Kit stared hard at the mirror as Jane came to stand on her other side. "It's true, Kit. You just need the right man. A *good* man. You've never had one of those before."

Kit laughed sadly and rubbed the goose bumps on her arms. "Maybe you're right. Maybe I should buy this dress," she said softly. "It'll be my symbol of hope. Hope that there's someone out there for me."

Layla and Jane squealed and jumped up and down while Kit grinned and joined them. A few minutes later after the sisters had settled down Kit frowned and stared at Layla.

"Wait a second, enough about me and Jane. We're here for you, Layla. Do you um. . . *like* that dress?" she asked, smiling with a wince at Layla's dress. It was an off white long, slim, column dress. Very sophisticated, very demure and *very boring*.

Layla glanced down at her dress. "Not really. I can't find

anything I like. They're all so, *not* me," she said lamely, looking sad all of a sudden. "We walk in and you two find your perfect dresses and I can't find even one dress I could see myself getting married in," she said forlornly.

Jane and Kit forgot about themselves and went to work doing what they should have been doing before. Helping Layla find the perfect dress. Because unlike them, she *was* getting married and soon. The wedding date was only a month away and this was the third bridal boutique they'd been to.

An hour later, Layla looked pleased because she'd found two of the cutest bridesmaid dresses for Kit and Jane. They were summery full pale, pink skirts with large bright pink sashes. The tops were buttery cream satin. They only needed slight alterations to fit.

After Kit and Jane purchased their dresses they walked out to Layla's car frowning guiltily. Layla had tried on at least twenty dresses and had turned her nose up at each one. Kit was starting to wonder if it wasn't the dresses and maybe it was Layla. Maybe Layla wasn't ready to get married and this was her subconscious way of letting the world know it?

"You know, Layla, you don't have to get married right now. No one would blame you if you decided to put the wedding off for a few months. I mean, this is a huge decision. I'd be nervous too," she said softly, touching Layla's arm as she pulled out of the parking lot and into traffic.

Layla glanced at her in surprise and laughed. "Oh, I'm not nervous about marrying Michael. I'd marry him in a pair of jeans and a t-shirt. No, I just want it to be perfect for him. He's been through so much heartache because of Ashley. Just in the last month, he's had to to sell his house and give her half the value of his business. It's been rough. I want him to look at me on our wedding day and see a woman who will love him forever. I want him to see his dreams come true," she said, her voice going soft the way it did when she talked about Michael.

Kit smiled at Layla and sighed, "*Wow*."

Layla blinked a couple times and looked at her curiously. "What do you mean, *wow?*" she asked, with a smile.

Jane laughed and leaned forward. "It just means, *wow,* Layla. Like, you're so in love it'd be pathetic if it wasn't the sweetest thing I'd ever seen."

Layla frowned at Jane in the mirror. "*Pathetic?* You think I'm pathetic?" she asked her eyes narrowing dangerously.

Kit rolled her eyes at Jane who was sitting back slowly, biting her lip. "No, not pathetic, Layla. What Jane *meant* to say was, that it's *wow,* because you and Michael have fallen so completely and totally in love with each other, that it makes *everything else* in this dim and disappointing world seem sad and pathetic. You're living life in Technicolor and we're all staring at this gorgeous rainbow of emotion and we're a little jealous," Kit said, glancing away from her sister and out the window at the gray clouds moving across the moody sky. "I made a wish today. *No.* I prayed today. I prayed that I'd be able to fall in love like you, Layla," Kit admitted, with a blush.

Layla smiled sweetly at her sister and reached over and put her hand over hers. "Then you're halfway there. And you've put your faith behind the prayer, because you bought the dress. I bet you you're married within the year Kit."

Jane laughed. "Layla, you cannot be serious. A year? She's not even dating anyone, and every guy who has asked her out in the last few months, she's turned down flat."

Layla shrugged, "One year."

Kit sighed and turned back to Jane to say something rude, but stopped when she caught sight of the dress bag lying over the back seat. *Her* wedding dress. One year. *Hmmm.* Maybe . . .

Chapter Two

BLIND DATES

As Jane and Kit carefully pulled their wedding dresses out of the car, Layla looked back at her younger sisters with a happy grin on her face. "Don't forget my engagement party tonight. Michael said you were supposed to bring dates by the way," she said breezily and jogged up the front stairs of their bakery as if she didn't have a care in the world.

Kit and Jane looked at each other with identical frowns. "Dates?" Kit asked, automatically feeling depressed.

Jane grimaced and slammed the car door with her hip. "She's teasing. She's just being mean because we have dresses and she doesn't."

Kit's face lightened for a moment and then she felt her phone vibrate in her pocket. She took it out as she walked slowly and carefully toward the stairs with her precious dress.

"Hi, Michael," she said, after looking at the screen.

Jane's eyes went wide and tense. "No!" she whispered desperately, shaking her head back and forth.

"Hey, Kit. My mom and dad wanted me to make sure I reminded you to bring dates so that the seating works. I told my mom it was kind of last minute to throw that at you, but she's kind of insisting. She's having it catered and wants everything perfect. You know how moms can be," he said, with an embarrassed laugh.

Kit groaned softly and closed her eyes and Jane's face fell in defeat. "Michael, I know you mentioned bringing a date last week, but I thought it was just a suggestion. I um, *we* don't have dates," she muttered.

Michael cleared his throat for a moment before speaking. "*Whoa.* That's so crazy. You and Jane are two of the most gorgeous girls in this whole town. You probably have lists of men waiting to ask you out. Can you just call up a couple guys and invite them? It is going to be amazing. My mom and dad's house is down by the beach. We're going to have dancing and a band. Low key, but fun. Come on, Kit. *Please*," Michael said.

Kit shook her head and shifted the now very heavy dress in her arms as she stared at Jane. Jane looked ill. Jane was shaking her head NO. *Great.*

Kit sighed. "Michael, you're the sweetest future, brother in law I've ever had, but I don't have a list of guys waiting to ask me out. I've kind of all told them no and to get lost. Listen, I've met your mom. She's darling. Just tell her that Jane will be my date."

Utter silence on the other end. . . . Kit felt her stomach turn over nervously. Michael could be stubborn sometimes. Layla was proof of that.

"Kit, you've given me no choice here. I'm setting you up. I don't want to hear any arguments about it either. You and Jane be ready to go at six, or you're in trouble. Got it?" he said, in a voice that she knew he used on his daughter Stella.

Kit frowned and scuffed her toe in the dirt. "I've never been set up on a date in my life," she said grumpily, as Jane's mouth fell open in shock.

Michael laughed. "It's your own fault and you know it. Tell Jane I have the perfect date in mind for her. See you later," he said and disconnected.

Kit shoved her phone in her pocket and stared moodily at her sister. "I hate weddings."

Jane raised an eyebrow and looked at the large and incredibly heavy dress bag over her arm. "Yeah, I know. So did I hear right? Is Michael seriously going to set us up on blind dates for the engagement party?"

Kit sighed and moved toward the front porch again. "You heard right. And Michael wants me to tell you that he has the perfect date for you."

She glanced at Jane and was surprised to see a look of interest. "You're okay with going on a blind date?"

Jane shrugged her shoulders and then opened the front door, pushing through and walking toward a table. She carefully laid her dress down and collapsed in a chair before looking at her. "Yeah, I guess I am. One of my best friends from college met her husband on a blind date. And Michael is awesome. Think of his friends. If they're anything like him, then count me in," she said, with a grin.

Kit laughed and put her dress down too, sitting down next to Jane. "Michael is thirty and you're only twenty-two. The men Michael knows might be a little old for you."

Jane looked at her like she was insane. "You have got to be joking. I'm twenty-two, not fifteen, Kit."

Kit winced. Jane was her younger sister and yeah, she still kind of thought of her and *maybe* treated her, like she was still fifteen sometimes.

"Fine, sorry. Hot older guys. Got it."

Jane relaxed back in her chair and studied her. "You look kind of nervous. What's the deal? Men are easy for you. They're powerless against your charm and beauty."

Kit frowned and kicked her feet up on an empty chair as she closed her eyes. "I hate to break it to you, *oh wise,* twenty-two year old, but I'm a big fake. I can flirt and smile and talk to guys, true. But only because it doesn't matter. I haven't let it matter. But now that I'm getting to a point in my life where it's starting to matter, all the fake stuff is no good. Making an actual emotional connection with a man is not something I'm really comfortable with. And it's definitely not something I'm good at," she said simply, raising her eyes to see Jane looking at her in surprise.

Jane blinked a few times and then nodded slowly. "*Okaaaay . . .*" she said slowly, with a look of alarm in her eyes. "But it's just a blind date, Kit. Like I said, no big deal. And I'll be right there with you along with everyone else. They're just forcing the date issue because of seating. After dinner, you can mingle and ditch the guy if he's a loser."

Kit nodded and relaxed. "You're right. It's a party. It's not like some weird, horrible. awkward dinner where I'm stuck staring at a stranger for an hour while we force ourselves to have a lame conversation."

Jane smiled and relaxed. "Exactly. Now we have one hour to get ready. Hop up, princess. Time to shine," she said, and disappeared out of the room, obviously excited about her blind date.

Kit followed much slower, feeling the weight of her wedding dress get heavier with every step. *What in the world had she'd been thinking?* Kit Kendall buying a wedding dress of all things because she was going to actually find a man worth wearing it for. And her two sisters standing there, egging her on. She could have spent that money on a weekend at a spa up in Seattle, or better yet, Hawaii. *But, no.* She'd spent it on a dress she could only wear once. At her wedding.

Kit felt a headache slip up the back of her head as she threw her wedding dress on her bed, looking at the large bag with disgust. *Ugh.* She turned and walked into her closet. She looked everything over and grabbed a little black bandage dress. She ignored all the fun and summery outfits that would have been perfect for an engagement party and slipped on the dress she had bought up in Seattle a few months back. She'd been planning on wearing it to her first art show.

"Time to break you in," she muttered, and grabbed her three inch stilettos. She stared at herself in the mirror and grimaced. She just couldn't bring herself to make her usual effort. She left her long red hair down in casual waves. She brushed her teeth, freshened her lipstick and eyeliner and called it good. She ignored her bottles of perfume and took one last look. She looked okay, but not like she was trying too hard. Perfect.

Now, time for her blind date. She was horrified to find that she was actually feeling a little sick to her stomach. She ran a hand over her stomach and made a detour to the kitchen to grab some Tylenol. If her sisters even realized how nervous she was they'd laugh themselves sick.

Layla and Jane were already in the kitchen. Jane was sitting at her laptop, wearing a darling lavender skirt and top with gorgeous platforms. Her hair was pulled up in a twist and she looked beautiful. Layla was stunning though. As the guest of honor and the bride to be, she had gone all out. She was wearing a glamorous red maxi dress with heels to match. And it looked like Michael had been generous lately because she was wearing a new necklace too.

Kit rushed over and lifted the necklace in her hands as Layla blushed and bit her lip. "What has Michael been up to, Layla?" Kit asked teasingly.

Layla grinned and looked down at the chandelier necklace with three rather large round diamonds. "Michael has been spoiling me," she admitted, with a soft laugh.

Kit hugged Layla hard. "And you deserve it. You've never been spoiled once in your life. Enjoy it," she said, knowing sadly, it was true. With the exception of Jane, they hadn't been spoiled at all. And Jane had only been spoiled in the sense that she'd had two older sisters to give her all the attention she wanted.

"So, what are we doing here? What is this? *Facebook?*" Kit asked, leaning over Jane's shoulder to see what they were looking at.

Jane shrugged and looked embarrassed. "It's Michael's Facebook page. He won't tell Layla who he set us up with so we're trying to figure it out. But Kit, seriously, look. All of his friends are gorgeous," she said excitedly.

Kit scanned through the faces and smiled appreciatively even as her stomach twisted harder. She just wasn't prepared for meeting a gorgeous guy tonight. What she really wanted was a large chocolate cupcake and a bubble bath.

Layla smiled, but then narrowed her eyes at her. "Kit, what's wrong? You're not mad that Michael is setting you up are you?" she asked worriedly.

Kit smoothed out her features and shook her head. "Nah, I'm looking forward to it. When's the last time Jane and I got to hang out with gorgeous men? Besides there's going to be dancing. You know I'd be a professional club dancer if I could get paid for it," she said, trying to lighten the mood.

Layla smiled and relaxed, picking her clutch up off the counter. "I still remember the last time you took me dancing in Seattle. I had to stay home from work the next day because I was so exhausted. But just to warn you, I don't think Michael's parents are hiring a band that plays the kind of music you're used to dancing to."

Kit and Jane exchanged sour looks and followed their sister to the front of the bakery and out onto the front porch. They sat on the large wooden porch chairs and waited for their ride as they looked out over their new town.

"Any regrets?" Layla asked, looking at her two younger sisters with love in her eyes. "Jane, you could be some hot shot accountant right now and Kit you could still be painting. Now we're bakers. Do you ever think you made the wrong decision?"

Jane shook her head immediately with a shudder. "*Never.* Being here in Fircrest with you two and baking and running our own business, is the best thing that's ever happened to me," she said fervently.

Kit nodded. "I wouldn't change a thing. It's weird though. I thought that was all I was, you know, a painter. But it turns out there's more to me. I'm the best darn sourdough bread maker in Washington, and I have a newspaper article to prove it," she said, with a proud toss of her head.

Layla laughed and leaned her head back on her chair. "That you do, Kit. And now I can't rest until I get my own newspaper article written about my macaroons."

Kit grinned. "You've got more important things on your mind, right now. Like marrying Michael," she said, as Michael drove up to their house.

Kit ignored Michael and watched Layla's face as she watched the man she loved, walk toward her. Her face came alive. Her eyes sparkled, her cheeks flushed and her smile was brilliant. *She glowed.* She'd always thought that term was so annoying. She'd heard it describe pregnant women and women in love, but actually watching her older sister's face soften and brighten, made everything worth it. Even if the bakery had turned out to be a total disaster, watching her sister fall in love was turning out to be one of the highlights of her life.

Kit turned and watched Michael walk up the stairs and of course, *as always*, his eyes were glued to Layla and there was the reason for the glow. Who wouldn't glow when a man's eyes were filled with adoration? He walked slowly toward Layla as she stood to greet him and he shook his head in wonder.

"You're too beautiful, Layla. What did I ever do to deserve a woman like you?" he whispered, reaching out a hand for her.

Layla took his hand and then put her arms around his neck as she kissed him. "I was just thinking the same thing. What did I ever do to deserve you?" she said, staring up into his intense eyes, as if they were the only two people in the world.

Jane's romantic sigh must have been too loud because Michael blinked in surprise and turned to glance at Jane and her.

"Oh, hi, ladies. You both look stunning tonight," he said, his cheeks turning red.

Kit laughed and walked over and kissed him on the cheek. "You are so cute, Michael."

Layla grinned. "In just a month from now we'll be married. Can you believe it?"

Michael's eyes narrowed. "I can believe it. I say we ditch the wedding and elope. We can be in Paris tomorrow," he said, looking hopeful.

Kit, Jane and Layla erupted in shocked horror and Michael laughed and held up his hands. "Sorry! Forgive me, please. What was I thinking?" he asked, as he escorted Layla down the steps to his car.

Jane and Kit looked at each other, feeling unsure and awkward. "Wait, Michael. Are we coming with you?" Kit called after them.

Michael shook his head. "Nah, your dates will be picking you up any minute. See you at the party," he yelled, and waved cheerfully before disappearing into his car and then seconds later they were driving down the street.

Kit sighed and flopped down on the chair again. "I feel like a teenager sitting on the porch, waiting for my date. Let's go back inside, Jane," she said, standing up.

Jane shook her head and pointed. Kit turned around and saw a silver Jaguar pull up in front of their bakery and closed her mouth. "Oh crap. He must be rich," she muttered.

Jane stood up next to Kit as a tall, large man eased out of the car and walked toward them with a slight smile on his face. He had large shoulders that weren't disguised very well by a suit and a face that could have made millions of dollars in the movies.

"*Wow*," Jane whispered just as the man reached the bottom step. "It's Bradley Cooper's younger brother."

"Hi, there. My name is Garrett, and I'm here to pick up Jane," he said, looking back and forth between the two women.

Jane held up a shaky hand and cleared her throat. "That, *um*, would be me," she said, in a high squeaky voice.

Garrett grinned at her, his warm, brown eyes gleaming in amusement. "Well, today is my lucky day. Would you do me the honor of being my date for the night?" he asked politely, holding his hand out to her.

Jane's eyes were huge as she turned to look at Kit. Kit grinned and nodded at her. "Have fun, Jane. I'll see you there," she said softly, watching her little sister walk down the stairs and take Garrett's hand.

Kit waved and watched them drive away. Wow was right. If Garrett had been her date, she would have been ecstatic. She turned and sat back down in her chair and crossed her legs as she sighed. Well, if her date never showed up, she'd be off the hook, since Michael had taken off without her. Of course she could just drive herself to the party. She could use this against friends and family the rest of her life. *Sorry, I don't do blind dates. I was stood up for my sister's engagement party and it traumatized me for life.*

Kit grinned to herself and crossed her ankles as she leaned back in her chair with a grin on her face. She'd even be able to miss half the party. And when she finally showed up, on her own, maybe a tear streak down one cheek, Michael would feel so bad, he'd probably want to buy her a necklace, very similar to the one he'd bought Layla. *Hmmm,* something to ponder.

Kit yawned and stretched a little before taking her phone out and glancing at the time. It was 6:15 now. A man who showed up fifteen minutes late for a blind date? *Had to be a loser.* Kit smiled happily, feeling better and better about the evening. If she'd been the one on a date with Garrett, she'd be twisted up in nervous knots. Losers? Familiar territory.

Kit looked at her phone one more time. In thirty seconds she was going to go back inside. She could watch TV for a half an hour and then head over to the party on her own. She was actually looking forward to torturing Michael for having the gall to force a date on her. As she slipped the phone back into her purse she heard a noise that had her stiffening in her chair. The gleeful smile she'd been wearing slipped a few notches as she recognized the distinctive sound of a motorcycle. She closed her eyes and groaned.

Please, no, Michael.

She opened her eyes and stared as a motorcycle drove up right in front of the bakery. The rider slipped off his helmet and stared up at her, not getting off the bike.

"You Kit?" he yelled at her.

Kit raised an eyebrow and stood up slowly. He had to be kidding her. He was yelling at her. *Really.*

"Yes, I'm Kit," she called out as she stood on the top porch steps staring unhappily at the man waiting impatiently for her. He looked like every man she'd ever dated. Kind of wild, kind of gorgeous and kind of thoughtless. He had long, sun tipped hair that started out dark blond at the roots and ended up white at the ends. He had dark sunglasses on and a slight sneer on his mouth. For the formal occasion he was wearing a button up shirt that was unbuttoned to below his chest and to set off his dark jeans, he was wearing cowboy boots. Of course.

"Hurry, babe, we're late. I had to finish my pool game. Michael's going to kill me if we miss dinner," he said, glancing at his watch.

Kit sighed and looked down at her bandage dress. It was form fitting and wouldn't stretch enough to accommodate a motorcycle. There. Was. No. Way.

"Look, I don't even know your name, but I'll just drive myself over, okay? I'll see you there," she said, and then turned around to head back inside. *Seriously?* What man picked up a date to a formal engagement party on a motorcycle?

"The name is Hunter and don't worry about your dress. I won't look, I promise," he said, with an obvious leer.

Kit turned back with a sneer. "Take off, Hunter. Not happening," she said, and pushed through the door, turning and locking it with a distinctive click.

She walked through to the kitchen, grabbed her keys and headed out the back. Her car was parked on the side. She could feel steam flowing out of her ears. Michael was no longer her favorite future brother in law. He picked the most gorgeous man on earth with class *and* a Jaguar to pick up Jane. And his choice for her? A pool playing loser. So maybe she had dated guys like that before. Well, she'd turned over a new leaf. Michael really should have realized that.

She hopped in her car and pulled out of the driveway, passing Hunter who was still sitting on his bike looking irritated. She waved sunnily to him and then zoomed off down the road. She took the invitation out of her purse and stared at the address. Easy. Fox Island. No way would she be on time now though. Not with traffic. But at least she had a good excuse and he was right behind her, following her every step of the way.

Kit ignored her escort and turned the radio up as she fantasized of all the different things she could and would be saying to Michael and Layla. *Stupid seating arrangements*, she muttered to herself as she pulled into the long driveway of Michael's parents a half hour later. It was gorgeous, she'd give them that. A beautiful, shake style house, with a steep roof. Living on an Island in the Puget Sound. *Life was so tough for some people*, she thought cynically.

She hopped out of her car and walked as quickly as she could in her three inch heels, making it through the door before Hunter could catch up. She squeezed past groups of people and immediately saw Jane talking to Garrett in a cozy corner. Her face was animated and she was using her hands to talk. Garrett looked attentive and interested. Kit relaxed a little and smiled. *Good.* She wanted Jane to be happy and have a good time. She'd take the loser. *Or not.*

She caught sight of Michael and Layla talking to a distinguished looking older couple and made a beeline for them. Just as she squared her shoulders and took the first step, a long, hard arm wrapped around her waist and pulled her back.

"Now, where do you think you're going?" asked a smooth, deep voice close to her ear.

Should she use her elbow or her heel? Just as she'd made up her mind to slam her foot down on the man's instep, he let her go.

Kit smiled dangerously up at the man, ignoring his tanned, blond, surfer looks. "Why, I was just going to thank my hosts for setting me up with you, of course," she said coldly.

Hunter grinned at her and shoved his hands in his pockets.

"That's what I thought. You wouldn't happen to be disappointed with me now, would you?" he asked, his eyes twinkling down at her.

Kit raised an eyebrow and sighed. "I'm sure you're a very nice man, Hunter, and you probably think it's really cool to pick up a woman for a date on a motorcycle, even though you *had* to know I was wearing a dress. It's just dinner, right?"

Hunter looked a little embarrassed and shrugged. "Most women love it when I pick them up on my motorcycle."

Kit stared at him and nodded slowly. *Riiight.* She caught sight of a man just behind Hunter and realized they were being watched. She blinked in surprise and saw it was Rob Downing. *Ergh.* She'd actually had high hopes for Rob, but he'd ignored every one of her signals that she was interested. So then why was he glaring at Hunter's back, as if he wanted to take a sledge hammer to it?

Kit looked down at her feet and bit her lip. *Hmmm.* Maybe Hunter would come in handy. Motorcycle and all.

"You probably have a few tattoos too, huh?" she asked, with a smile for Rob's sake.

Hunter grinned and opened his shirt up wider to show a large expanse of tanned and toned pectoral muscle. "None yet, although I was thinking of getting one of Spider Man or Iron Man, now that you mention it."

"Charming," she murmured as he let his shirt fall back into place. "So, how do you know Michael?" she asked, actually curious now. Hunter seemed the exact opposite of Michael in every way.

Hunter smiled and glanced over at Michael. "We were college roommates for a while. He left school to take care of his daughter and I went on to become a programmer."

Kit's eyes widened. "A *computer* programmer?" she asked doubtfully, looking him up and down. He looked more like a bouncer or male stripper.

Hunter laughed and shoved his hands in his pockets. "Yeah.

I've sold a few games. Have you heard of *Call of Duty*? I was part of the team that did the graphics," he said, trying to look modest but failing completely.

Kit grinned. "I'm impressed. Graphics, wow. I'm an artist too, but I'm a painter. Well, I *used* to be. Now, I'm a baker, so I paint in my spare time when I can," she said, noticing that Rob was completely ignoring his date so that he could listen in to their conversation.

Hunter nodded and smiled shyly. "Well, yeah, *I know*. That's why when Michael called and told me about you, I was kind of excited to meet you. It's nice to talk to someone who understands the creative process."

Kit smiled at Hunter and relaxed. Hunter was just a nerd underneath it all, trying to be a cool, bad boy. He had the look down perfectly, that's for sure. *Okay, she could do this.* And maybe she wouldn't have to kill Michael, a month before his wedding.

"I agree, Hunter, I haven't talked to a fellow artist since I moved down from Seattle. This will be great," she said, as Rob bumped into Hunter's back.

Hunter turned around and saw who it was and grinned. "Rob! Dude, it's so good to see you. I haven't seen you in over a year," he said, throwing his arms around Rob and squeezing him hard.

Rob grinned and thumped on Hunter's back, hard. "Hunter, man, it's been too long. I didn't even recognize you. The last time I saw you, you were skinny and pale. Now look at you. What have you been doing? Training for the Olympics?"

Hunter blushed furiously and glanced at Kit in embarrassment. "Nah, but I did hire a personal trainer, chef *and* image consultant."

Rob grinned and shook his head. "Well, you look fantastic. We should have a game night one of these days before Michael gets married. Maybe for his bachelor party?"

Hunter looked excited and nodded his head quickly. "Oh, man, I would love that. I just designed this new game I'm really excited about. We could give it a run through. I've gotta tell

Michael," he said, and without another word for her or Rob, hurried toward the man of honor.

Kit smiled ruefully after her date and looked back at Rob who was now staring at her with a faint frown.

"You and Hunter, huh? I guess it makes sense. *Kind of*," he said doubtfully, with his eyes narrowed and a frown on his face.

Kit shrugged and smiled at Jane as she walked by. "Oh, totally. He's got the wild look I go for, but underneath it, he's just a sweet guy. He's perfect really," she said breezily, as she waved to Michael who was now talking to Hunter, but looking at her nervously. Yep, they were still going to have a talk. She nodded her head and pointed a fake gun at him, pretending to shoot him.

"A woman like you could never be satisfied with Hunter though, *could you?*" Rob asked, pulling her attention back to him.

Kit's smile disappeared as she turned to stare at Rob. She raised an eyebrow and said nothing as Rob turned red and looked at his shoes.

"That came out wrong. I mean, a woman like you, who *um*, is beautiful and sophisticated and talented. Hunter looks like a wild guy now, but he's happiest with a bag of chips and an x-box."

Kit nodded and looked away, feeling tired all of a sudden. "Why do you care anyways, Rob? Why should my choice in dates bother you? See, now I'm looking at your date, waiting patiently over in the corner for you to stop talking to me. Let's turn the tables on you. *Rob*, is a cute, little, shy girl like that, really the woman for you? Do you really want a woman content with waiting in the shadows for you?"

Rob winced and glanced over his shoulder at his date before looking at her. "Marryn is an amazing woman. She's a paralegal and volunteers at the animal shelter on the weekends."

Kit smiled at the shy, cute woman, staring longingly at Rob's back. She was wearing a conservative, blue skirt and a short sleeved, white button up shirt. Her glasses gave her that sexy librarian look that guys went for, and her short brown hair completed the package. Rob's ideal woman. *Safe.*

"I'm not surprised. Listen, let's make a deal. You don't worry about my love life, and I won't worry about yours," she said, with a cold, hard smile before turning to walk away.

Rob's hand shot out and grabbed her arm though, stopping her. "I'm sorry, Kit. I don't know why it bothers me. *But it does.* I think of the two of us as friends. And I owe you. Without your bread, the Iron Skillet would still be under the radar. I want to see you happy, Kit," he said, stepping closer and looking down into her face searchingly, his warm brown eyes urging her to melt.

Kit's breath hitched in her chest as she tried to look away. "I *am* happy," she snapped, trying to pull her arm away.

Rob shook his head. "You're like me, Kit. I know you are. I recognized it the first day we met. You're used to the excitement and the fun of the city. You're used to men falling at your feet and now you're here in Fircrest and getting up at four in the morning and working hard. I know you get bored and wonder if there's more to your life than constant work. I know you think about love and a family," he said, with something suspiciously like pity in his voice.

Kit felt like he'd slapped her. *How dare he assume to know her heart?* "You're projecting, Rob," she said softly ,with a good imitation of his kind smile. She patted his cheek with her hand. "Don't worry. You'll find your way," she said, and walked away enjoying the look of utter shock on his face.

Jerk.

She let her fake smile fall away, and some of the anger she was feeling flowed out and down into her hands, making her shake. *How condescending could you get?* He was flat out rude. He'd basically been pitying her and her pathetic love life. *Caring about her happiness?* What a joke. She'd made it so obvious that she'd wanted to go out with him but he'd ignored every single one of her openings. And now he was worried about her? He wanted to see her happy? Running him over with her car right now would make her delirious.

"Uh, Kit? Please tell me that glare isn't for me."

Kit turned and speared Michael with her hot, hazel eyes. "Just the man I wanted to have a *long* talk with," she purred.

Michael's eyes went wide and he turned to search the crowd for Layla.

"No one here to save you, Michael. It's just you and me," she said, knowing she was going to take her anger at Rob out on Michael. She didn't even feel bad about it.

"You *forced* me to accept a blind date, and the guy shows up late, and on a motorcycle."

Michael swallowed and nodded as he lowered his head guiltily. "It was kind of last minute, Kit. I only had an hour to find you a date and I actually thought you guys would hit it off. He's a super, sweet guy and he um . . . *looks* like some of the guys you used to date, *but* he's a boy scout underneath. And I thought I'd make his life. He's always dreamed of dating a woman as gorgeous as you,"

Kit rolled her eyes, but had to admit that was kind of sweet. Of course Michael was playing her, but it was effective. "Now, Jane's date. *Garrett?* He's perfect. Why couldn't you have set me up with someone like him?" she asked, pouting as Jane and Garrett walked by ignoring everyone but each other.

Michael looked at Jane and Garrett and grinned. "Sorry, Kit, but Jane is perfect for Garrett. Garrett just retired from the marines. He's running a landscaping business now. He once told me when he was home on leave from Iraq, that he was so tired of evil and war and hate that when he got home he wanted to find a sweet innocent girl and fall in love. I've been meaning to set them up for weeks now."

Kit's heart melted as she stared at Garrett with compassion. Jane was someone's dream come true. *Okay, that got her.* She let all her anger slip away and she gave in and smiled.

"*Fine*, I'll forgive you. But don't you have a friend whose dream come true is *me*? I mean, *besides* Hunter," she added quickly.

Michael laughed and put his arm around her shoulders as they turned and watched the party. Well-dressed, beautiful, successful people talking and laughing and celebrating the love of two people.

"I know a lot of men who would take one look at you and think they'd won the lottery. But now that I'm your brother, I absolutely know most of them aren't good enough for you. You might want to take a deeper look at Hunter. He's one of the nicest guys I know."

Kit looked up at Michael and put her arm around his waist. It was kind of nice to have a big brother. *Who knew?* "Thanks, Michael. You're a good brother," she said, and leaned up on her toes to kiss him on the cheek. "You better get back to Layla before one of your friends steals her away," she said, as she noticed Layla surrounded by three tall, good looking men over by the water fountain.

"You have got to be kidding me," Michael muttered, and then left her without a backwards glance.

Kit laughed and then stepped back into the shadows. She watched the party quietly for a few moments with a wistful smile on her face. She kind of felt like Cinderella, invited to the ball, but still on the outside.

Chapter Three

HUNTERS AND GATHERERS

Kit spent most of dinner listening to Hunter talk about his new game he'd designed. She could have forgiven him for that if he'd even once asked her about herself, but he seemed so intent on impressing her that he didn't spend any time getting to *know* her. It was almost as if he was going down a check list of his credentials and checking them off one by one.

Michael's parents' house was a large beachfront home with a beautiful view of the water and the lights from Tacoma. As the party grew louder and the night darker, Kit began to relax and enjoy herself. She even dragged Hunter out to the dance floor. If there was music, she was going to dance. The band was actually a pleasant surprise, playing current songs and doing it well.

The band began singing, Bruno Mars' *24K Magic*, and she couldn't resist.

"Kit, *please*. You don't understand. *I don't know how to dance,*" Hunter whispered desperately, in her ear.

Kit frowned and looked at him impatiently. "It's no big deal, Hunter. It's not like the waltz. You just move to the music.

Hunter blushed and ran his hands through his beautifully highlighted hair. "Tony, my image consultant hasn't found me the right dance instructor yet. We haven't gotten that far. Kit, I don't want to look like an idiot, who doesn't know what he's doing," he said, all hints of bravado gone.

Kit smiled compassionately at Hunter and stepped forward, putting her hands on his shoulders. "Hunter, forget about your image and looking cool. Right now, *tonight*, you're a good looking, successful man and you're on a date with *me*. We're going to have fun dancing. Nobody is going to judge you. We're just going to relax and have fun."

Hunter looked at her doubtfully and then looked at all the couples now dancing and laughing. Michael and Layla were dancing in the middle, laughing and talking, as they just used it as an excuse to put their arms around each other. Jane and Garrett were dancing toward the edge and from Jane's delighted giggles and Garrett's uninhibited dance moves they were having a good time.

"See, look at that guy," she said, pointing to one of Michael's friends. "He can't dance at *all*. He's just moving side to side. Does anyone care? *No*, because no one cares what they look like. They're having fun," she said, leaning up to talk into Hunter's ear.

Hunter sighed and straightened his shoulders as if he were facing a root canal. "Okay, I can do this," he told himself, and walked with her onto the dance floor.

Kit smiled encouragingly and started moving to the music. She'd always loved dancing. Her biggest dream as a teenager had been to be on the drill team, but her mom never had the money for it. Rent had always been more important for some reason. So she put all her energy and dreams into her art. *And then went clubbing as much as possible.*

She grinned at Hunter and felt her heart melt at the vulnerability she saw on his face. She'd been born with confidence and a touch of feistiness. But Layla wasn't the only one who championed the weak and abused. Kit had made it her hobby to go after school bullies. No one had wanted Kit angry at them. Whichever jock she'd been dating at the time, would make it a priority to seek out the bully she wanted stopped and have a talk with them after school. That had always cleared up the problem quickly, she found.

She studied Hunter's tense face and had a sudden image of someone picking on him and felt a strong urge to protect him. He was trying so hard to be cool. Well then, she would do her part and help him.

"Hunter, just look at me and ignore everyone else here," she said, moving to the music effortlessly.

Hunter shook his head and blushed. "That makes me even more nervous. You're so beautiful and I acted like such an idiot when I picked you up. Tony told me to show up late and bring the motorcycle. I'm really sorry about that," he admitted.

Kit smiled and stopped dancing as she stepped closer to Hunter. She put her hands on either side of his face and looked into his eyes. "Forget Tony. *You're good enough,* Hunter. You're brilliant, talented and good looking. Just be yourself and relax. Okay?"

Hunter's shoulders relaxed and the tense anxiety left his eyes. He grinned down at Kit and nodded. "Okay. I like that. *I'm good enough.* Tony's always telling me that I have to change everything. Sometimes it's exhausting trying so hard to be someone I'm really not," he admitted sheepishly.

Kit couldn't resist. She gave Hunter a hug. "Well take it from a *real* image expert. I've dated legitimate bad boys. I've even dated some of the hottest men in Washington. But you're worth ten times any of them. And if you ask me, you should fire Tony."

Hunter looked down at Kit and smiled so innocently, Kit felt her heart warm. He really was kind of cute.

"Kit, you're so sweet. Maybe I could use you as an unofficial image expert?" he asked shyly.

Kit nodded her head and started dancing. "I would love to. But let's go a step further. Let's be friends. When I need a guy friend or a computer expert, I can call you. And when you need help with anything to do with women or your image, you call me. *Not Tony*. That guy is an idiot," she said fervently.

Hunter studied her for a moment and then nodded his head. "I would really like that. A lot."

Kit grinned and then instructed Hunter on how to do some cheesy dance moves. For the next hour she showed Hunter how to do the sprinkler, the shopping cart, the butter churn, the window cleaner and even the Dougie. They had so much fun, dancing and laughing that a crowd of people joined them doing all the dance moves together. Before she knew it, she was the center of attention and the entire engagement party was surrounding her following every move she made. She flipped her hair to the side and glanced over the crowd, noticing that Rob and his date were standing stiffly to the side, watching everyone else have fun. It looked like Rob was trying to encourage her to join in, but Marryn wasn't having it.

When a slow song came on she breathed a sigh of relief. A break would be nice. Hunter pulled her into his strong capable arms and moved into the slow moves of the box step.

Kit smiled up into Hunter's face. "Hey, you're pretty good," she said, moving with him around the floor.

Hunter nodded proudly. "I practiced forever to get this right," he admitted.

They moved gracefully among the couples and at the end of the song, Kit had to admit she was having a really good time and that was largely due to Hunter. He was a sweet, shy guy underneath his carefully constructed image. She had to admit she liked him.

At the end of the night, Hunter stood by her car door looking nervous. "Kit, would you like to go out, like on a *real* date sometime? I would pick you up on time and bring my car and everything. I promise."

Kit closed her eyes and lifted her face to the breeze coming off the Puget Sound before answering. "Hunter, you're a lot of fun. Yeah, let's go out sometime," she said, looking up at him. In the moonlight, Hunter looked pretty dang good. But more than that, he was nice. Probably the first nice guy she'd been on a date with.

"Okay, then. *Wow*, that's so great. I'll call you then and . . . thanks for being so cool about tonight. You could have just ignored me, but instead you were really sweet and um, I had the best time of my life," he said softly, looking at her with gratitude.

Kit grinned and hugged him. "You are adorable," she said, and gave him a quick peck on the lips. Hunter's eyes went wide in surprise and then his eyes gleamed down at her.

"We're definitely going out," he said, in a strong voice that surprised her.

Kit watched as he walked away and mounted his motorcycle. He turned in a circle and revved his motor a little before taking off down the road in a plume of dust.

"Kissing on the first date?"

Kit frowned and turned around to face Rob. *Again*.

"What is this, Rob? Every time I turn around, you're there. I hate to use the word *stalking* . . . What's going on?" she asked, deciding on a direct confrontation.

Rob shoved his hands in his pockets and stepped forward out of the shadows. The moonlight shone down on his chiseled features and his dark and dangerous eyes.

"I can't stop thinking about what you said earlier. About me projecting. I guess it kind of hit home. I want to apologize," he said, walking even closer until he was standing right in front of her.

Kit frowned and took a step back, coming up against her car. "*Okaaay*," she said softly, feeling nervous all of a sudden.

Rob stepped forward again, until they were nose to nose. "You looked like you were having a really good time with Hunter tonight," he said, sounding irritated as he stared down at her.

Kit smiled easily. "He's really cute. I like him," she said honestly.

Rob frowned and shook his head. "You know what I was

thinking as I was watching you dance with Hunter?" he asked quietly.

Kit shook her head and bit her lip as she felt his hand come up and grasp her waist.

"I was thinking you should be dancing with *me*," he said, and then leaned down and kissed her gently, tipping her chin up as he tilted his head down. Kit was so surprised, she didn't respond and tried to pull back, but he followed her and deepened the kiss. Kit kissed him back instinctively and blinked in surprise when he finally pulled back.

As they stared at each other in silence, Kit felt slightly irritated. She'd been dreaming of kissing Rob, *literally*, but the reality was not living up to her dreams. All the chemistry she'd imagined between herself and Rob had turned to dust when he'd put his lips on her.

"*Rob* . . ." she said, but he shook his head.

"Kit, I've been fighting this since the moment I met you that first day in my restaurant."

Kit frowned and looked down at her feet. "Why would you fight being attracted to me?"

Rob shook his head, his hands falling away from her waist. "I made a decision that I would find a woman who was loyal, faithful, kind, good and who loved me. I made a list of all the qualities I wanted in a partner. . . *a wife*. I swore I'd only date women who measured up. I can't do the night life and the clubbing and the fake, shallow relationships I used to have. I don't want that life anymore," he said, almost angrily, looking at her as if *she'd* done something wrong.

Kit felt a wave of coldness wash over her and she stood up straighter, her hands clenched at her sides. "Which means you think *I'm* fake and shallow. You're upset that you're attracted to me because you think I'm just a sports bimbo like all of the other women you used to date. Is that what you're trying to say?" she asked, in a deceptively gentle voice.

Rob swallowed and looked away. "That's not what I said, Kit," he said tonelessly.

Oh, yes it was.

"*Hmmm*, well it's too bad you've sworn off bimbos, Rob. But if it makes you feel any better, I've sworn off cruel, thoughtless jerks. So we're both off the hook," she said, and then pushed him back hard, making him stumble.

He stared at her wide eyed as she slipped into her car and drove away. She waved out the window in farewell as she left him standing in the dust her car made and let her smile slip into a snarl. *He thought she was a bimbo.* A fake, gold digging, shallow, trashy bimbo.

She hated Rob Downing.

Chapter Four

REVENGE

Kit woke up the next morning in the worst mood ever. She pitied whoever got in her way today. She turned on her side and stared at the clock. 3:59am. She closed her eyes and groaned as she turned off the alarm before it could go off. She stumbled to the bathroom and turned the shower on high. Images from the party last night tried to push in past her morning fog, but she pushed them back harder and focused all of her energy on one thing. Waking up. Not easy when she'd stayed up way too late the night before.

She dragged herself to the kitchen to find Layla and Jane already hard at work. She grunted at her sisters and got everything out she would need for sourdough bread. It would be a busy day at Rob's restaurant since it was Saturday so she would need to make a double batch. *And then deliver it.* Her frown deepened as she measured her ingredients. She glanced at Jane and wondered what she would have to do to bribe her to make the bread delivery for her. Or Layla for that matter.

Kit watched Layla dance around the kitchen to Imagine Dragons', *Natural* and smiled. Layla was so happy she wouldn't need to be bribed.

"Layla, could you make my bread delivery today for me? I

need to get started on that cake for the Leavitt's anniversary party," she said, with an innocent smile.

Layla looked at her questioningly. "The Leavitt's party isn't for another week."

Kit glared at her sister and then tried smiling again. "Yeah, well, I want to sketch it out."

Layla stopped what she was doing and walked over to her sister, looking suspicious. "*Uh, huh.* I'm not buying it. What did Rob do this time?" she asked, putting her hands on her hips with an amused smile on her face.

Kit sighed and turned the bread mixer on and then walked over to the fridge to grab a water bottle. "Nothing, really. He just kissed me and then told me that he only wanted to date a woman who was loyal, faithful, kind, good and who would love him. *But* he was tired of fighting his attraction to me. He was really upset with himself as if he'd failed or something. As if, *I* was the opposite of all the things he wanted in a woman," she said sadly, pinching the bridge of her nose with two fingers.

Layla and now Jane were standing in front of her with their mouths hanging open in shock.

"I *hate* Rob," Jane whispered fiercely.

Layla nodded her head slowly. "I hate him more. How dare he insinuate that you're not good enough for him," she breathed out, her blue eyes turning to cold fire.

Kit grinned at Layla and felt better. The one thing she could always count on in this world, was Layla tearing apart *anyone* who messed with her little sisters. "It's okay," she said, trying to sound like she was being brave. "It's just ever since we moved here, I kept hoping that he would like me back, you know. But this whole time he was judging me because . . ." Kit paused for a moment, and shocked herself when she really did feel real tears pushing against her eyes. She sniffed and bit her lip. "Because he thinks I'm trashy."

Jane's soft brown eyes turned to hard slits and her jaw hardened. "I'll make the bread run today," she said quietly.

Kit's eyes widened. *Whoa.* Her sweet little Jane looked like she wanted to kill Rob.

"No, Jane, *we'll* be making the bread run today. It'll be our last one," Layla said grimly.

Kit's mouth fell open and she saw what judges used to see when they met Layla in the courtroom. Someone willing to do anything to protect another person. *Rob was toast.* Kit swallowed nervously and shook her head.

"Layla, I don't want to lose our business relationship with Rob over this. It's okay. *Really.* I've got thick skin. It doesn't really matter what Rob thinks about me," she said firmly, although . . . *it kind of did.* It hurt a lot.

Layla watched her carefully and nodded her head. "Kit, *it's done.* Besides, there are plenty of restaurants dying to do business with us. There's a new French restaurant down by Point Defiance. I'll stop by and talk to the owner today. I'll give him a couple loaves of your sourdough and see what he thinks," she said, walking away from her sisters and back to her éclairs. "We don't need Rob, half as much as he needs us."

Kit closed her eyes, feeling sick. She'd had no idea Layla would react so harshly to Rob's treatment of her. But she should have known. Nobody messed with her sisters. *Nobody.*

Jane still stood in front of her, looking at her sadly. "I'm so sorry, Kit," she said, and took the two steps toward her and hugged her. Kit hugged her back automatically, but when Jane wouldn't let go, she gave in to the comfort her little sister was offering her.

"I really thought that someday he and I would be together. I hate that I was so stupid. *Again,*" Kit said, around a few lingering tears.

Jane rubbed her hand over Kit's hair and pulled back, revealing a few tears running down her cheeks. "I did too, Kit. You're not stupid! Layla thought the same thing."

Layla looked over her shoulder and nodded, still stiff with fury. "We all thought it, Kit. *He's* the stupid one. He has no idea who you really are, if he can say crap like that to you. No idea. You're smart and amazing and talented and sweet and decent . . ." she muttered to herself, fading off into her own thoughts.

Kit wiped her eyes and grinned at her sisters. "Dang, it's good to have sisters," she said, and hugged Jane hard before walking over to her big sister and wrapping her arms around her waist, leaning her head against Layla's back.

Layla's shoulders relaxed and she turned around and hugged Kit so hard she felt her back crack. "Someday you're going to meet the most amazing man ever, Kit. I promise. A man who will thank Heaven every morning that you were born. Someone smart enough to recognize the genuine, *good* woman, you are," she swore, her voice sounding shaky with emotion.

Kit sighed and squeezed Layla back one more time. "Well, this guy Michael set me up with last night isn't too bad," she said, letting go of her sister and heading back to her bread. She kept Layla and Jane enthralled for the next half hour as she told them how Hunter had picked her up for their date on a motor-cycle and then everything up to the point where she'd kissed him good night. She had them laughing and giggling within minutes and felt better. She hated upsetting her sisters. Soon they were all back to singing and dancing in the kitchen but two hours later when the bread was done, both Jane and Layla were picking up the bread trays in their arms with icy glares and eyes filled with fire. *Rob was still going down.*

Kit watched them drive away, as she went to turn the sign to OPEN, and tried to feel a little sympathy for Rob.

And then she thought better of it.

She pulled the blinds up and looked up at the bright, sunny August morning. Today was going to be a good day. Kit helped all of the morning customers but kept glancing at the clock hoping Layla and Jane would return soon. Their morning clerk had called in sick and she was being run ragged. *Finally*, Layla and Jane walked into the front store, arranging their aprons around their waists and began helping her with the line she had.

Kit ran to the back to get more trays of croissants and muffins and hurried back. She studied Layla and Jane's expressions trying to guess how it had gone with Rob but they both had professional smiles on. She wouldn't know what happened until they had a break.

An hour later, when the last customer walked out, she turned to ask Layla what had happened with Rob. But just as she opened her mouth, the bell rang over the door signaling a new customer. Kit groaned softly in impatience and turned to smile.

Rob.

He was not smiling.

Kit's own smile faded as she felt Jane and Layla come to stand on either side of her.

"I thought I told you, you weren't welcome in our bakery anymore," Layla said, in a soft, yet dangerous sounding voice.

Jane hissed as she stared Rob up and down, as she set a tray of her cupcakes down on the counter. "How dare you show your face here, after what you said to Kit," she said ,sounding offended and seriously ticked.

Rob held up his hands. "I'm just here to apologize to Kit. However, I think what I said and what Kit told you, are two *very* different things. I never called Kit trashy. I think this is all a horrible misunderstanding. Which just goes to show you, I was right to keep my distance from Kit. *Nobody* needs drama like this."

Kit's mouth fell open as she stared at Rob, wondering what she'd ever seen in him. Okay, yeah, his dark good looks, granted. And yeah, he'd been a professional athlete and it still showed. Okay, he looked like her dream come true. *But everything that actually counted?* Pathetic.

"Did you just call my sister a liar?" Layla whispered, her hand shaking, as she reached over and picked up a large chocolate cupcake.

Rob looked furious as he continued to look at Kit,

completely ignoring Layla. "Jeez, Kit, all I did was kiss you and you sic your sisters on me?"

Kit shook her head in unbelief. "You were *angry* you'd kissed me, Rob. You told me about the perfect woman you had planned on finding, and you were so stinking disappointed to find that you were attracted to me," she said, wincing at the memory.

Rob put his hands on his hips and stared her down as if she were playing for the Red Sox. "Well, if it makes you feel any better," he said, his eyes narrowed cruelly, "whatever attraction I *was* feeling for you last night, was momentary at best, and is *completely* gone now. So, if we can get back to business, I'd appreciate it. This emotional soap opera, you and your sisters are playing, is a poor example of how to run a business."

Layla pulled her arm back, winding up, before letting the moist cupcake covered in mounds of fudge icing, fly right at Rob's head. Since he'd been staring at Kit the entire time, he was completely caught off guard as the big cupcake exploded against his head, sending chocolate crumbs flying everywhere as the icing stuck like glue to his face.

Rob blinked slowly and turned to stare at Layla in shock. Layla picked up another cupcake just as Jane let hers fly, hitting Rob on the other side of his head. All three sisters had played Softball in high school. Their aim was never off. Kit grinned at Rob's dazed expression before Layla hit in him in the center of his chest, whooping loudly as if she'd just won a prize at the fair.

Rob's face contorted in rage and he took a step toward the sisters, just as Kit let her cupcake soar, hitting Rob squarely in the nose. Jane hurled the last cupcake, determined to get the last throw in. Kit winced when she saw where Jane had aimed, but let out a helpless giggle too, covering her mouth with her hands as all three sisters burst out into laughter. Rob let out a moan as he bent over for a moment before turning to walk out of the bakery with as much dignity as he could muster.

Just as he was about to disappear out the door, Layla called out, "And good riddance! Don't you ever come back again!" she shouted, pushing her hair out of her face and grinning gleefully.

Jane and Layla gave each other high fives and laughed gleefully as Kit quietly went to get the mop. Layla and Jane were still laughing ten minutes later, when Officer Matafeo walked into the store, looking grim.

Jane cleared her throat and stepped forward as Kit wheeled the mop bucket back to the kitchen. Tate Matafeo was a regular at Belinda's Bakery. He'd started coming around from the very beginning but now only came in occasionally. Jane had asked him out on a date and he'd turned her down flat. Since then, things had been awkward to say the least.

"What can we do for you, Officer?" Jane asked, in an overly polite voice, as Layla washed her hands in the sink.

"I've just received a report of an assault. Rob Downing called in and said that you three woman assaulted him, by throwing cupcakes at him. I just talked to Rob down on the street, and he's covered in chocolate. He's threatening to press charges. Seriously, what is it with throwing food at people you're mad at? It's childish and it's going to end up with one of you getting arrested one of these days," he said, eyeing Layla cautiously, before looking at Jane with a raised eyebrow.

Kit walked back into the store, having heard everything and leaned up against the counter, crossing her arms over her chest, her face expressionless. *Rob had called the cops on them.* It was official. The man was a loser.

Layla dried her hands and walked slowly toward Tate, not blinking as she came out from around the counter, coming to stand directly in front of him, in full older sister mode. Which was terrifying and yet beautiful thing to witness.

"Tate, you know us. You've known us ever since we moved to town. Don't you think there would be a *really* good reason for us to pelt that idiot with cupcakes? *Hmm?* Do you think we just throw food, that we work hard to make, at customers *for fun*? Or, because we want to lose business or have the cops called on us?"

Tate frowned and shook his head. "Just tell me what happened, Layla," he said quietly.

Jane stepped forward and put her hand on Tate's arm, gaining his complete attention. "Tate, he insulted Kit. He made her cry," she said, imploring him with her eyes.

Tate glanced at Kit and she nodded her head jerkily, still not saying anything. Tate sighed and ran his hands through his hair. "Pretty bad insult, I take it?" he asked, looking back to Jane.

Jane sniffed and nodded. "He implied she wasn't a good woman and that she wasn't good enough for him," she said quietly.

Tate's eyebrows rose an inch and his mouth fell open. "Oh, man, *what an idiot*," he muttered. "Okay then, ladies. I'll let you get back to work," he said simply, and smiled gently at Kit, before turning and walking out of the bakery.

Layla sighed, her shoulders relaxing as she turned to look at the now clean store. "Maybe I shouldn't have thrown that first cupcake," she said, with a faint smile.

Jane winced and picked up a stray crumb of chocolate, Kit's mop had missed. "You're probably right. And I *probably* shouldn't have thrown the second."

Kit grinned and came around the counter. "Well, I disagree, because when I threw my cupcake, it was the best feeling in the world," she said, hugging her sisters and yanking on their hair. "Of course, that last cupcake Jane threw, could get her sent away for a long time," she said, walking to the glass fronted door to peer out. Tate was still talking to Rob who was gesturing angrily at the bakery.

Layla and Jane joined her as they watched Rob bluster and try to wipe the cupcake mess off his face. Every time he tried though, he just ended up smearing it instead. After a few minutes, Tate obviously at the end of his patience, got in Rob's face and started to do some pointing himself. Tate's Samoan heritage came in handy when dealing with irate people, his tall powerful physique could speak louder than any shout. And what-

ever Tate was saying, was effective because Rob's face immediately went still and his body motionless. Kit watched his face
carefully, and then . . . she saw it. *Shame*.

Thank you, Officer Matafeo.

"And that's that," she said quietly, as a customer started
walking up the porch steps. "Back to work," she said, and walked
back behind the counter.

Chapter Five

REGRET

Rob watched Tate's police car pull away from the curb and sighed, crossing his arms over his chest. He hadn't messed up this bad in years. Possibly even a decade. The closest example he could think of, was in the eighth grade, when he'd had a crush on Jennifer Hahn, and she'd liked his best friend, Jason instead, so he'd teased her unmercifully the entire year in revenge. He'd been your typical, immature idiot.

Looks like he still was.

He stared up at Belinda's Bakery and watched as a couple walked down the steps holding bakery bags, smiling and talking. He was now blacklisted from the bakery. No restraining order yet, but he wouldn't hold it past them. And he'd been told bluntly to get the bread for his restaurant somewhere else, because Belinda's Bakery would no longer be working with The Iron Skillet.

Rob sighed and felt sick to his stomach. Kit's sourdough bread was so incredible, one of the harshest critics in the Pacific Northwest had written a rave review about his restaurant and put his restaurant in the spotlight. And how did he repay the favor? He'd crushed Kit with a few thoughtless words. Well, more than a few actually.

He walked slowly over to his car, wincing at all the messy chocolate sure to get everywhere. He drove away seconds later, and headed to his restaurant. His home was the second story of his restaurant. His own private sanctuary. He trudged up the stairs and let himself in, heading straight to the bathroom. He took a quick shower and then put on sweats and an old Mariner's t-shirt from back in the day. He collapsed on the couch, but instead of turning on a game, he just sat there. *Thinking.*

He had totally messed up. Now that he thought back to every word he'd said to Kit the night before, he could see why she'd been furious. Most women would have blown it off easily though. No big deal. The only reason it could have hurt her so much, would have been if she'd had feelings for him. Rob closed his eyes and sunk lower on the couch, covering his face with his arm.

She must hate him now.

He'd basically told her that he'd wanted a good, wonderful woman but that he couldn't help being attracted to her. Jeez, *he should be shot.* And to make matters worse, he'd stood there on the street, blustering about being assaulted, while Tate stared at him like he was a pile of dirt. Being lectured on how to treat a lady, by a man younger than him . . . *that had burned.*

He *knew* how to treat a lady! When he'd been living the good life up in Seattle, during his baseball years, he'd been famous for spoiling the women in his life. The best restaurants, jewelry, vacations to Europe and the Caribbean. Nothing had been too much for the woman in his life. Of course he'd been all about flashing his cash back then. Back then, he'd thought he had to go all out, in order to date models and actresses.

And then everything had changed. When his shoulder had gone out on him, and his contract wasn't renewed, all the money had gone too. Soon, followed by Chloe. He'd bought her an engagement ring and told her his dreams of starting over and opening a restaurant. She'd laughed in his face and began dating one of his buddies from the team, the very next week.

He'd learned a few hard lessons that week. Lessons he'd never forget. And every small success he celebrated, he thought of her. The last time he'd heard, Chloe was now living in Boston, since Brent had been traded last year. Yeah, well he wished them well.

Except he didn't.

Rob lowered his arm and thought of Kit's face as she'd stood there in the bakery an hour ago, staring at him like he was the biggest loser she'd ever had the misfortune to meet. That had hurt almost as bad as Chloe walking out on him. He still remembered seeing Kit for the first time. It had been like a punch to the gut, she was so beautiful. All that fiery red hair and her mischievous hazel eyes. She had that smile that was so mysterious, it made you want to get closer and find out all of her secrets.

But he'd taken one look and had put her firmly in the category of, *Way Too Dangerous.* And he'd done everything he could to keep his distance, except he'd failed horribly. If she was in the same room, he found a way to stand next to her. If she was making a bread delivery, then he'd be the one to sign off. He hated to go a day without seeing her. He didn't want to look too closely at why that was.

Everything he'd learned about Kit proved he was right about her though. He'd asked around and had a buddy who knew of her. He'd confirmed every suspicion he'd had about Kit. She was a flighty artist who had spent her time in Seattle dancing and dating and trying to get a showing for her work. The exact opposite of the type of woman he wanted to settle down with.

Of course, when she'd moved here to Fircrest with her sisters to take over her grandmother's bakery, she'd settled down. But how long could that last before she went crazy and moved back to Seattle? He didn't want to gamble his heart on the answer.

But last night, at the party, when he'd watched her dancing with Hunter, he'd been mesmerized. She'd been so sweet, showing that goof, Hunter, how to dance. They'd laughed and had a great time, while he'd been miserable with his date. Bored out of his mind, to be honest. And he'd wished with all of his heart that it had been him dancing with Kit. And so, idiot that he was, he'd told her that and then done something even dumber. He'd kissed her. It had been better than he'd imagined it would be.

He was so infatuated with Kit, that he didn't even know how to control what came out of his mouth anymore. And he'd messed everything up. The sad thing was, he was *still* infatuated with Kit. He'd wanted to beg her forgiveness, but his pride had gotten in the way. And instead, he'd been pelted by cupcakes. *Hard.* He winced at the memory of the last cupcake, thrown at him by Jane.

He'd think twice before insulting a Kendall again. *That's for sure.* But now what? How in the world was he going to fix this mess?

He stared at his cell phone and picked it up off the couch. There was one small possibility. He went through his contacts and selected Michael Bender.

"Hey, buddy. You got time for lunch today? My treat."

Chapter Six

WINSTON

Kit turned the sign to CLOSED, as she waved goodbye to Mandee. *Today had exhausted her.* It had been excruciating, smiling and chatting with all the customers, when what she really wanted to do, was hole up in her room and watch movies and cry.

Jane patted her on the shoulder and took the apron from her. "You look like you could use a bubble bath and a good book."

Kit smiled. "Your cure for everything Jane. But you're right. That sounds pretty good right now," she admitted readily.

Layla finished wiping the glass case down and stood up tiredly. "I have a bottle of the most amazing bubble bath, Kit. I insist you try it," she said, walking over to her sisters.

The bell over the door had all three women turning around with identical frowns on their faces. Layla's face relaxed immediately when she saw who it was.

"Michael! I was just getting ready to change and come over," she said, walking over to reach up and kiss his cheek.

Michael grinned down at Layla and pulled her into his arms. "I hate waiting even five extra minutes to see you," he said, kissing her quickly.

Layla sighed and snuggled into his side as Kit and Jane

exchanged smiles. Michael finally noticed them and smiled. "Hey, guys. Um, I was wondering if I could take all three of you out for a quick dinner. How does Thai sound?" he asked, with a serious look in his eyes.

Layla frowned and stepped back from Michael. "What is this about, Michael? Is Alex Foster pestering you with more offers to show us?" she asked, glancing at Kit and Jane.

Michael shook his head. "Nah, I haven't heard from Alex in a while. This is a different matter altogether," he said mysteriously.

Kit looked at her feet as a suspicion entered her head. *Rob.*

"Michael, I'm a little tired tonight. It's been a rough day for me, so I'm going to pass. I'll let Jane and Layla fill me in later," she said with a wave of her hand, before hurrying toward the door.

"Wait, Kit."

Kit slowly turned around and stared pleadingly at Michael. Michael was standing there, looking at her exactly the way an older brother would, who was caught in the middle of a friend and a sister. Uncomfortable, concerned and determined to fix things.

"It's important that you come," he said.

Jane stared at Michael hard and shook her head. "Rob put you up to this, didn't he, Michael?" she asked softly, moving to stand between him and Kit.

Michael nodded immediately. "You're right. He's asked me to talk to you. He's one of my best friends and I owe him," he said, looking at Jane and Kit imploringly.

Layla looked torn. She'd do anything for Michael, but she was incapable of not sticking up for her sisters. She looked up at Michael with a frown and stepped back from him.

"Kit doesn't have to listen to you if she doesn't want to, Michael. Jane and I will come, but Kit shouldn't have to. Not after the way he's acted," she said, her voice going hard.

Michael blinked in surprise and looked at Layla with a frown. "*Layla?* Come on, honey. Don't make this into something big and ugly. It was just a misunderstanding. Let's talk it out and work through this like adults. There's no reason to burn bridges," he said, looking at her quizzically.

Kit could see the situation blowing up and causing problems between Layla and Michael and she hated the idea of Rob causing anymore heartache than he'd already done. She walked forward and put her arm on Layla's arm.

"I'll listen, Layla. It's okay. I can always have my bubble bath and book later," she said softly, with a smile for her sister.

Layla shook her head and rubbed Kit's back soothingly. "You don't have to, Kit. *Really.*"

Kit shook her head. "It's no big deal. Besides, I could use some Thai food. Jane? You hungry?" she asked, looking at her younger sister.

Jane rolled her eyes. "Fine. Let's get this over with," sounding way more hostile ,than either she or Layla had.

Michael's eyebrows rose in surprise, as he followed the women out the front door and to his car. The ride to the restaurant was completely silent, but Kit was happy to see that Layla was holding Michael's hand.

After ordering their curry dishes, Michael sat next to Layla, with his arm around her shoulders as he stared at Kit and Jane.

"Rob feels horrible, Kit. We had lunch this afternoon and he's just sick about it. He'll do *anything* to make it up to you."

Kit stared at Michael silently as Layla snorted rudely and Jane shook her head in disgust.

"Michael, do you even *know* what happened?" Jane asked, as she glared at him.

Michael held up his hands, not used to being the target of their wrath.

"First things first. I am on *your* side here, so please don't get angry at me. I'm here to help Rob *and* Kit and everyone else, move past this and get back to being friends."

Layla ran her hands through her long blond hair and then took it upon herself to fill Michael in. Jane couldn't resist jumping in here and there to give her opinion or clarify a point. When Layla came to the end, their waiter showed up with their meals, cutting the conversation off.

After everyone had taken a bite or two, Michael cleared his throat and took a drink of water. "Ladies, I'm probably the best one to stand here for Rob, because I understand him the best. We've been friends forever, and when he came back to Fircrest to start over, he was a heart broken wreck of a man. Chloe, his ex-girlfriend tore his heart out. And ever since, he's been suspicious of beautiful women. That in no way excuses what he said to you, Kit, but if you can look at it from his point of view, here's this guy who's determined to fall in love with a woman, who is steady and trustworthy and loyal, and someone who would never cheat on him or leave him. And then you show up, and remind him of all the beautiful, exciting women he left behind with his old life. I think everyone who has been in the same room with you two will attest to all the sparks that fly," he said, with an imploring smile at Kit.

Kit frowned at him.

Michael winced and looked at Layla and Jane and saw identical frowns on their faces too.

"He's been fighting his attraction for you for months, Kit. He's been desperately dating every single woman in Fircrest and Tacoma, trying to find the perfect woman for him. But he can't. He told me that, last night, when he saw you dancing with Hunter, he had to restrain himself from cutting in. He's tired of fighting it, Kit. Last night, he made a mess of things, but what he was *trying* to say was, *that he likes you.* That he wants to take you out. He wants to give this thing between the two of you a chance," he said, smiling hopefully at Kit's frozen face.

Kit looked down at her lap, no longer hungry and feeling sick again. She was his second choice. He couldn't find the woman he really wanted, so he'd settle for her, even though she reminded him of every shallow and empty woman he'd ever known.

Jane's eyes were slits and Layla's hands were now fists on the table. Michael cleared his throat nervously as the seconds turned into minutes and the atmosphere at the table turned deadly.

"Michael, thanks for dinner, but Kit and I have somewhere we need to be. Layla, we'll see you back at the house later," Jane said in a cold voice, as she stood up, taking Kit's hand firmly in hers. Michael stood up, but Layla yanked him back down firmly.

When Kit was pulled out of the restaurant and into the sun, she sighed in relief and then embarrassed herself by bursting into tears. Jane immediately threw her arms around her sister's shaking shoulders and rubbed her back.

"Just forget about him, Kit. What an idiot. I have no idea why Michael is friends with such a jerk, but hopefully Layla will set him straight. Come on, let's get you home. You have a bubble bath and a good book to look forward to tonight," she said, as she stared in irritation at the parking lot.

Michael had been their ride. They had no choice but to go back in the restaurant or call a cab. Kit wiped her eyes and hugged herself. "Great. Now we get to hear more about poor misunderstood Rob, and his magical search for the perfect woman. Poor guy failed so bad, he's willing to make do with me," she said morosely.

Jane made a furious hissing sound and shook her head, taking out her phone. "I'll call Garrett. He told me to call him if I was ever in trouble. He meant it," she said simply, holding her cell up to her ear.

Within seconds, she was smiling and giggling into the phone. They walked across the street to a book store and waited for ten minutes until Garrett showed up in his truck. Jane sat next to Garrett in the front seat while she was squeezed up against the door. Garrett smiled at them curiously, but didn't ask any embarrassing questions, for which she was overwhelmingly grateful. Fifteen minutes later, she was inside and walking up the stairs to her room as Jane talked to Garrett.

She spent the rest of the night taking an extra-long bubble bath and then relaxing with the six hour Pride and Prejudice

Mini-series. Colin Firth was the best medicine for any heartache. Honestly, a man who would do anything to help the woman he loved, even when he didn't think she returned his affections, was a man to dream about.

The next day was Sunday, their day off, so she slept in until the decadent hour of eight o'clock, only giving herself an hour to get ready for church. When she skipped down the stairs, wearing a cute navy blue and white striped skirt and white top, she found Layla and Jane talking quietly in the kitchen, as they nibbled on leftover croissants from the day before and drinking orange juice.

"Hey, guys. Any croissants left for me?" she asked, with a carefree smile on her face.

Layla looked up and smiled kindly. "Of course. We saved you two. Jane, why don't you pour Kit a glass of juice?" she directed, as Kit walked over.

She sat down and ate as Jane and Layla talked about Garrett. When they'd moved to town months ago, Jane had set her heart on winning over Officer Tate Matafeo, but he wasn't budging, and she had lost all patience. Kit grinned as she listened to Jane's impromptu date the night before.

"And then he stopped by a flower shop and bought me roses," she said dreamily, leaning her chin on her hands.

Kit sighed with her. The Kendall sisters were suckers for roses. Layla smiled cautiously at Jane. "From what Michael has told me, Garrett is transitioning pretty well back into regular life."

Jane blinked and nodded. "Oh, of course. He retired from the Marines last year, when he got home. He's doing amazing, Layla. We're going out again tomorrow night. He asked me to go sailing. I can't wait," she said excitedly.

Jane hurried out of the room to grab her purse as Layla watched her with worry in her eyes.

"What aren't you saying, Layla? Is there something about Garrett we should know?" Kit asked quickly, before Jane could come back in the room.

Layla shook her head with a frown. "Michael mentioned Garrett's being treated for PTSD, Post Traumatic, Stress, Disorder. He's doing great, but it just takes time and continued care and therapy and sometimes medication. I just don't think Jane is aware that Garrett is only showing her one side of who he is, right now. She needs to see the whole picture, before she gives her heart to this man."

Kit frowned at Layla. "Layla, he's a Marine. He gave years of his life to our country. He's a great guy. Jane won't care if he suffers from PTSD. She'd do anything she can to help him heal. You know her," she said curiously.

Layla smiled and shrugged. "Of course, I know that, Kit. It's just, you know me, it's my job to worry."

Kit grinned and hugged her sister as Jane walked back in the room. "I'm very aware, Layla. You're the best older sister a girl could have. I hope you didn't give Michael a hard time yesterday after we left," she said, taking another bite of her croissant.

Layla blushed and looked down at her feet. "I might have. Let's just say, that Michael and I have agreed to disagree on Rob. He's determined to see the best in his friend. And I'm determined to run him over with my car, if he ever comes near you again," she swore, her eyes gleaming dangerously.

Kit winced and took a sip of juice. She was actually starting to feel a little bad for Rob. She finished her croissant and they left for church, sitting in the back pew together. Michael and Stella were sitting in the front row, but they'd gotten there early. Stella kept turning around in her seat and waving at Layla, blowing her kisses continuously.

Rob was there too, sitting next to his mother and his two sisters, Taryn and Bailey. Kit tried to listen to the talk on forgiveness, but couldn't seem to concentrate. Her eyes were drawn over and over to Rob's bowed head and his gleaming dark hair. She felt like pulling her own hair out, when she realized what she was doing. Acting like any typical teenage girl, with a crush on a guy, who would never take her seriously.

After that, she was determined to ignore Rob. Later when they were walking back home, arm in arm, Jane cleared her throat. "Rob came up to me at church today and apologized. He was actually kind of sincere," she said.

Kit's head snapped up and she stared at Jane in surprise. "*Really?*"

Layla looked over at Jane and frowned. "It's an act, Jane. Don't buy into it. He judged Kit based on her looks, and didn't even bother to get to know her, before putting her in the *trashy and fake* category."

Kit winced and tried to keep smiling. "It's okay, Layla. Really, it's for the best if we all forgive Rob and move on. Making a bigger deal of this dumb situation, just makes Rob a bigger deal than he really is. *And he isn't.* He's just some speck of a man, who I admit, I would have loved to have dated. It's true, I had thought that someday I'd be in a relationship with Rob. But, I've put Rob into the trashy and fake category, and I'm ready to move on, and meet a man who is about more than appearances," she said, in a determined voice.

Layla stared at her with wide eyes and a smile. "Wow, Kit. You're a better woman than me."

Kit snorted. "Yeah, right. Not in this lifetime. I just know that the best revenge, is living well. And I still have that wedding dress in my closet. By the end of the year, I'm going to be wearing that dress, and Rob will be invited to the party."

Jane laughed. "Kit, that's perfect. I can't wait to see his face."

Layla sighed. "I would absolutely love that. And I'm glad you're feeling mature about things with Rob, because his mother and sisters cornered me at church and invited us over for dinner this Wednesday. You know Anne. No one's ever said no to that woman and lived. *I might have agreed we'd be there,*" she said, in a confused voice.

Kit sighed and ground her teeth. "*I'm* perfectly capable of saying no, to Anne. But it's no big deal. I can go to dinner with Rob's family. It won't bother me at all," she said casually.

Jane and Layla exchanged impressed smiles, and the rest of the walk home was happy and lighthearted.

The rest of the day they relaxed until Layla left around six to go watch a movie with Michael and Stella. Garrett came by unexpectedly and asked Jane to go for a ride, leaving Kit all by herself. Kit wandered out onto the front porch and pulled her knees up to her chin as she rocked back and forth. She closed her eyes as she let the silence of the evening overtake her.

The sound of a motorcycle made her wince though and open her eyes. She stared in surprise, as Hunter pulled to a stop in front of the bakery. He pulled his helmet off his head, whipping his hair out of his eyes, before smiling hopefully up at her.

"I hope tonight's a better night for a motorcycle ride?" he asked, grinning up at her.

Kit stood up and smiled down at Hunter. He looked amazing, *thanks to his stylist*. But facts were facts, the man looked good. He was ripped, tanned and his sun tipped hair set off his blue eyes and cheek bones. She'd be crazy to say no.

"Sure, Hunter. Why not?" she called out as she slipped on her tennis shoes and walked down the porch steps. Wearing jeans and a plain white t-shirt, she was ready for a ride this time.

Hunter handed her an extra helmet and she hopped on, wrapping her arms around his waist as he revved the motor and took off. He took her for a long ride over onto Vashon Island. Riding over the bridge was exciting and feeling the wind and the power of the machine she was on, along with holding onto a strong, good looking man, was enough to put a genuine grin on her face.

When Hunter came to a stop in front of a magnificent, beachfront home, with an amazing view of the Sound she looked around in confusion. He took his helmet off, so she took hers off too.

"Hunter, why are we stopping here? The owners of this house

probably don't want us trespassing on their property," she said as she stepped off and turned around in a circle as she stared at the gorgeous house and the natural landscaping surrounding the home. She could see a dock behind the house and kayaks tied up. *Wow*. What would it be like to live here?

"Ah, we're not trespassing. This is my house. Want a tour?" he asked hopefully.

Kit stared at him in surprise but then relaxed and smiled. She should have known. Many young and talented computer geniuses were making millions in the gaming industry. "I would love a tour Hunter. Lead the way," she said, grabbing his elbow as he led her inside.

Although the exterior looked like a typical Pacific Northwest home with natural colors and materials, the interior was designed with Hunter in mind. Very high-tech, modern and masculine. There was a lot of chrome, reds and blacks and modern art work scattered liberally along all surfaces. She was surprised to find that she loved it.

"I like your house, Hunter," she said, smiling as he kept looking back at her for her reaction as they walked through all the rooms. When they got to his family room, she could tell he'd made a lot of personal touches himself. There were large game posters all over the walls that he'd worked on or designed. And on one wall, there were pictures of Hunter as a child with his family and later on as a teenager and a college student. She'd hit the mother lode.

"Kit, come check out my soda fountain. You can have any fountain drink you want," he said, sounding uncomfortable and nervous. "You, uh, probably don't want to look at all of those old pictures," he said, sounding like he was embarrassed.

Kit shushed him and bent over to look closer. She felt her heart warm as she saw Hunter and his mom and dad standing in front of a small book store. He must have been three or four. He had the cutest little blond bowl haircut and bright, happy blue eyes. The next picture, he was about nine or ten and she could see a little bit of the nerdiness he had told her about. Scruffy dark, blond hair, a Spiderman t-shirt, and a large dog at his feet. *He was adorable.*

The next few pictures, she could tell it was Hunter, but he didn't look anything like he did now. He was tall and super skinny and very pale, as if he never went out doors. He still had a smile on his face, but he looked more cautious about it now, as if he realized he was a geek, because someone had made sure to point it out to him. The last picture she looked at, was a picture of him and some friends at a convention. She blinked in surprise as she realized one of the guys was Michael, smiling and clapping Hunter on the back. Hunter looked ecstatic. She looked closely and saw that he was holding an award in his hands, and there was a huge banner behind his head. *Game of the Year, Totally Gaming Awards.*

She glanced around the wall but didn't see any current pictures of him, now that he was toned, tanned and sexy. Interesting.

"Pretty nerdy huh?" Hunter asked quietly, already wincing as if he were expecting an insult, or worse, a laugh.

Kit looked at him curiously. "You say that like it's something to be embarrassed about. Nerdy to me, just means someone who has spent more time using their brain than their body. Look at Bill Gates. Biggest nerd in the world. Rich, successful and happy. He spends his time now, on figuring out ways to help other people. He's amazing."

Hunter shrugged and touched the edge of a picture frame as he looked away from her. "Yeah, but would you want to *date* Bill Gates?"

Kit laughed and stood next Hunter. "Well, he's married and has kids now, *so no.* But I think I'm mature enough to realize that I need to be attracted to what's on the inside, before the outside matters."

Hunter looked at her and smiled shyly. "A year and a half ago, I started working out and um, you know, hired Tony. I realized that as successful as I was in my career, I had no personal life really. No one to care about or love. I know women are attracted to physically active men and so I started making changes. In the past six months, I've been dating a lot. Mostly women Tony has set me up with, but I haven't found anyone I've liked very much," he admitted, in disappointment.

Kit patted him on the shoulder. "Welcome to my life," she said, with a grin.

Hunter's eyes brightened and he motioned her to follow him. "End of the tour. But I want to show you my favorite place," he said, and opened the door to his back deck that looked out onto the water. The sun was starting to set and the colors of the sky were heartbreakingly beautiful. She closed her eyes and tried to drink in the color through her pores, as she felt for the first time in weeks at peace.

"You're the most beautiful woman I've ever seen," Hunter said quietly, looking at her with hopeless eyes.

Kit opened her eyes and grinned at him. "Why do you sound so sad about that," she asked, feeling her heart warm at the sincere compliment.

"Because, a woman like you, would never take me seriously," he said simply, smiling a little, before turning his body to lean against the railing, as he looked out over the water.

Kit stared in silence at the man in front of her and took a few moments to look deeper. She could see past the shiny new exterior, Hunter was wearing, to the slightly shy, insecure but brilliant man underneath. She leaned her arms on the railing next to him and bumped his hip with hers.

"Hunter, I've been judged by my looks this last week, and it didn't feel so good. I might not take the motorcycle and the unbuttoned shirts seriously, but the nerdy, little genius underneath it all. . . *I like*."

Hunter looked down at his hands before looking at her in the softening light. "Do you mean that? I know we don't know each other that well yet, but I'd *like* to get to know you . . . on a real level. *Not,* just as friends," he clarified, as his cheeks turned slightly red.

Kit turned her head and smiled at him and felt something inside her urging her to say yes. "What's your last name, Hunter?"

Hunter grinned sheepishly, looking away. "Hunter. My name is actually, Winston C. Hunter."

Kit smiled and looked out over the water. "Did Tony tell you to go by your last name?"

Hunter laughed and shook his head. "Nah, all my friends call me Hunter. The first game I sold was all about this Vampire soldier, who hunted werewolves. Anyways, that's what I answer to these days."

Kit turned to say something, and then changed her mind and ran a hand down a strand of long blond streaked hair. "All right then, Hunter, would you like a haircut? I used to make extra money in college by giving haircuts."

Hunter smiled but looked nervous. "Tony said this was the best style for my face shape and personal style, but it does get on my nerves. I have to put it in a ponytail when I work. *Which I hate.* If you promise I won't look like an idiot, I'll say yes."

Kit pulled on his arm and they headed back inside. "I wouldn't do that to you."

A half an hour later, Kit stood back proudly as she ran her hands over Hunter's broad shoulders, brushing the hair off. Hunter was staring at himself in the mirror with a happy grin as he ran his hands through his short, slightly spiky hair. She'd cut his hair so it was longer on top, in the middle, and had ran a little hair gel through the ends, giving him a modern, edgy look, which fit him *so* much better than the male stripper look, his stylist was pushing him towards.

Kit stared at him in the mirror and felt a little flip in her stomach. *Holy crap.* Winston was hot. She looked quickly down at her hands as she realized two things. Hunter was a genuinely sweet guy. *And, she could be in trouble.*

Hunter stood up and turned around, plucking the scissors out of her hands before putting his hands on her shoulders. "*Hey.* Look at me," he insisted.

Kit looked up, suddenly shy now for some reason. Hunter looked down at her, his clear blue eyes, traveling over her face slowly before he leaned down closer. "Thank you."

Kit bit her lip and smiled back at him. "For what?"

Hunter ran his hand through her long red waves and then touched his finger to her eyebrow, tracing the curve before answering. "Because you're kind. You looked past all of my stupid pretenses and saw *me*. You never once laughed at me. And you still like me, in spite of everything," he said, pausing as if he weren't sure what to do next.

Kit sighed as she put her hands on Hunter's waist and went up on her tip toes and kissed him lightly on the lips. "Not, inspite. *Because.*"

Hunter's eyes turned bright before pulling her back and taking charge of the kiss. He kissed her with more finesse and skill than Kit imagined a man who'd spent most of his life designing video games, should have.

When Hunter pulled back, she stared at him in surprise, willing her heart rate to slow down. "*Wow,*" she whispered, and then kissed him again.

On the ride back home, Kit had a good half hour to think, as she held tight to Hunter's rock hard stomach. She'd been able to see through Hunter to Winston. Why hadn't Rob been able to see past her exterior, to the real her? Underneath her looks, was just a vulnerable woman who was tired of being hurt. *Just like him.*

Hunter on the other hand, looked at her like she was the most beautiful, incredible woman in the world. Now that she thought about it, it was almost exactly the same way Michael looked at Layla. She blinked in surprise and felt a tremor race down her spine. She leaned her head against Hunter's back and wondered for a moment. Life really could be surprising.

Chapter Seven

THE CONTRACT

Kit spent the next two days working, and trying to put the subject of men to the side. Rob had sent a few large bouquets of flowers to the bakery with beautifully written apologies. She had read them with Layla on one shoulder and Jane on the other and hadn't felt any emotional response to the flowery words.

"I bet you a million dollars his mom or one of his sisters wrote these," Layla said with a derisive sniff, before walking to the back room.

Kit frowned at the loopy handwriting and rolled her eyes. Seriously, *what adult man has their mother write their apologies for them?*

Jane snatched the card out of her hand and threw it in the trash. "The flowers are pretty though. I'll give Rob credit for those," Jane said, before grabbing the broom and sweeping the store.

Kit stared at the card in the trash and sighed. She was so *under*whelmed by Rob that she could barely remember what it felt like to be in the same room with him and be so attracted to him, that she couldn't even remember her own name. That seemed like forever ago. But Jane was right. *The flowers were gorgeous,* she thought with a smile and then got back to work.

Layla breezed back into the store with a tray of Jane's straw-berry cheesecake cupcakes. "He's only crawling on his hands and knees because he wants your bread. He's more worried about money than he is your feelings. If he was worried about your feelings, he would have written the stinking cards himself," she said coldly, as she began to place the cupcakes on the glass shelves.

Kit frowned and looked at her feet. *Ahh.* She should have known. So strange, a man being more worried about himself than her. *Not.*

"No worries, girls. I've got Rob's number now. I've seen the real Rob and no amount of bouquets will erase the memory," she said firmly and with a bright smile.

Layla nodded at her proudly. "That's my girl," she said, and ran a hand down Kit's long red ponytail.

Jane nodded sadly. "I still think it's just so crappy though. I really, *really* wanted you two to end up together. Why do good looking guys have to be so ugly on the inside?"

Layla snorted. "Really, Jane? Because Garrett is gorgeous and from what Michael tells me, he's even better looking on the inside."

Jane sighed and grinned happily. "He is an exception to the rule, isn't he?"

Layla laughed. "There is no rule. There are beautiful men who are beautiful, and ugly men who are ugly, and ugly men who are gorgeous on the inside and beautiful men who are hideous on the inside. No generalizations. Look at Michael," she said, and then closed her eyes with a small smile on her mouth.

Jane and Kit shared a laughing look and got back to work. Now that the wedding was so close, Layla spent all of her spare time smiling, thinking about Michael and Stella or *talking* about Michael and Stella.

With ten minutes till closing, a Fed Ex guy walked in with a small package. "Kit Kendall?"

Kit frowned and walked toward the man holding the clipboard out to her. "If this is another gift from Rob I'm going to throw it in the garbage," she muttered, as Jane and Layla joined her at a table. Kit thanked the Fedex guy and then started tearing the box apart.

She took out a long, black box and went pale. If he had bought her jewelry she was going to be furious. *What an idiot*, she thought, already getting mad as she opened the heavy box.

It was not jewelry.

It was a pair of bright, gold hair cutting scissors. Kit picked up the scissors in her hand and snipped the air with them, as a grin split her face in half. Now Hunter was a man who knew how to give a gift. She put the scissors down and picked up the box. There was a tiny, white card on the bottom. She pulled out the card and read,

Turns out the way to a man's heart, is not his stomach.
It's his hair.
– Your biggest fan,
Winston

Kit laughed as she remembered cutting Hunter's hair.

Layla looked at Kit's face and her eyebrows went up an inch. "Jane, notice what happens when a man writes his own notes."

"Who the heck is *Winston?*" Jane asked, with a curious smile on her face.

Kit sighed and picked up her new hair cutting scissors again. "Winston is Hunter, my blind date from Saturday night. He's one of those men who are beautiful in *both* ways," she said softly.

Layla looked doubtful. "Michael told me about Hunter. He's not exactly the kind of guy you're used to going out with, Kit. He's a genius geek. Cute, granted, but can you really see yourself with a guy who will talk your ear off about levels and points and all that gamer stuff?"

Kit looked at Layla with a frown. "Does Michael talk your ear off every night about liens and offers and addendums?"

Layla narrowed her eyes at Kit and put her hands on her hips. "Well, no, of course not, but Hunter is like a King in his little video game world. He has fan sites that get thousands of hits a day. He's big time, Kit. And you're a baker. I just don't see what you two have in common," she said bluntly, watching her sister's face closely for her reaction.

Kit glared at Layla hotly and crossed her arms. "You don't even know Hunter, Layla. He's the sweetest man I've ever met. The only time he bored me with all of his big time gamer life, was at the party and he only did that because his image consultant told him he had to brag about his success in order to impress girls. As soon as I told him he didn't need to impress me, he showed me who he really is. *A sweetheart.* He's kind, good, thoughtful *and real.*"

Layla grinned and shook her head. "Well, I wanted your honest opinion of Hunter and you just gave it to me. He has my blessing. Just don't use those scissors to kill Rob. They're too easily traceable," she said, as she switched the sign to CLOSED.

Kit took her scissors and her card from Hunter upstairs, leaving the large bouquets of flowers ignored in the store. She flopped on her bed and pillowed her head on her arms as she thought of the two men in her life. Rob had pulled at her heart for months, but now she was cutting herself loose. Hunter on the other hand, was a big, happy, wonderful surprise. One she wouldn't take for granted.

When Wednesday arrived though, Kit found herself a little tense and anxious. She'd bragged to Layla and Jane about not caring if she had dinner with Rob and his mother, but the truth was, she'd rather do *anything* other than go to the Downing home and be in the same room as Rob and his mother. She couldn't even imagine a more awkward dinner. But at least she would have her sisters with her and Layla wouldn't allow anyone to bully her. She just had to realize that this was all about the bread. Anne and Rob had one goal tonight and one only. To do or say anything they had to in order to get her bread back in their restaurant.

She'd overheard Michael tell Layla how horrible the bread was they were using now. It would start affecting business eventually, unless they got back in the Kendall sisters' good graces. She was trying so hard to be mature. There was really no reason to turn their back on a lucrative business relationship, because the owner of the restaurant was an insulting idiot. *Really*.

She went through her day in a very serene mood, but when it came time to close up shop and get ready for dinner, she felt a little short of breath. Jane and Layla looked at her worriedly as they took off their aprons and locked up. Kit sighed and straightened her shoulders and put on a big smile.

"Can't wait to see what Rob and Anne cooked up for their big suck up dinner. I hope it's amazing, because I'm starving," she said, with a casual smile.

Layla's face relaxed and Jane laughed softly. "Kit, I was thinking we should cancel. I was thinking dinner with the Downing's has to be a disaster," Jane said.

Kit winced and silently agreed but tried to laugh. "No biggie. Let's just get this over with and then we can get back to normal. How are we going to handle their groveling? All they want is our bread back. Should we be gracious or cold and Godfather-ish?"

Layla ran her hands through her hair and considered. "Michael is convinced that we'll handle this in a mature and logical manner. I couldn't bring myself to guarantee it though," she said, with a wicked grin. "Rob says one thing to upset you ,and he'll never see our bread again in this lifetime."

Kit hugged Layla. "You're the best. Now, if you'll excuse me, I've got to go primp so he suffers just a little, knowing he could have been with me, but threw it all away."

Jane smiled sadly at her sister. "Poor guy. Worst decision of his life."

Kit changed into slim, white capris and a bright lime green square, cut t-shirt with white sandals. She pulled her long red hair up into a deceptively simple looking bun and made sure her makeup was perfect. She looked casual yet amazing. *Perfect.*

An hour later, as they walked up to Anne's modest home, Kit sighed tiredly. The sooner this night was over, the sooner she could shut the door on Rob and all of her useless daydreams about the two of them being together.

Anne opened the door before Layla even touched the door-bell. She was wearing a bright red shirt and black skirt and her dark hair was poofier than usual. Her lipstick matched her shirt and her eyes were bright and alert. She was ready for battle.

"Hello! Come in, come in," she said, waving her hand in the air like a traffic cop on steroids.

Jane looked back at Kit with a raised eyebrow. Kit ignored her and kept her serene smile in place. She would smile throughout the whole evening even if it killed her.

"Come into the dining room. Rob is just about done setting the table," she said, smiling brightly at all three women.

Kit followed Layla and Jane into the small dining room and glanced around. The home must have been built sometime in the seventies, but had been remodeled recently. The table was beautiful cherry wood and the chairs were exquisitely carved and obviously expensive. Looked like Rob enjoyed spoiling his mom.

Rob walked in carrying a platter of steaming, grilled salmon. Their eyes collided and his eyes went large. He breathed in deeply and set the platter down.

"Hi," he said softly, looking at her with a half-smile, calcu-lated to charm.

Kit nodded her head and gave him an impersonal smile. "Hey, Rob. Smells great."

Rob blinked in surprise and nodded before greeting Layla and Jane. Anne and Rob had them seated and served within minutes, being courteous and more solicitous than even the Iron Skillet's best waitress.

As soon as they picked up their forks, Anne folded her hands on the table and leaned forward.

"Girls, let's stop messing around here. What will it take to fix this misunderstanding? Now, as a woman, I *know* how annoying men can be. And from what Rob has told me, he really put his foot in it. But he's sorry. Kit, you *have* to know how sorry he is. He's just sick that he hurt your feelings. So let's just put this in the past and move on, shall we?"

Layla put down her fork, patted her lips with a napkin and then copied Anne by folding her hands and leaning forward.

"Anne, we realize that not having our bread in your restaurant must be hard. Especially since it was because of *our* bread, that Rob got a good review. I already have a new contract for our bread at Jacque's, a new place down by the Point . So, the fact is, we don't need The Iron Skillet. And we especially don't need to work with someone who demeaned my sister. We appreciate that you invited us over for dinner, but from where I'm sitting, I don't see the point in continuing a relationship with Rob *or* his restaurant."

Anne's mouth fell open and she swallowed hard, before looking at Rob. "Baby, you're on your own. This one's tough," she said, staring at Layla with a surprised frown.

Kit snorted lightly and looked down in her lap with a grin. Layla was still ticked. *Wow.*

Rob cleared his throat and patted his mom's hands. "It's okay. I'm the one who messed up. What kind of man would I be, to let my mother fix my problems," he said pleasantly.

"Kit, please forgive me," he said, ignoring Layla, Jane and his mom, and staring at her, as if it were only them in the room.

Kit looked away from Rob's intense gaze, and stared down at her plate. "Sure, Rob. It's no big deal," she said simply, and smiled at Rob, before picking up her fork and taking a bite of salmon.

Rob's face twisted in confusion. "*Wait*, um . . . I thought you were mad at me, because of what happened at the party?"

Kit shrugged. "I was really shocked at how you acted and the things you said to me. I admit, I was pretty upset that first night, because I was under the impression that you were a nice guy. But now that I know who you really are, it's no big deal. I've made my peace with it and moved on," she said lightly, smiling at Anne to include her in the talk too.

Anne's face mirrored her son's face, as they both looked taken aback. They had obviously been expecting to find her eaten up over Rob's opinion of her. Kit grinned lightly as Jane's foot kicked her under the table. She glanced at Jane and Jane looked like she was about to burst out laughing.

Anne shook her head back and forth slowly. "Wait, I thought you were in love with my boy? Rob, you said Kit was crazy for you and mad because you called her trashy?"

Rob groaned and leaned his head in his hands as Kit continued to eat peacefully. She could actually sense Layla stiffening beside her and feel Jane vibrate with anger.

"Let me clarify the situation, Anne," Layla said, in that cold, smooth voice of hers, that always meant someone was getting ready to get a beat down. "Kit is not, *nor* has she *ever* been, in love with Rob. Although she was shocked at being talked to so disrespectfully, as you can see, she's quite unaffected by Rob's attitude toward women. We're hoping he gets counseling. As a matter of fact, she's involved in a loving, respectful and *mutually* satisfying relationship with a man who we all look up to."

Rob's head whipped up and he glared at Layla furiously, before turning to stare at Kit. "I don't believe it," he said flatly, daring her to speak.

Kit cleared her throat as she kicked Layla under the table. Layla was a pit bull and sometimes had to be reined in.

"Rob," she said softly, in a kind voice that people used with children and the elderly, "Although I admit that I *used* to find you attractive, that is no longer the case. And Layla's right. *I do not love you.* I'm not sure where you got the idea that I did. I'm happy to let you know that I'm dating a wonderful man now, who I . . ." she paused, and looked over Rob's shoulder, as she thought of Hunter. She immediately thought of her golden scissors and grinned before continuing, "Who I really like. He makes me happy. He makes me feel special. I'm actually pretty relieved that everything has turned out the way it has," she said simply, and then smiled at everyone around the table.

Rob tried to smile, but ended up snarling instead. "*Hunter?* Is *that* the man you're talking about? *Are you joking?* He's a loner, a geek, *a nerd.* There is *no* way the two of you could *ever* be together," he stated firmly, and with a decisive nod to his head.

Kit looked at him and laughed at his expression. "Well, we've already deduced that you *don't* know me. I mean, since you thought I wasn't good enough for you to date, how could you know me well enough to know what kind of man would make me happy? Now, I don't really like talking about my personal life, so I think it's time to change the subject. I think you and your mom invited us here tonight to talk about the bread for the restaurant. Not me. And not my love life."

Rob looked stunned and turned to stare at his mom in shock. Anne's eyes were wide and she bit her lip nervously.

"Okay then, honey. Looks like Rob was a little confused about a few things. You're right. Let's just focus on your bread and what we have to do to get our working relationship back on track."

Layla opened her mouth to speak, but Jane jumped in first. "Anne, we've raised our prices fifteen percent in the last week. If you still want to do business with Belinda's Bakery, we'll agree to start bread deliveries tomorrow, *if* you sign this contract accepting the new price," she said, pushing a paper across the table.

Rob snatched the paper off the table, glaring at it so hotly it should have burst into flames. "Insult the Kendall's and get a price hike? That's pretty pathetic business ethics," he said, glaring at Jane and Layla one at a time.

Layla shrugged and stood up. "You're welcome to say no, Rob. I prefer you do. If it were up to me, I wouldn't work with you at all. I had Jane work up a contract because Kit wants everyone to be friends again. I'm not so forgiving though. And my business ethics? I guess that's the perks of being a small business owner. You insult my sister, *you insult me.* Take it or leave it, Rob and stop whining," she said coldly, pushing her chair into the table.

"Thanks for dinner, Anne, it was delicious," Layla said, ignoring the fact that she hadn't taken more than one bite of her food.

Jane stood up too, nodding her head in agreement. "We'll be on our way," she said firmly, and walked over to stand by Layla.

Kit took one more bite of salmon and stood up slowly. If they'd just given her ten more minutes, she could have finished her dinner. She looked over her shoulder at her sisters and winced before looking back at Rob and Anne. "No hard feelings, right? Good luck to you both," she said, and pushed her chair in.

As the three sisters moved toward the hallway leading to the front door, Anne stood up so fast, her chair went flying. "*Wait!* Please, wait, girls. We'll take the price hike. We'll take it. We *have* to have your bread."

Rob ran his hands through his hair and took the paper in front of him and a pen out of his pocket, signing the contract with a flourish. He stood up and walked slowly around the table, coming to stand directly in front of Kit. He held the paper out to her, but pulled it back right as her fingers touched the edge.

"On one condition. You go out with me. I don't believe for a second that you have feelings for another man. I think it's been you and me from the very beginning. No computer geek is going to walk in at the last minute, and steal you away from me. Just give me one date, Kit. And if you can tell me that there are no sparks and that you feel nothing for me after that, then fine. I'll back off. But I demand a chance to redeem myself."

Kit's eyebrows went up an inch and she turned to look at Layla. Rob reached out and grabbed her chin gently between his finger and thumb and shook his head. "No, Kit, this is just between you and me. I want your bread, but I want you more. I don't care what Layla or Jane have to say. I want to know what *you* have to say. A date, Kit. You and me," he said softly, stepping closer to her.

Kit swallowed and frowned, thinking immediately of Hunter. She shook her head, but was stopped when Rob put his hands on her shoulders, making her look up at him.

"Please, let me make it up to you. I was an idiot," he whispered, staring so intently into her eyes, she couldn't even blink.

"*Okay*," she said, before she knew what she was doing.

Rob grinned and let go of her, as Layla put her arm around Kit's shoulders, glaring hotly at him. Jane snatched the contract out of Rob's hands and glared too.

"Talk about ethics," Jane muttered darkly, and pulled Kit out of the room.

Layla and Jane hustled her outside and to their car silently, not saying anything until they were halfway home.

Jane hissed out a breath. "If he even thinks of stepping out of line with you, I'm going to have Garrett break him in half," she swore, looking at her clenched hands, as if she'd be willing to do the job herself.

Kit sighed and leaned back in her seat, frowning. "It's just a date, plus we get our fifteen percent and they get their bread. I feel a little cheap though, like I'm being bartered for money or something," she said, feeling a little freaked out.

Layla's hands clenched the steering wheel so tightly, that her knuckles went white. "You're *not* going. We have a new contract with Jacque's and we don't owe the Iron Skillet or Rob anything," she said, in a murderous voice.

Jane and Layla growled and complained and snarled the rest of the way home. Kit ignored them for the most part and went upstairs to her room, flopping on her bed with a groan. *Why couldn't life just be simple?*

Chapter Eight

CHOICES

Kit rolled on her side and grabbed her phone, so she could check her messages. She saw a new message from an email address she didn't recognize, monsterhunter 562@ . . . Kit clicked on the email and watched an image appear on her screen. *It was her!* In cartoon form, but still, *that was her.* Kit watched as her cartoon image did the Floss dance move and then jumped up, and the screen was filled with giant robots. Her cartoon character started throwing loaves of bread at the robots. Every time she hit a robot with her bread, the robot exploded in sparks and hearts.

Kit grinned, mesmerized by her computer screen. And then her character jumped up again and when she landed, she was wearing a long flowing white dress and holding a paintbrush in one hand. Kit grinned as her image began to paint enthusiastically on a large canvas. When her image was done seconds later, she turned the canvas around and looked right at her. Kit's breath hitched in her throat as she read the words,

You're amazing. I had no idea my new barber was the same artist who painted this . . .

Kit gasped as the words on the canvas disappeared and what looked like a painting she'd done two years ago, named

Choices, appeared on the screen. It was a painting she'd done of a woman, swaying in the wind, surrounded by twelve arms in different positions. It almost looked like she was dancing, except for the look on the woman's face. Torn and confused. It had been a self-portrait, not that she'd realized it at the time. It had been one of her favorites and she'd hated to part with it. She'd sold it to a man who had been purchasing artwork for an office building. It had been sell or starve. She'd picked survival.

Kit reached out and touched the screen and the image disappeared. Now the screen slowly lightened until the new image was a picture of Hunter, standing in front of her actual painting, smiling.

What?

Under the picture of Hunter were the words, *Call me. I need help hanging my painting.*

Kit closed her eyes as she felt a sense of joy overtake her. She'd get to see her painting again! And a man she liked and respected, now owned it. Her paintings were like children, her creations. She'd get to see it and touch it again.

Today was a very good day.

"Yay!" she squealed, and jumped off the bed, grabbing her phone as she ran for the door. She hopped in her car less than a minute later and called Hunter. He answered immediately.

"Hunter! You have my painting!" she practically yelled, in the phone.

Hunter laughed, "Yes I do. Come see me," he said simply.

Kit grinned and drove faster. "I'm in my car right now."

"I'll expect you in twenty minutes then," he said, and disconnected.

Kit threw her phone on the seat and turned the music up loud. She took the pins out of her hair, letting it fall all around her shoulders as she sang as loudly as she could to *Cake* by Flo Rida and then moved on to *No tears left to cry,* by Ariana Grande. By the time she reached Hunter's house, she was in such a good mood, she ran to the front door, ripping it open and going in without even waiting for Hunter to open the door.

"*Where are you?*" she yelled, with her hands up to her mouth.

"I'm in my room. Come on up," Hunter shouted, from upstairs.

Kit took the stairs two at a time and reached Hunter's bedroom, breathless and grinning. She scanned the large, light filled room and saw Hunter holding her picture in his arms against the far wall. He glanced back at her and raised an eyebrow.

"What do you think? Is this a good spot? It's been empty forever. I wanted the perfect painting and now I have it," he said, with a shy smile.

Kit's eyes warmed as she put her hands on her hips and stared at her painting. She felt a happy sigh leave her, as she stared at the painting that had haunted her and even defined her at times.

"Are you sure you want it in your bedroom? It's kind of an intimate place, and this painting *is* . . ." she stopped, looking away as a blush washed over her cheeks.

Hunter's smile faded as he leaned the painting on the floor and looked at her quietly. "*You?* Yes, I know. If you're uncomfortable having your painting in my room, I'll hang it somewhere else," he said, smiling at her.

Kit relaxed and shook her head. "No, you hang it wherever you want to. It's yours," she said, walking over to him. She stood next to him and touched the frame, tilting the painting back and staring at the face she knew so well. "You'll never know what this means to me that you have this painting and it's not in some soulless office building somewhere, being ignored or mocked."

Hunter put a hand on her shoulder and cleared his throat. "Well, that soulless office building ,was mine. When it came time to decorate the office, the team I hired to design and decorate, was given the instructions to buy edgy, passionate and unique artwork. I've stared at this painting for *years* wondering about the artist. And then when I met you at the party, I kept thinking about this painting. So I went up to Seattle this morning for a meeting, and I went right to it. I knew it was you," he said, with a satisfied grin.

Kit smiled back and leaned up and kissed Hunter on the cheek. "You, Hunter, are an angel. Hold it up and I'll tell you if it's straight or not," she said, stepping away and walking back to the opposite side of the room.

"Nope, go a few inches to your right. *Hmm*, maybe one inch higher. No, you went too far. *Okay!* Right there. Stop," she ordered loudly, clapping her hands together as Hunter carefully marked the spot and then set the painting down. He hammered the nail in place and hung her painting carefully on the wall. He walked over and stood next to her as they looked at the painting together.

"I remember the first time I saw it. It was like a punch to the gut," he said, his arm draped casually around her shoulders.

Kit looked up at him curiously. "What did it make you feel?" she couldn't help asking.

Hunter shrugged and ran his free hand over the back of his neck. "The woman is so lost. She's coming undone. It made me feel sad, but mostly protective."

Kit closed her eyes and let her head fall forward, her red hair curtaining her face. She took a deep breath and wondered what in the world she was going to do with a man who could see her that clearly. Hunter moved in front of her and pushed her hair back, tilting her face up by her chin.

"Hey," he said softly, caressing her cheek. "I didn't mean to make you sad. You're not that woman anymore, you know. When I look at you, I see someone determined and strong. And beautiful," he said, before kissing her gently on one cheek and then the other.

Kit nodded, looking up into his crystal, blue eyes. "Thank you," she said simply, not knowing what other two words would fit.

Hunter's eyes crinkled at the sides as he studied her. "For what?"

Kit shook her head a little. "For seeing me back then, and seeing me now, and finding something to like in both of us," she said slowly, trying to make sense of what she was feeling.

Hunter sighed and pulled her into his arms, hugging her warmly and securely in his arms. "The pleasure is all mine. Come on, let's go celebrate. My mom brought me over a home-made, peach pie this afternoon. Let's go have a piece on my back deck," he said, taking her hand and leading her out of the room.

Kit watched Hunter serve up two huge pieces of pie and followed him outside to his deck. She sat down on his oversized lounge chair and took her plate. She took a quick bite as Hunter sat down and froze. It was sweet and fresh tasting as if the peaches had just been picked that morning. The light syrup was so tangy and flavorful she closed her eyes and groaned as Hunter laughed at her reaction.

"Your mom is the one who needs to open a bakery," she said, licking her lips and looking over at Hunter, who was watching her intently. He shook himself and took a bite of his pie before answering.

"She's thought about it, but she doesn't want the hassle of running a business. She loves baking pies though. You should taste her cherry pie. Every pie she makes is from the fruit she grows from her own trees. Completely organic. You should meet her. I think you'd like her," he said carefully, looking at her quickly to gauge her reaction.

Kit smiled and nodded. "I would love to meet your mom. At the very least to offer her a job at Belinda's Bakery. But mostly to tell her that she must be an amazing mom, because she raised one of the nicest, sweetest men I've ever known," she said, smiling at Hunter's flustered expression.

"Kit, I'm not trying to be nice or anything, I honestly *do* think you're an incredible artist. Not to put down your baking skills, but what in the world are you doing making bread, when you could be painting?" he asked, with a frown.

Kit sat back and took another bite of pie. After a few moments she smiled at Hunter and shrugged. "Have you heard the term, *starving artist*? It's a saying for a reason. It's almost impossible to actually support yourself with your art. Heaven knows, I tried. Every time you're lucky enough to get a showing, you pray that an art critic will stop by, who will usher your way into the spotlight. Or, you sell a few paintings, and you're living the dream. Life is perfect. And then, bam. *Nothing*. You go a year without selling anything and you begin to doubt yourself. You doubt your talent and your purpose. *And you lose hope*," she said sadly, laying her plate down on the deck, and then sitting back as she stared at the moody clouds, floating overhead.

Hunter stared at her silently for a while, and set his plate down too. He turned his body so he was facing her and leaned his arms on his knees as he leaned forward.

"I hate that you ever once doubted yourself or your talent," he said softly, reaching out to touch the back of her hand with his finger.

Kit smiled and shrugged off his pity. "It's okay. I've made my peace with it. And I really love baking and working with my sisters. In my free time, I've been painting, so I haven't lost that part of myself. It's just not my *sole* purpose now like it used to be. I actually think I'm a better painter now because of it," she admitted.

Hunter looked at her doubtfully. "*Sure*."

Kit laughed and turned on her side to face him. "I was trying so hard and focusing everything I had into my painting. I was desperate and it wasn't fun anymore. And it started to show. Now, when I paint, it's a treasure. A treat. I relish every second I spend painting. And it brings me joy again. It's good, Hunter. Don't feel bad for me. I have it all now. Income, a home *and* painting in my free time. Which I have a lot of," she said ruefully.

Hunter tilted his head and smiled at her expression. "Why do you have so much free time?"

Kit laughed and pushed her hair away from her face. "I don't have much of a social life. I look at my older sister, Layla, and all of her time is spent on Michael and Stella. Which is awesome and she's so happy, but it doesn't leave her much time for a hobby. Even Jane is dating now. You might know him? Michael's friend, Garrett?"

Hunter nodded. "I've met him a few times. Super nice guy. He gave me some workout tips and offered to go to the gym with me," he said, as he looked away over the water. "You know, Kit, you could have a social life *and* paint. You'd just have to pick a man who understands that painting is a part of who you are. Someone who would love to see you use your talent," he said, now looking at her intensely.

Kit looked back and then blushed. *Okay.* Hunter was going somewhere with this conversation. But was she ready for where it was going?

"Speaking of dating," she said, changing the subject and using Rob as an excuse. "You wouldn't believe what I got myself into today," she said, and then told Hunter everything about her situation with Rob and the fifteen percent hike and the date she was now stuck going on.

Hunter's eyes narrowed and he looked angry for a moment before his face cleared and he smiled at her, even though his eyes looked dark. "Rob really said that to you?" he said, shaking his head in disgust.

Kit shrugged, still bothered by it, if she was being honest. "Yeah. I have to admit that when I first moved to Fircrest, I kind of liked him. I'm starting to think I might have bad taste in men."

Hunter stood up and held out a hand to her, pulling her over to the railing so they could look at the boats on the water and the sunset beginning to turn the sky orange.

"Let's do an experiment then. How about you start dating *me* and see how that goes? I'm not a jerk and I would treat you like you deserve to be treated. After dating me for a while, you might find that you enjoy dating a man who respects you, and is in awe that you even exist," he said, staring at her so earnestly and sweetly, that her heart stuttered and she felt her mouth fall open.

"*Hunter* . . . ," she began, and then looked away. "You're too nice for me. I'd probably run over you and through you," she said, with a shake of her head.

Hunter stared at her like she was insane and shook his head. "You'd be an adventure. Loving you . . . I *mean,* dating you, would be like stepping into one of your paintings. Lots of light and edges and passion and life. *I want that,*" he said, reaching out and pulling her toward him.

Kit's eyes went wide and she looked over his shoulder at the water turning choppy and dark. "Hunter, I don't know what to say. I like you. *A lot,* to be honest. I don't know that I've ever actually liked any of my past boyfriends. But you're so different from me . . ." she said, and stopped, seeing that Hunter's face had turned hard and his eyes withdrawn.

"You don't want to date me because you're not attracted to me? Is that what you're trying to say?" Hunter asked softly, with pain in his eyes.

Kit winced and shook her head fiercely back and forth, reaching up to grasp his shoulders in her hands. "No! It's not that, at all. I think you're very attractive. *I'm* very attracted to you. I just don't . . . *hmmm,*" she said, and paused as she looked away, thinking for a moment.

Hunter's eyes went sharp and he pulled her face back to his. "*What?*"

Kit blushed. "I guess what I'm trying to say is, *why not?*"

Hunter looked at her in stunned silence for a moment, before grabbing her and twirling her around making enough loud whooping noises for a football game. He held her tightly and then slowly let her down as he stared wonderingly down into her face.

"Are you sure? I'll probably drive you crazy. I've already designed a character for my newest game based on you."

Kit laughed and ran her hands through his newly trimmed hair before stepping back. "I promise I'll drive you just as crazy. I'm already planning on setting up my easel right over there, so I can paint. I'll get in your way all the time, and I'll probably force you to be my model."

Hunter laughed and ran his hands down her long, red hair. "Let me know when you get to something negative. Those things all sound wonderful to me," he said, smiling down into her eyes before he looked at her seriously. "But there is one thing I'd have to insist on. I'm kind of an old fashioned guy. If we were together, I wouldn't want you to date anyone else. Just like, I wouldn't date anyone but you."

Kit's grin faded as she nodded her head. She looked down and realized her arms were securely wrapped around Hunter's waist. Exclusivity. Monogamy. *No Rob then*. She smiled and relaxed against Hunter's chest, as she laid her head against his heart.

"Then it's settled. Winston, you're now my honey."

Kit felt a kiss on her hair and closed her eyes as a sweet peacefulness enveloped her. Before, when she'd dated, she'd always gone into the relationship on edge, unsure of herself and insecure. Being with Hunter was a new and wonderful feeling. Kit looked up into Hunter's bright, happy eyes and grinned before he leaned down and kissed her, wrapping her in his arms so securely, she felt utterly safe and cherished.

They spent the rest of the evening talking about art and kayaking. Hunter was already planning on taking her out Saturday. Kit found herself asking him about the video games he designed and the world of gaming.

"We have huge conventions all over the country. I show up and say a few words about the next game I'm designing and answer questions. Kids and adults will come dressed up as their favorite characters from my games. It's a lot of fun. The next convention I'm going to is in a few weeks up in Seattle. It's one of the bigger ones. It covers everything from games to movies to comic books. And everyone dresses up as a character."

Kit sat next to him on the large, comfortable couch in his family room, as she played with the buttons on his shirt and traced the veins on his hand and ran her hands through his hair. She'd never been touchy feely before. In every other relationship she'd had, she'd always been a little cold and distant, unsure of whether or not she could trust the guy. One man she had dated for a few weeks, had even called her an ice princess. But it wasn't that she was cold. She'd just always been unsure and nervous. Uneasy. Now, with Hunter, she was so completely at ease and comfortable, she could relax and be herself. Turns out, she was kind of playful.

"So, who are you going to dress up as?" she asked, leaning back into his arms and wrapping her arm around his waist.

Hunter obviously felt it was his turn to play, because he began pulling his fingers through her hair as if he were fascinated by the texture and length and feel of it. "I'm going as a classic, Gandalf, from Lord of the Rings. Last year, I dressed up as Spider Man and the year before that, I went a little dark and went as Loki."

Kit laced her hand through his and laughed a little. "I would actually love to see that. Who should I dress up as?" she asked.

Hunter leaned his head back as he considered it seriously. "I've always had a thing for Princess Leia, to be honest and your hair is long enough to do the side buns. Maybe you should come with me," he said softly, almost hesitantly.

Kit turned and looked at him. "Of course, I'll go with you. Where else would I be?"

Hunter traced the ridge of her nose, coming down to lightly touch her lips. "You make me happy," he said softly, smiling slightly as his eyes softened.

Kit stared back into Hunter's eyes, and saw something there

that made her heart ache. She kissed him lightly, but pushed him back when he leaned forward to kiss her again.

"Hunter, we're just starting out, so of course everything is new and wonderful and perfect. But, if I ever start making you miserable, I want you to promise to tell me."

Hunter frowned and shook his head. "Fine, I promise, but there's no way that could ever happen."

Kit sighed and stood up, stretching her back. "Well, my boyfriend, I must depart. I have to get up at 4:00. Why don't you walk me to my car?"

Hunter stood up and walked her outside, both of them lost in their thoughts. Kit lifted her face to the cool breeze off the water and turned to hug Hunter. He had a way of wrapping his arms around her that made her feel adored and yet safe.

"Text me when you get home so I know you made it back safely," he said, opening her door for her.

Kit raised an eyebrow and laughed. "You have got to be kidding me."

Hunter looked sheepishly down at his shoes and put his hands in his pockets. "Sorry, I guess that could come across as annoying. In my defense though, I've never actually had a girl-friend to worry about. I've dated and socialized and all that stuff. But yeah, uh, *you matter*," he said, looking embarrassed.

Kit grinned and gave Hunter a light kiss before sliding into her seat. "That's so sweet, I think I might actually text you when I get home," she said, turning the key.

Hunter leaned down and rested his arms on her window as he smiled at her. "If you don't, I'll probably stay up all night wondering, but sure, if you get around to it."

Kit looked down at her steering wheel for a second before looking back up at Hunter. She stared into his blue eyes, still shocked that they'd just agreed to be together.

"You make me happy too," she said simply, and watched as his eyes did that funny thing where they crinkled at the edges and started to sparkle like someone had just lit a firecracker.

Hunter leaned in and kissed her lightly. "That's kind of the way it's supposed to be. Good night, Beautiful," he said and stood up.

Kit watched him in her rearview mirror as he stood there in the last of the light, watching her car drive away and felt her heart flip over. *Wow.*

Chapter Nine

REVIEWS

Kit woke up the next day so full of energy, she skipped down the stairs. She flipped on the light and began the bread, smiling at her sisters as they both yawned and nodded at her silently. She docked her I-pod and selected Layla's favorite ,the Lumineers, and hummed along as they worked efficiently in their three separate corners of the kitchen. It always took about an hour for everyone to fully wake up and begin talking and singing and in most cases, dancing.

Eventually, Layla walked over and selected Taylor Swift's newest and Kit grinned her approval. She had to sing as loud as she could to hit the high note, but this was a morning for joy and she was going to hit that note or die trying. At the end of the song, Kit opened her eyes and noticed Layla and Jane were staring at her with their mouths open.

"What in the world has happened to you, Kit? You're singing and dancing around the kitchen like a New York musical. She's lost it, Layla. The woman is crazy," Jane said suspiciously.

Layla tilted her head and looked at her closely. "Not crazy. *Happy*. Spill it, Kit. What's going on that you haven't told us yet?"

Kit checked her bread, already rising and shrugged. "I don't know, I guess it's just kind of nice to be off the market. To not have to wonder or care if you're asked out or not asked out," Kit paused, and leaned against the counter as she looked at her feet for a moment. "It's just so nice to know that there's someone out in the world who cares about you and whether or not you make it home safely," she said, sighing with a soft smile on her face.

Layla's smile faded as she star,ed at Kit with a frown. "*You're kidding me.* I'm a little surprised I guess. I was shocked when you said okay to the black mail, *but this?* This is a little much. Rob is such a jerk. I thought you were through falling for idiots."

Jane shook her head in disgust. "I'm not having it, Kit. I'm not watching you get hurt again. He doesn't even know you!" she yelled, and then flung her hands in the air in disgust before turning and stomping away from her sister, to the opposite side of the kitchen.

Kit blinked in surprise and stood up, holding her hand up as if she were in class and needed to be called on.

"I think there's been a little misunderstanding. I was talking about *Hunter*," she said, and watched with a smile as Layla and Jane rushed back to her, yelling, laughing and jumping up and down as they demanded all the details.

Kit grinned and went over to the fridge to grab a water bottle. As her sisters joined her, she told them about the email and her painting and everything that followed.

Layla sat back with a satisfied smile and sighed. "I love Hunter. That man *sees* you. He sees all the incredible sharp and beautiful facets of your soul."

Jane nodded leaning on her arms as she looked at her sister. "I would have never called you ending up with a computer genius, but it works. We need to have Hunter over for dinner. I think Layla and I should have a chance to interview your young man and make sure he has good intentions," she teased.

Kit shrugged and stood up. "He would probably love that. He's already mentioned that he wants me to meet his mom. And I tasted her peach pie last night. You. Would. *Die.* It is so good."

Layla paused and then laughed out loud, biting her lip as more giggles threatened to come out. "Oh, my word, Kit. What are you going to do about Rob? What about our 15% price hike and that date you said you'd go on? He is going to be furious. He was already ticked when he found out you were *dating* Hunter. What's he going to do when he finds out you're *together,* together?"

Jane's eyes narrowed and she smiled coldly. "He's going to realize what an idiot he was. Kit, you are *not* going on a date with him. I won't allow it," she said firmly.

Kit snorted and shook her head. "You're my little sister. What do you mean, *you won't allow it?* But regardless, Hunter has already made it very clear that we are exclusive and monogamous and everything else. He wouldn't want me to date Rob. Even for fifteen percent," she said, and turned the ovens on to warm up.

Layla nodded her head. "We'll take it down to a ten percent hike, and leave it at that. No dates. I'll text Rob and let him know."

Kit put the lid on her water and got back to work. Sounded good to her. Last night when Rob had been staring at her and insisting on having a second chance to redeem himself, she had wondered if he'd only been interested in her because he couldn't have her now. Maybe Rob was one of those men who were interested in the chase and the unattainable. Now that she was out of reach, he was actually putting forth an effort. She'd left Anne's house last night feeling cold. But now? It was over. Her crush on Rob was gone and her life was now open to bigger and better things. Mainly, Hunter.

When the store opened up a few hours later and the sign had been turned, they were ready. She said hi to their morning clerk and then headed back to the kitchen to work on her design for a wedding cake coming up. Layla had volunteered to make the bread delivery that morning so she was free to sketch and google images and ideas. The bride was twenty-three years old, just out of college and very bright and bubbly. She had requested a three-tier cake with the bottom in bright pink fondant, followed by a bright orange middle and topped with a small striped cake in different shades of hot pink and bright orange. She also wanted molded zinnia flowers in yellow pink and orange scattered all over it. It could end up a hot mess or fun and young. She was hoping for spectacular.

An hour later, Jane wandered back to the kitchen and peeked over her shoulder. "That is so cool," she said quietly.

Kit glanced up and smiled. "I hope so. Hey, why the frown?"

Jane shrugged and glanced back at the store area. "We haven't had any customers this morning. Not one and it's almost ten," she said, her voice laced with worry.

Kit put her pencil down and stared at Jane. "Are you kidding me? We always do our biggest rush in the morning," she said, standing up and walking quickly into the store. Mandee, their clerk, was leaning on her elbows, texting on her phone. She was the only person in the store.

"Something is going on," she said quietly, walking over to the front door and looking out on the quiet street.

Nothing.

Layla walked in a few minutes later from the back and joined them at the front door. "Why are we so dead? What's going on?" she said, sounding exactly like Jane.

Jane frowned and hurried to the kitchen. Kit and Layla followed right behind her and watched as Jane grabbed her laptop and pulled it toward her. Kit stood behind her stool and watched as Jane googled the words, *Belinda's Bakery*. The first thing that popped up was the newspaper article mentioning their bread and Rob's restaurant. Following that were a few mentions of their ad in the papers and a few coupon offers.

Jane put her finger to an article halfway down the page. "That's it."

Kit and Layla leaned forward, practically pushing on Jane as she clicked on the yelp review. Kit gasped and put her hands over her mouth.

What's worse than over-priced muffins and cupcakes? Getting food poisoning from their underdone brownies. I did some digging and these women aren't even professionally trained bakers. They just took over their grandmother's bakery and figured they'd make some money. I'm all for the American Dream, just don't kill me in the process.

Kit glanced at Layla. She looked like she'd been slapped. Jane's shoulders were slumped over and she was leaning her head on her hand. *This was not good.*

"What's the person's name?" Kit demanded.

Jane looked at the screen and clicked the article. "The person who posted the review is listed as anonymous."

Kit sighed and ran her hands through her hair. "This is a disaster. What are we going to do? Even if we post a rebuttal of some sort or find a few friends to put their own reviews up of our bakery, it will take something huge to erase this smear. Who would do that to us?" she asked softly, turning away.

Layla sat down tiredly on a stool and shook her head. "Quite a few people actually. There's Alex Foster. There's our own father, Landon Kendall."

Jane stood up and shut the laptop, turning to face her sisters. "And Rob. He was furious that we didn't sell him our bread this week. And then with the price hike, he could be out for revenge."

Kit's mouth fell open. "No, not Rob. He's Michael's best friend. We got him his good review. There's no way it was him."

Layla pursed her lips and turned to look at Jane. "I wouldn't put it past him."

Jane stood up and untied her apron. "You know I haven't seen Alex around lately. It's been at least a week and a half since he's been in, pestering me to go out with him. Maybe he got sick of hearing no? Plus, he's always been very upfront about us selling to him. He could be trying to ruin us so that we're forced to sell."

Kit sighed and rubbed her head. "Then that means our dad is

involved too. He wants his share of the bakery. He wants half of the money we'd get from selling to Alex."

Layla shook her head. "I bet it's Rob, Kit. We humbled him and a macho guy like that wouldn't take something like that lying down. This is revenge, pure and simple. When I delivered the bread this morning, I was treated like a leper by his employees. He wants to make a statement."

Kit groaned, feeling sick to her stomach. Whoever said running a business was easy though? Kit told Mandee to go home early while Layla made a huge sign for their front window. *Bake Sale! Buy one, Get one Free.* They started getting customers after that and even though they didn't make up half of what they usually sold in a day, at least it wasn't a total waste. Layla took the leftovers to the battered women's shelter and Kit and Jane finished cleaning and mopping.

What started out as a good day, was quickly turning bad. Kit glanced at Jane's laptop and bit her lip. There had to be something they could do. "Jane? Would you mind printing me off a copy of that article? I want to show Hunter. He's a computer guy. Maybe he can find out more about the person who posted it. And if this is Alex, maybe we could sue him for slander or something?"

Jane nodded her head and put her broom down. She opened her laptop and googled the words Belinda's Bakery. But instead of seeing just one bad review pop up, *there were now three.* Kit's mouth fell open as Jane sniffed back tears. "This is a disaster," she whispered.

Jane printed off all the reviews and handed them to Kit. Kit read them, frowning darkly. "I'm no expert, but it feels like these were all written by the same person. This one is signed *Donut Lover* and this one is signed *Chocolate Chip.* Still anonymous. I think we need to show the police. What do you think?"

Jane winced and nodded. "You might be right. I'll call Tate and see what he thinks," she said, sounding stoic.

Kit glanced at her curiously and then walked up the stairs to her room to change into a pair of shorts and a t-shirt. It had been such a stressful day, she needed to paint for a few hours. After calming down, she'd call Hunter and get his take on the situation. He might have insight into their problem.

She grabbed her large case of paints and brushes and the canvas she'd been working on for weeks and headed outside to the lush and fragrant backyard. It was one of her all-time favorite places to paint. It was quiet, serene and all hers. Well, except for Bubba. Bubba greeted her with a friendly howl and then went back to sleep in the shade. She walked over and made sure his dishes were full of water and food. He was good.

Her new painting was called *Fallen*. It was a picture of a woman bursting free from black feathers. It was one of her darker paintings, but it made her feel good. Anytime she was hurt or in pain, painting helped her get it out of her system so it didn't swim around poisoning her. Kit worked until the light started fading and then started cleaning up. She smiled tiredly as she climbed the steps to the house. She set down her paint box to open the door, when someone beat her to it.

Rob.

In her house.

"Hi, Kit, let me help you there," he said reaching for her painting.

Kit stepped back automatically, frowning. She didn't like other people touching her canvasses until they were sold. She was very territorial.

"No, that's okay. Rob, *what are you doing here?*" she asked frowning as she moved to step past him into the house.

Rob smiled charmingly at her and followed her into the kitchen. She carefully set her painting on the counter and turned to face him. Someone had to have let him in. Dang, she could have used a little warning.

"I came over with Michael. I just made myself at home. I hope you don't mind," he said, smiling in such a way that let her know there was no way she could have a problem with it.

"Okay. So did you get Layla's text about dropping the hike from fifteen to ten percent?" she asked, watching him as he walked toward her.

"Yeah, but I'll just keep the fifteen percent hike and have the date with you. I'm determined to have my second chance with you, Kit. And you told me you would yesterday. You said, *okay*," he said slowly, moving closer.

Kit scooted away and frowned. "Rob, we took it down to ten, because I'm not going to be going on any dates with you. Things have changed since last night."

Rob's eyes narrowed and he crossed his arms over his chest, highlighting the toned muscles of his arms. "What could have possibly changed in twenty four hours?"

Kit shrugged and moved further away from Rob. "I have a boyfriend now. And he's made it clear that we're exclusive. Out of respect for Hunter's wishes, I'm going to pass on our date," she said, with a friendly smile.

Rob looked up at the ceiling and shook his head. "I'm telling you, Kit, you *can't* be with that guy. He's not the one for you. You need a take charge kind of guy. A man who knows how to be a man. You need me, not that wimp. I don't care how much the guy can bench press now. He doesn't know anything about women," he said, in a hard cruel voice.

Kit felt anger burn in her chest as she stared at Rob. "He knows a lot more than you. I think you should leave now," she said, standing up straight and looking him in the eyes.

Rob glared at her and shook his head. "*No*. You *owe* me. Just one date. One chance for me to show you the difference between Hunter and me. The chance to show you what you're giving up, by being with that geek."

Kit sneered at him and shook her head. "Forget it."

Rob tilted his head and put his hands in his pockets. "You were slammed today in all the papers with bad reviews. What if I could help you fix your little publicity problem?" he asked, in a coaxing voice.

Kit's mouth fell open in surprise. *"It was you,"* she breathed out, her hazel eyes turning to golden fire.

Rob shook his head and held up his hands. "No, Kit, I wouldn't stoop that low. But, I've been in business longer than you girls. When I first started, I got a few bad reviews. I know how to turn things around if you're interested. We'll call it a business dinner," he said, smiling again.

Kit frowned and looked away feeling sick and pulled in two different directions. "As long as it's just business . . . *I'll think about it*. Look, I'm not trying to be mean here. I actually really like Hunter. He makes me happy," she said simply, trying to get Rob to back off.

Her words just seemed to make Rob even angrier though and he left quickly.

Kit turned around and leaned her arms on top of the counter. Almost immediately she felt two strong hands massaging her shoulders. She squeaked and reared back, turning around in fright.

"Hey."

Kit relaxed and melted into Hunter's arms.

"I take it Rob doesn't like the word, *no*, huh?" he said dryly.

Kit pulled back and pushed her hair out of her eyes as she tried to smile. "You could say that. How much did you hear?" she asked, her arms still around Hunter's waist.

Hunter shrugged, but his eyes looked dark and angry. "I would have to say, everything. You won't believe this, but I thought me and Rob were friends. I guess I know how he really feels about me now," he said, with a shake of his head.

Kit reached up and put her hands on both sides of Hunter's face, bringing his face down to hers. She kissed him softly and then looked in his eyes. "I think we both know that Rob is a horrible judge of people. He thought I was trashy and he thinks you're a nerd. He's clueless."

Hunter grinned and hugged her gently. "Actually, I am a nerd, but to say I don't know anything about women? Come on. I found the most intelligent, beautiful and talented woman I could find, and now she's mine. I'd call that a home run."

Kit laughed and shook her head. "I'm sure Rob would appreciate the baseball reference. And you're so right. Did you happen to hear everything *I* said to Rob?"

Hunter nodded and looked down into her eyes, all teasing and laughing gone now. "I'm glad I make you happy and I'm glad you told Rob that we're together, but I don't want you going out with him. Even for a business dinner. I heard him, Kit. He's determined to win you back from me now. It's almost like a game or something. I knew he was competitive, but this is crazy," Hunter said, looking honestly upset.

Kit winced and rubbed her hands up and down his arms. "Nothing he could do or say could win me back. It's would just be a business dinner and he says he can help us. Hunter, you would not believe what happened to us today. We were trashed in a bunch of reviews. Come look," she said, pulling him over to where Jane's laptop was and picked up the papers she'd printed out for him.

Hunter took the reviews and read over them quickly, his face turning grim and serious. "This looks a lot like sabotage, Kit. Someone is trying to ruin you and your sisters. *Why?*"

Kit groaned and sat down on the bar stool as Hunter massaged her tense neck muscles. "We have three contenders," she said and ran down the list, telling him about Alex Foster, her father and even Rob.

Hunter squeezed her shoulder and sat down next to her. "We'll figure something out. I'll do whatever I can to help you, Kit."

Kit leaned in to his side and closed her eyes as his arm came around her. Just hearing him say those words somehow made it all better. "Come on, you look like you could use a walk on the beach and an ice cream cone. What do you say?"

Kit smiled and stood up. It sounded perfect. Twenty minutes later they walked hand in hand up and down the shoreline, talking and relaxing. Kit had never really had a boyfriend before who was the hand holding type. It was kind of nice. As the stars began to come out, they found a large boulder to sit on as they finished eating their ice cream. As soon as she finished, she lay down with her head on his legs and her hair spread out. She stared up at the sky and felt strangely peaceful.

"How is it, everything can be falling apart, but I feel so happy?" she asked softly, looking up at Hunter's face.

Hunter smiled, his eyes crinkling as he played with her hair. "It's probably because for the first in your life, you're with a man who honestly cares about you and would slay all your dragons if he could."

Kit grinned, her eyes sparkling with hints of green shining through. "It could be that or it could be the ice cream," she teased.

Hunter narrowed his eyes at her and leaned down to kiss her. "Ice cream?"

Kit sighed happily. "You," she said softly.

They walked back to his motorcycle and he drove her home quickly since it was past her bedtime. He walked her to the door but stopped her before letting her walk through.

"It's going to be okay, Kit. I'll figure out what's going on, I promise."

Kit smiled over her shoulder at him and nodded. "I know. And even if it's not okay and we go out of business and end up in the gutter . . . it'll still be okay."

Hunter's eyebrows went up and a bright smile lit up his face. "And why's that?" he asked hesitantly.

Kit turned around and slid her arms around his shoulders as she looked up into his face. "Because, I've realized that there's more to life than money or success or fame."

Hunter leaned down and kissed her lightly as he looked at her intently. "Like what?" he asked, sounding hopeful.

Kit laughed, "You're kind of persistent, aren't you? *Fine.* I guess, everything will be okay, because I've finally found you," she said, and then kissed him to shut him up.

Hunter pulled her tightly against his chest and tilted his head to deepen the kiss. Moments later he pulled away and stared intently down into her eyes. "Wait, I thought *I* was the one who found *you*."

Kit shook her head and pulled away and walked through the front door. "It's all about perspective, Hunter. Good night," she said, and walked in laughing. She smiled at Hunter's face on the other side of the glass. He was so cute. She watched him walk down to his bike and locked the door.

She sighed happily and turned on the light switch. Seconds later, she heard the sound of Hunter's motorcycle fading off into the night as she walked over to the doorway leading to the kitchen and paused.

Click

She looked over her shoulder at the counter by the cash register and felt a sizzle of adrenaline burn down her veins.

Someone was in the store with her.

She swallowed and kept walking as if she hadn't heard anything. As soon as she reached the hallway though, she ran for the stairs as fast as she could. She felt the pounding of feet right behind her and screamed as loud as she could, right as she reached the railing.

Two arms grabbed her around the middle and dragged her back from the stairs, twisting her around so she hit the wall with a loud thud, smacking her head so hard, she felt lightheaded.

"*Kit?*" she heard Jane call from the top of the stairs.

Kit rammed her elbow back as hard as she could, coming into contact with her attacker's face. She heard a grunt of pain and then felt a large hand cover her mouth. He began dragging her back toward the front store area. She struggled and fought him every step of the way, biting and kicking and finally when her mouth was free again, she screamed for her sisters.

What seemed like an eternity later as her attacker reached

the store, pulling her roughly after him, she heard yelling and saw Layla and Jane rush into the room. She heard a loud whacking sound and within seconds her attacker screamed in pain and dropped her, letting her fall hard on the tile floor, before he ran for the door, wrenching it open and running into the night.

Jane rushed to her side as Layla ran after the attacker.

"*Kit!* Kit, are you okay?" Jane screamed, sounding hysterical and close to tears. "I saw that man grab you and I ran for Layla. She beat the crap out of that guy with her metal baton. Oh, my word, Kit. Are you okay?" she demanded, running her hand over her face and arms.

Kit closed her eyes and nodded. "I'm okay," she mumbled as Jane tried her best to soothe her. Kit was happy to just stay where she was. She felt frozen, as if she moved, she'd break into a hundred pieces.

Layla ran back into the bakery and fell down beside them. "Is she okay?" she demanded, breathing hard as she touched Kit's face.

Jane wiped the tears off her cheek and shook her head. "I don't know! She won't talk. I think she's in shock."

Layla pulled out her cell phone and dialed 911 and within ten minutes they had two police men in their bakery. Kit licked her lips and opened her eyes, trying to focus on the men asking her questions instead of the pain in her head.

"My head . . . my head hurts," she muttered, and then closed her eyes again.

Someone, it sounded like Tate Matafeo, made the call for an ambulance and after that, she didn't remember too much. As she was being lifted onto a stretcher, she grabbed Jane's arm. "Call Hunter. *Please*, call Hunt . . ." *And then she was gone.*

Chapter Ten

HEADACHES

When she opened her eyes, she lifted her hand up and felt a bandage around her head and frowned.

"It's kind of da,shing. Makes you look like a pirate."

Kit turned her head slowly and smiled when she saw Hunter sitting next to her bed. *"Hi,"* she said, her voice sounding scratchy. And then her attention was caught by bouquets of every kind of flower imaginable. She closed her eyes for a second as the colors were almost overwhelming.

"I might have gone overboard at the florist's. I wasn't sure what kind of flower was your favorite so I just ordered everything," he said, as he scooted his chair closer to her bed. He gently took her hand in his and kissed her palm.

"You scared me to death. I got a call from your sister just as I reached the bridge telling me you were attacked. I went a hundred miles an hour getting back to you. I'm so sorry, Kit," he said, his voice breaking as he stared at her. "I can't believe I just left you and there was a man inside the store waiting to hurt you."

Kit reached out slowly and touched his dark blond hair. "Hey, it's not your fault," she whispered. "You couldn't know that. *I didn't know it.* It's okay. I'm a little banged up, but I'll live," she said, trying to smile.

Hunter lifted his head to stare at her and bit his lip. "I'm so sick inside, I don't know what to do. I feel like hunting the guy down who did this to you and killing him or just picking you up and taking you out of here and moving to Alaska. We'll live in a cabin and we'll both learn to fish and fly planes."

Kit grinned and then winced. *Dang,* even smiling hurt. Hunter saw her expression and grimaced before closing his eyes. "Your new security system wasn't full proof, it turns out. The guy knew which wires to cut and just walked in, locking up behind himself, so you wouldn't suspect he was there. He forgot to cut the wire to the camera though. Your security company sent the tape over this morning. Layla and Jane let me watch it with them. Layla is pretty tough. I'm surprised the guy isn't in the hospital right now. She hit him at least three times with that metal baton of hers. She had to have broken something."

Kit closed her eyes and then began crying, holding her hands up to her face as what happened started to sink in. That, and knowing that her sister had saved her, when she couldn't save herself. Hunter sat on the edge of the bed and pulled her onto his lap, careful of her head and cuddled her against his chest as she sobbed her heart out. She had always been proud of her feisty personality, but the fact was, she'd never even been in a school fight. Layla had always been there looking out for her. She sniffed a couple times and then relaxed against Hunter's chest as more tears wet his shirt.

"It's okay, sweetheart. I've got you now," he murmured softly, as he rubbed her back.

Kit raised a shaky hand and tried to wipe her cheeks. Hunter grabbed some tissues from off the small rolling table next to them and gently wiped her face and nose for her.

"I've never had anything violent like that happen to me before. I think I understand what the word, traumatized, means now," she admitted.

Hunter rocked her back and forth as if she were a child. "Of course you're traumatized. *I'm* traumatized," he said, with a half-smile, as his eyes turned stormy and sad.

Kit reached a hand up and touched his cheek. "Don't be sad, Winston," she whispered, and then turned as she heard someone clearing their throat loudly.

She turned her head very slowly toward the door and saw Layla and Jane standing in the doorway, smiling, but looking sad too.

"Mind if we come in?" Layla asked, smiling at Hunter, as he turned slightly red.

Kit nodded. "Of course, silly," she said as Hunter moved her from his lap back to the bed.

Jane and Layla both hugged Hunter and then sat on the bed next to her as Hunter sat back in his chair.

"You okay? You scared me to death," Jane said, as she took Kit's hand.

Kit began to nod but Layla started talking. "Kit, when I saw that guy dragging you, I just lost it. I really thought I was going to kill him."

Kit grinned and closed her eyes for a moment. "I'm surprised you didn't. You must have been tired."

Layla laughed and then burst into tears, throwing her arms around Kit so hard, she gasped as the sudden movement hurt her head a little. Hunter stood up looking worried, but Kit shook her head slightly, as she patted her sister's back.

"Layla, I'm okay. I promise, I'm okay," she said softly, against her sister's fine, long blond hair.

Layla pulled back and stared at her, her eyes red and wet. "You might not have been, Kit. If he'd gotten you outside and taken off with you. . ." she stopped, closing her eyes.

Kit frowned and shook her head. "Layla, please be okay," she whispered, knowing her tender hearted sister would take all of her pain on herself, if she could.

Layla got up to blow her nose and Jane took her place. Jane

reached over and kissed her very gently on the cheek. "Kit, I was so scared for you," she said, her voice shaking with emotion. "I saw the footage of you. We saw you run out of the store when you realized someone was there, and we could hear you screaming and fighting. Even though he'd hurt your head, you were still fighting him off. You were amazing, Kit."

Kit blinked back tears and nodded. "Thanks, Jane. I'm no Layla, but I think I did okay. I want to get a metal baton like you though," she said slowly, looking up at her grim older sister.

Layla nodded. "You'll have one, Kitten. I could see on the film that you were trying to do your self-defense moves on that jerk. If you hadn't banged up your head, you would have had him easy."

Kit smiled and then looked over at Hunter who had been silent through the whole conversation. He was just sitting there, looking at her silently with his heart in his eyes. Her breath caught in her chest, and she held a hand out to him. He moved closer and took it in his.

"So, now what? What do we do? Have the police been looking for the guy? Do we know who he is?" she asked, as Layla and Jane stared at her with big eyes as they looked back and forth between her and Hunter.

Layla began to speak but was interrupted by her nurse poking her head in the room.

"Officer Matafeo is wondering if now would be a good time to talk to you," a nurse in green scrubs said, from the doorway.

Layla and Jane frowned but nodded their heads. "Send him in," Layla instructed.

Hunter frowned worriedly. "Are you up for this, Kit? Maybe you should rest first?"

Kit nodded her head as Tate walked in with his partner. He smiled gently at her and looked at Layla, Jane and Hunter before speaking. "I need to interview Kit. If you could wait outside or in the waiting room, I'd appreciate it," he said, all business.

Layla grumbled and Hunter glared. "Kit, I'll leave if you want me to, but if you need me, I'm staying," he said, ignoring Tate.

Tate sighed as Kit shook her head. "No, Hunter, it's okay. Really. I'll be fine."

Kit watched everyone file out of the room and Tate took the vacated seat next to her. "Kit, I'm so sorry this happened to you," he said, sounding more like a friend than a police officer.

Kit tried to smile but winced again. She would need some pain medication soon. Her head felt so tender like it might explode if she moved it too fast.

"It's okay, Tate. Let's get this over with," she said.

He walked her through the entire evening and recorded everything she said. His partner asked a few questions, but Tate did most of the talking. And by the time she was done, she was so tired, she lay back with her eyes closed. Before Tate left, he promised to keep her up to date on the investigation. The nurse then came in and helped her go to the bathroom and gave her some pain meds. The doctor came in shortly afterward and by then she was so exhausted she fell asleep, not waking up for two hours. The doctor suggested keeping her one more day for observation but since it was just a concussion and there was no bleeding on the brain, she wanted to be home.

Kit was surprised that Hunter stayed at the hospital the entire time with her. And then again, she wasn't. Every time she expected him to act like the typical men she knew, he surprised her and was tender, caring and sweet. When she was checking out, she insisted he go home and get some rest.

After the twenty minute ride from the hospital in Tacoma, Layla and Jane helped her walk into the house from the back kitchen. She'd been lying around so much in the hospital though, she didn't want to go back to bed, so they helped get her settled in the small family room upstairs and handed her the Netflix remote.

Kit smiled. "You guys are spoiling me. And you didn't even

open the bakery today. I feel kind of bad," she said, as she scooted back against the pillows Jane had placed around her.

Jane and Layla exchanged a dark look before smiling at her. "No worries. You come first," Layla said, and handed her a Coke Zero, her favorite.

Kit smiled happily and took a long sip. It was good to have sisters. "I love you guys. Thanks for everything. Thanks for taking care of me and beating up the bad guys for me and getting snacks and a Coke. You two are the best sisters in the world," she said, blinking back the tears, so she could smile.

Layla nodded her head but couldn't speak and had to leave the room. Jane gave a watery laugh and sat down by her feet though, massaging them automatically.

"You really scared Layla. You know she went into social work thinking she could save everybody and when she couldn't, it almost killed her. And then our sister gets attacked, right in our own home. It's really thrown her. All she's ever wanted is for you and me to be safe," Jane said wonderingly.

Kit frowned too. "I wonder why? I mean, why be so worried about it? Life happens. Violence happens. Did something happen when we were little? That we don't remember?" Kit said softly, looking away.

Jane's eyes went big and she stared at Kit. "Oh, my heck, Kit, I bet you're right. We all know our father was into drugs before he left us. Maybe something happened? Maybe Layla saw something that has affected her and how she sees people and the world. Not that it's wrong. I mean, the world needs all the social workers it can get. And Layla *is* good in a fight."

Kit grinned. "No doubt. That poor guy will think twice before attacking the Kendall sisters again, that's for sure. But poor Layla. We have to find out, Jane."

Jane sighed and looked away. "Well, our mom is gone and so is our grandma. That only leaves two people who would know. *Layla and our father.*"

Kit bit her lip and leaned her head back. "Hmm, maybe we could convince Layla to go through hypnosis?"

Jane shook her head immediately. "She'd never go for it and it might be traumatic and bring all the horror back. No, I think we should hunt our dad down."

Kit shook her head. "We tried finding him a couple months ago with no luck. That man needs rehab like no other," she said sadly.

Jane's brown eyes turned dark and sad and she nodded. "Well, we just need to keep trying. I bet Hunter would help us," she said hopefully.

Kit smiled. "He would help me with anything, Jane. I think I love him," she said softly.

Jane gasped as she stared at her sister. "You. Are. Lying."

Kit shook her head slowly back and forth. "I. Am. Not."

Jane laughed and stood up holding her arms out in a classic Cheerleader pose. "Yay!" she yelled, and then did a few kicks and jumps.

Kit laughed as she watched her sister act silly. "Stop it!" she ordered, with a smile on her face. "Layla will hear you and want to know what's going on," she hissed at Jane.

Layla poked her head in the door. "Too late. What's up?" she said, walking all the way in the room as she studied Jane's happy expression.

"Let me guess. Garrett wants to take you out again?" she asked patiently.

Jane shook her head. "No, although I would love that. No, this is all about Kit. Kit? Do you want to tell her or shall I?" Jane asked, with a laughing smile.

Kit shrugged and held her hand out for Layla. Layla walked over, kneeling down beside the couch and took her sister's hand in hers. "Layla, I think for the first time in my life, I really think . . . I believe that it's possible, that I *might* be . . . in love with Hunter," she said carefully, and slowly, as if she were trying to get the words out from the bottom of her soul.

Layla's eyes went huge and her whole face lifted up before she closed her eyes and shook her head. "That makes me so happy, Kit. I was so worried that you'd never find a man you could trust with your heart. But you did. Oh, Kitten, I'm so, so happy for you," she said softly, and kissed her forehead gently.

Kit grinned and hugged her sister as Jane erupted into another loud cheer.

"What in the world is going on here?"

Kit and Layla pulled apart and turned to see Michael and Stella holding Bubba's leash. Layla let out a whoop and rushed over to Michael who grabbed her in his arms and held her tightly, kissing her quickly, but with enough passion to make Kit and Jane turn their heads away. As soon as Michael let Layla out of his arms, he walked over to Kit and kneeled down next to her the same way Layla had,, and touched her cheek.

"Kit, you know I already feel like you're my own sister. I was so worried about you. I want you and all of your sisters to move into my house until the police find the guy who attacked you. I'll move in with my parents until after the wedding. I just want you all safe," he said, looking back at Layla.

Layla bit her lip and looked down at her feet. Kit glanced at Jane, but Jane was looking away with a frown. Kit patted Michael's hand covering hers and shook her head.

"This is my home, Michael. We've never really had one before. It was always apartment after apartment. Move after move. My grandmother, for whatever reason, *I choose to believe it was love*, designed my room with *me* in mind. And I have a job here. But most of all, I'm happy here. Thank you, my dear, gorgeous brother, but *no*. Besides, with Layla looking out for me, who would dare attack me now?" she asked, with a grin to her sisters.

Michael's face turned hard and he stood up walking over to the window. Stella took his place immediately, touching Kit's forehead softly before giving her a light kiss on the cheek.

"I'll help you get better, Kit," she promised,, and gave her a drawing she'd been holding behind her back.

Kit felt her heart melt as she saw Stella had drawn a picture of Bubba surrounded by a field of bright yellow flowers.

"Stella, I love it! You're going to grow up to be an artist just like me," she said, touching her soft caramel brown hair.

Stella grinned and jumped up. "I want to be a baker like my mom, but I could be both," she said, running to hug Layla.

Kit laughed happily at the glow on Layla's face, every time Stella called her mom.

As Michael stood by the window silently, everyone realized at the same time, *he wasn't happy.* Layla walked over and touched him softly on the arm.

"Sweetheart, what's wrong? Are you upset?"

Michael turned around, his face looking harsh and his eyes furious. "You could have been hurt too, Layla. Jane showed me the tapes. I sat there and watched you beat the living crap out of that guy and then. . . *then you chased after him!* You could have been killed!" he said, in a loud voice that made Stella flinch and look frightened.

Layla put her arms around Michael's waist and hugged him hard before turning around. "Would you guys watch Stella for us? I think we need to go take a ride and have a talk," she said, looking at Kit and Jane with a raised eyebrow.

Jane and Kit nodded their heads quickly and silently and Layla pulled Michael out of the room quickly. Jane knelt down in front of Stella so they were eye to eye and smiled softly. "I was thinking about making Kit her most favorite dessert in the whole world. Would you help me out? You'd need to wear an apron and do the mixing though. Can you do that?" she asked, with a hopeful smile.

Stella grinned and jumped up and down in a good imitation of Jane's earlier moves. "Yes, yes, yes!" she yelled.

Jane looked over her shoulder at Kit with a small smile. "I'll be back in about an hour with chocolate chip cookies. Text me if you need anything," Jane said, and took Bubba's leash and left.

Kit frowned as she stared at the ceiling for a moment. Life was fragile and so precious. Seeing Michael's torment at just the *thought* of Layla getting hurt, made her realize that love was a serious business. Love meant wrapping your whole soul around the other person, so you felt every pain they felt, you hurt when they hurt, and you died a little when they died. Calling your loved one, your other half, was actually truer than she'd ever realized before. She surprised herself and said a little prayer for Layla and Michael, and for their happiness and safety. Because what she'd seen in the depths of Michael's eyes was a love so true and strong, that it couldn't bear to be broken.

Chapter Eleven

THE DEAL

Kit took the day off from baking to finish recuperating but was back at work Saturday, their biggest day. She thought she'd be up to it, but two hours in, she felt a little lightheaded and headachy and had to take a ten minute break. Layla and Jane were very understanding and took up the slack but she still felt bad.

Tate Matafeo came by at eleven to pick up a few muffins and check on her. She watched as Tate leaned over the glass case, his long powerful form, creating a beautiful line. She smiled and wondered if Tate would ever let her paint him. She turned to mention it to Jane, but Jane was lost in her own thoughts. Kit frowned as she saw a deep longing on her sister's face that told a story. Jane might be dating Garrett, but she was still head over heels for Tate. Kit felt her heart break a little for her younger sister and sighed. She'd spent three months pining for Rob and what a waste of time that had been. Sometimes, something better was just around the corner. *But then again . . .*

"Tate, have you made up your mind?" Kit asked, walking forward to help him, so Jane wouldn't have to.

Tate looked up with a grin and shook his head. "They all look amazing. I swear this bakery is my Nirvana," he said, with such love in his voice that she had to laugh.

"How about I give you a free sample on the house? I owe you, since you're hunting my attacker," she said, leaning down and picking the largest, chocolatiest muffin they had. She handed it to him on a wax paper square, and watched his face light up like it was Christmas.

"How did you know that's the one I was thinking about?" he asked, looking at her suspiciously, as if she were a mind reader.

Kit snorted and leaned against the counter with her arms crossed. "I have eyes, Tate."

The bell rang over the door and Garrett walked in, holding a large bouquet of flowers in his hands. Kit watched the scene unfold in front of her, as if she were at the movies. *Garrett sees Jane, his eyes light up. Jane rushes to Garrett's side, leaning up to kiss him on the cheek. Tate turns around slowly, with death in his eyes.* Kit grinned and took out a water bottle to enjoy the show.

Garrett put one arm around Jane's shoulders and smiled warmly down into her face. "I've missed you. I came over as soon as I heard about your trouble," he said, frowning worriedly.

Jane kept her arm around Garrett's waist as she looked at Kit. "We're hanging in there. Kit was hurt though," she said softly.

Garrett kissed the top of her head and let go of her as he walked over to Kit, holding out the large bouquet to her. Kit blinked in surprise and took the flowers automatically.

"These are for you, Kit. If there's anything you need, I want you to call me."

Kit smiled and smelled the blooms. "Thanks, Garrett. How thoughtful."

"I swear, if I ever find the guy who hurt you, he'll wish he'd never been born," Garrett said, in a voice so low and full of violence, that Kit believed him.

Tate must have heard the truth in his statement too, because he walked over and cleared his throat. "Hi, there. I'm Officer Matafeo, and I'm in charge of the investigation into Kit's attack. It's probably not a good idea to walk around making threats like that. Citizens need to leave the investigation in the hands of the authorities," he said firmly, but politely.

Garrett turned slowly and looked Tate up and down with a clear direct gaze. Kit looked back and forth between the two men and swallowed. If these two ever got in a fight, it would be a toss-up who would win. They were both huge, tall, powerful men, with a streak of violence in them you could sense, but never wanted to see.

"I'll keep that in mind, Officer. I'm Garrett Murphy," he said, reaching his hand out to shake.

Tate immediately shook Garrett's hand, smiling politely, although his eyes remained watchful and cold.

"Nice to meet you, Garrett."

Garrett relaxed and leaned against the case as Jane walked behind the counter to stand by Kit. "I'm Jane's boyfriend. I haven't seen you around. Are you new here?" Garrett asked, in a pleasant voice.

Tate stiffened and he stood up straight, turning his head to pierce Jane with a look of anger, and what might have been betrayal. Kit felt Jane stiffen next to her.

"*Boyfriend?* I didn't realize Jane was seeing anyone seriously," he said, looking back at Garrett with a frown.

Garrett, quick on the uptake grinned at Tate and slapped him on the shoulder. "Well, I don't think she had much choice. I took one look at her and realized that Jane was one in a million. Sweet, kind and beautiful. *And,* she cooks like an angel. She made me a pineapple coconut cake last week, that brought me to my knees. I begged her to marry me after the first bite," he said, grinning over his shoulder at Jane.

Kit's eyes went round and she turned to stare at her sister. Jane had turned a bright red color and was busy wiping the counters down.

"Garrett, you're such a tease," she said lightly, not meeting anyone's gaze.

Garrett laughed. "Who's teasing?"

Kit turned back and noticed Garrett's calculating smile, and Tate's devastated expression. *Time to take matters into her own hands.*

"Garrett, Jane's due for a break. She was telling me all morning long how she was craving a taco like nobody's business. Why don't you two take off and I'll watch the store?" she said with a smile, untying Jane's apron and pushing her toward Garrett.

Garrett nodded immediately. "I'm always hungry. Let's go, Gorgeous."

Jane nodded, and walked toward Garrett. She paused first though and looked at Tate. "Bye, Tate," she said, in a sad voice, before disappearing out the door.

Kit and Tate watched the door shut and then they both turned and looked at each other.

"*Really?*" Tate asked.

Kit nodded with a wince. "Tate, you had *so* many chances with her. You know you did. She even asked you out herself. I saw her face just now. She's *still* hung up on you, but she's trying to get over you now," she said softly, not wanting to twist the knife.

Tate nodded and looked down at his feet. "It's for the best. She needs to be with someone like her. We're complete opposites."

Kit snorted and shook her head. "Well, actually, Garrett isn't *anything* like Jane. He's a Marine back from Iraq, who has seen it all. He's had a hard time adjusting to regular life. Layla thinks he's dating Jane, because he thinks she'll erase all his nightmares," she said softly, feeling her heart break a little for Garrett, but at the same time, wondering if another person could really be someone else's cure.

Tate looked on edge and bothered but didn't say anything. He shook his head as if to clear his thoughts and then spoke. "Kit, as far as the investigation, none of the prints we lifted came back as belonging to anyone in the system. That just means this guy wore gloves or has never been caught before. We lifted hair samples too, but with this being a public bakery, that might not help us. We've gone through the footage, but because the man wore a mask, we're stuck. We need to look at motive. That's our only hope of tracking this guy down."

Kit sighed tiredly and touched her fingers to the side of her head where it was still sore and tender. "Layla and Jane told you all about those bad reviews we got. We've been sabotaged from day one, it feels like. I don't think it's a coincidence, Tate. I think it's all connected, and if that's true, then you need to be looking at Alex Foster and our father. Alex used to come in daily to bug Jane, but he hasn't been in for nearly two weeks. Something's up. Is there any way you can investigate him?" she asked, as Tate took a big bite of his muffin.

She had to wait for him to open his eyes and stop chewing, but when he did, he was all business.

"I'm already looking into him. According to Alex's secretary, he's on a business trip. From what I hear from other sources though, he found a lead on his wife and daughters and took off to try and track them down. He's in Michigan right now. I made some calls to the police in that area and Alex checked out of his hotel this morning. He should be home later tonight or tomorrow. Looks like she got away again," he said, with a small smile.

Kit felt queasy for a moment and frowned. "What in the world did Alex do to his wife that would make her run like that?" she asked softly.

Tate looked at her sadly and shook his head. "I can't say, but off the record, Alex Foster is a man that would stoop to the lowest of lows to get his way. But the facts are, he was out of town. That doesn't mean he didn't put somebody up to doing his dirty work for him. And as far as your father, wherever Alex goes, your father follows. He wants his money from you girls and he'll take whatever road he can to get it. Right now, he thinks his ticket is Alex."

Kit shivered and rubbed her arms.

"Hey," he said softly, walking over to her. "I'm upping my patrols of this area and Michael assures me your new surveillance system will be up and operational by tonight. Don't worry Kit."

Kit nodded her head and began to speak, but was surprised when Tate pulled her in for a hug. She smiled and relaxed in to the hug, even hugging him back a little when she heard the bell over the door sound.

Kit and Tate turned to see who it was. Kit's smile faltered, but Tate smiled easily.

"Hey, Rob, how's it going, man?" he said, with his arm still over Kit's shoulders.

Rob looked at Tate in angry surprise, as he walked over to stand next to Kit. "First Hunter and *now* Tate? Dang, Kit, I'm sure you can fit me into your dating schedule," he said, sounding angry.

Kit felt the punch of the insult, but refused to show it. She glanced at Tate and was glad to see he was glaring hotly at Rob. She moved away from Tate and Rob and walked around the counter to put distance between them.

"Rob, *what's the matter with you?* I swear you've gone from a decent guy, to a complete jerk," Tate said, with a look of disgust. Rob glared back at Tate but didn't say anything in response, just turning his back on him.

Tate shook his head and looked at Kit with a gentle smile. "I'm going to take off, Kit. Call me if you need anything *or if you need a restraining order*," he said coldly, looking at Rob one more time, before walking out the door.

Kit stared after Tate, wishing he had just stayed until Rob had left, but he was too angry. She looked at Rob with a frown and sighed.

"What can I get you, Rob?" she asked politely, with as little expression on her face as possible.

Rob ran his hands through his hair and walked over to stand in front of her. "Look, that came out wrong. Everything I've said to you lately has been coming out wrong. And I hate that. I'm sorry, Kit. *I'm sorry.* I just came over today, to check up on you, and make sure you're okay. I heard you got hurt the other night," he said, looking her over ,and smiling when he didn't see any obvious injury.

Kit nodded her head. "I'm fine, Rob, thanks for thinking of me. You should try Jane's red velvet cupcakes today. They're divine," she said, walking over to the case holding all the cupcakes.

Rob followed her, ignoring the cupcakes. "If you're feeling up to it, I'd like to take you out to dinner tonight. Just you and me, Kit. I promise I'll be on my best behavior. I won't give you a hard time about Hunter or Tate or any of your *other* boyfriends."

Kit stared at him, her mouth falling open slightly. He really did believe she was a promiscuous, party girl. "What other boyfriends are you talking about?" she asked curiously, with a smile that didn't reach her eyes.

Rob shrugged and looked away. "Well, when I figured I'd go ahead and let this thing between you and me happen, I asked one of my buddies up in Seattle, who's deep into the art scene, about you. He said you dated around a lot and that you went through men like tissue. I'm not going to judge you, Kit. I had my party days and I'm not proud of it. I know that I've matured and I'm making good changes in my life. I know that you can too. Although, the way you act with Hunter and Tate, it makes me wonder," he said, looking at her searchingly.

Kit let a long breath out and closed her eyes for a moment, trying to control the shaking in her hands. "Can I ask who your friend is? I mean, just out of curiosity. It sounds like we've been hanging out in the same circles," she said carefully, wondering who had lied about her to Rob.

Rob shoved his hands in his pockets and shrugged. "Jake Crawford. We used to hang out in the clubs back in the day."

Kit nodded and touched her head, which was pounding now, making her feel weak and tired. "Jake Crawford is my ex-boyfriend. We were together for a few months, before I caught him cheating on me with a sculptor," Kit said dryly, stepping backward to lean weakly against the counter.

Rob's eyes went wide and his mouth opened a little in surprise. "*Whoa.* I guess his opinion of you is a little biased. But you can't blame me for checking up on you, Kit. I've been burned before. I check and double check the people I date. But I decided to date you anyways, *even knowing everything.* Well, I mean, even hearing everything Jake said about you, which wasn't good. Trust me," he said, with a smile.

Kit closed her eyes, feeling weak all of a sudden. She had to sit down soon, or she was going to collapse. She'd overdone it, and now she was paying for it. She reached for her phone and texted Layla, who was just in the back kitchen to help her.

She put the phone back down on the counter and licked her lips. "Rob, I can't really talk to you about this right now. I'm not feeling very well," she said faintly, touching her forehead again.

Layla hurried through the doorway took one look at Rob, and ignored him as she rushed around the counter with a squawk, as Kit began to collapse to her knees.

"Jeez, Rob, why can't you leave her alone," Layla said furiously, under her breath as she took Kit in her arms carefully, feeling her pulse.

"Sweetie, you're as white a sheet and your skin is clammy. Why didn't you tell me you were having a hard time? Where the heck is Jane?" she asked, in a hard voice.

Rob walked around the counter cautiously, staring down at the two women, frowning as he saw Kit's white face.

"Look, I didn't mean to upset her. I was just telling her what my buddy, Jake Crawford told me. I didn't know it would make her physically ill," he said curiously. "I guess her feelings for me are stronger than I thought," he said wonderingly.

Kit kept her eyes shut as wave of anger swept through her. She was just too weak to tell Rob off.

Layla turned and stared at him for a moment, before her mouth snapped shut. "You cocky little . . . *ugh! She has a concus-*

sion, you idiot. She's just overdone it, is all," she said, grabbing a rag off the counter and wiping Kit's sweaty forehead.

Rob winced and looked a little taken aback. "Oh, man, I didn't know she was hurt that bad. I walked in and she looked fine. She was standing there draped all over Tate Matafeo for crap's sake. I bring up Jake, and she goes all woozy on me. Don't blame *me*," he said, holding up his hands.

Layla growled and then ignored him, grabbing her cell phone. She went through her contacts and sent out texts to a few people, before she slipped her phone back into her pocket.

"Hey, why don't I pick her up for you and I can carry her to her room or something, so she can rest?" Rob asked, moving toward Kit.

Layla glared at him. "No. I don't think so. I think the best thing for you to do, is leave, okay?"

Rob glared at her and put his hands on his waist. "Look, *what is your problem?* I've bent over backwards for you and this bakery, and all you do is glare at me and treat me like crap. Kit needs help. *I'm here.* I can help her. Now move out of the way so I can pick her up," he ordered, pushing his shirt sleeves up over his elbows.

Layla sneered at him and held up a hand. "You treated my sister like crap, and you *continue* to treat my sister like crap. If you touch her, I'll come after you with my baton," she warned, making Rob's eyebrows go straight up.

"*Treat her like crap?* All I've done for the past week is beg her to forgive me for asking her out, in a less than romantic way. All I've been trying to do, is tell her how much I like her, *and for that*, I've gotten nothing but a headache and a price hike. *I'm the victim here*, not Kit. You're crazy, Layla," he said, with a disgusted shake of his head.

Layla glared fiercely at Rob and pointed a finger at him. "You're not half the man Hunter is. He treats her like a queen. Every chance you get, you tell her what a *favor* you're doing her, by even being interested in her. You've trashed her self-esteem and I think you're a macho jerk."

Rob's face turned red at the mention of Hunter and the muscles in his neck and arms seemed to expand ,and his eyes turned to furious slits. "Hunter isn't even a real man. He's a *fake* man with his *fake* muscles, his *fake* clothes and *fake* life. If you took all the fakeness away, what would you have? A computer geek and his computer," he said, with a sneer.

Kit could feel Layla on the verge of exploding. "Well, guess what, Rob, there's one thing that isn't fake about Hunter. *His heart*. Too bad *you* can't say the same."

Michael took that moment to clear his throat loudly. He was standing in the doorway shaking his head back and forth in disgust.

"Rob, I don't even know what to say to you, right now," he said coldly, as he walked around Rob, to get to Layla and Kit. He picked Kit up easily in his arms, moving quickly around the counter.

Kit opened her eyes and stared at Rob as she was carried past him. He looked chagrined and a little shamed. He stared at her silently as she disappeared through the doorway. Michael leaned down and kissed her cheek.

"Dang, Kit, you're tearing my heart out here," he said, as he carried her easily up the stairs.

Moments later, Jane rushed through her doorway, just as Michael laid her down on her bed.

"Kit! I'm sorry! Layla is so furious with me, she could barely speak," she said in a rush, as Michael walked into her bathroom and came back moments later with a cold wet rag. He wiped her face gently as Jane smoothed the hair away from her face.

Kit licked her dry lips, feeling a little better. "It's okay, Jane, *really*. I just got a little lightheaded there for a moment. I think I overdid it a little," she said, closing her eyes again.

Jane groaned and took the rag from Michael. Michael stood up and stared down at Kit for a moment.

"Kit, just for the record, Rob is wrong about Hunter. He's one of the most amazing, genuine sweet guys I know. He just happens to be a computer genius and goes at life a little differently. He decided he wanted to settle down a couple years ago and got tired of getting dumped so he hired an image consultant. He might have gone a little over the edge listening to everything Tony said, but he had good intentions. He's one of my closest friends. I wouldn't listen to anything Rob has to say about Hunter," he said, and touched her cheek one more time before he walked out.

Kit tried to smile and looked up at Jane. "You better get back down to the store. Layla told me we had to let Mandee go because business is so down."

Jane shook her head looking scared. "I am not going down there until Layla calms down. She's so angry her eyes are like two red, demon fires," she said, with a theatrical shiver.

Kit laughed softly. "Stay with me then. I'll protect you," she said softly, patting the bed beside her.

Jane scooted over and lay down beside her sister. "Garrett told me he thinks Tate is interested in me," she said quietly.

Kit turned slowly on her side and looked at her little sister. She reached over and touched a glossy strand of deep brown hair and sighed. "Garrett happens to be right. But it doesn't matter. If Tate's not willing to let go of whatever is holding him back, then the best thing you can do is move on. You can't spend your life waiting for love," she said, thinking of Rob.

Jane nodded but sighed sadly. "I really like Garrett. I think it would be nice to fall in love with him. *But I can't*," she said, sounding frustrated.

Kit smiled. "That's because your heart is still with Tate. Sometimes it just takes time. Besides, you just barely started dating Garrett. Sometimes love take years to develop. Some of the best relationships do."

Jane turned on her back and stared at the ceiling. "Layla sure didn't take years. Michael took one look at her and he was totally snagged. And, holy cow, look at Hunter. When Layla and I walked into the hospital room, we just stopped. Kit, the way he was looking at you. It was *so* . . ." Jane paused, and her forehead wrinkled as she searched for the right words. "Beautiful. Tender. So exquisitely emotional, it hurt to see," she said softly.

Kit closed her eyes and smiled. "I love him," she said, and opened her eyes as she took a deep breath. "And, I think he loves me too," she said, feeling shaky again, but for a different reason this time.

Jane grinned at her and hopped off the bed. She ran to Kit's closet and walked in, turning the light on. She came out seconds later, holding the wedding dress Kit had bought just weeks before.

Kit grinned and struggled to sit up. "Jane!" she said, just as Hunter rushed through her bedroom doors.

Kit's mouth fell open in horror as Jane dropped her dress in shock. She squeaked loudly and picked it up quickly, looking at Kit apologetically. "I was um, . . .just showing Kit a dress *I* bought the other day."

Hunter ran a hand through his short, spiky hair and nodded. "It's really pretty, Jane. I didn't know you were getting married though. I thought it was Layla. Do you mind if I talk to Kit?"

Jane shook her head back and forth. "Oh, no! Of course not. I'll just take *my* dress back to my room," she said, and rushed past Hunter.

Hunter shut the door behind Jane and hurried to her side, sitting down and taking her hand in his. "Baby, when I got Layla's text, I was too far away to help you. It kills me that I can't be here when you need me."

Kit smiled weakly and touched her head gently with her hand. "What exactly did Layla's text say?" she asked curiously, leaning back down against her pillows.

Hunter frowned and shook his head. "She just texted that you needed me. And I wasn't there. Kit, I *need* to be there for you. I need that," he said softly, leaning down and touching his forehead to hers.

Kit closed her eyes and felt a warmth steal over her heart, healing all the cracks and breaks and tears, sealing all the holes and emptiness that she'd ever felt. She didn't know what would happen in the future between them, but right now, right at that very moment, she was loved, and it was the most amazing feeling she'd ever felt.

"Hunter," she said, opening her eyes and looking into his. "I'm in love with you," she said, staring into his eyes as she tried to gauge his reaction.

Hunter blinked in surprise and swallowed before he could speak. "Kit . . . *Kit*," he said, and kissed her with so much intensity, she felt her heart burst from the emotion.

"Kit, I adore you. What I feel for you goes so far beyond love. I can't even describe what I feel for you. No man has ever felt this emotion before," he said in a rush, touching her cheek with his hand.

Kit smiled brilliantly at him, laughing as a little joy slipped out. "I think that's what everyone says, who falls in love."

Hunter shook his head slowly back and forth. "Not like this, Kit. *Never* like this," he said, and kissed her again.

Kit pulled away as she fought to breathe. Hunter frowned and pulled back. "Sorry, sweetheart. You're not feeling good and so I figure I'll just kiss you until you pass out. I think I have a lot to learn about being a boyfriend."

Kit smiled, still trying to get her breathing under control. "You're the best boyfriend I've ever had, if that makes you feel any better."

Hunter grinned and straightened a blanket over her legs. "Amazingly, it does."

Kit smiled at him, not saying anything. She just wanted to remember everything about this moment for the rest of her life.

Hunter smiled back at her, his mouth tilted up on one side as his eyes crinkled. "You know, I've never been in love before.

Well, not like this anyways. I think I might have been in love with Charity. I tutored her in chemistry, in college, but it was *nothing* like how I feel for you. This transcends everything. Like, if this was one of my games? I've just reached a level I didn't even know existed," he said, grinning at her.

Kit laughed. "That is a beautiful image. I'll treasure it."

Hunter looked down for a moment and then looked seriously into her eyes. "Was that sarcasm? I know I'm this geeky computer guy, but that's the language inside of me. It's how I think and express myself," he said somberly.

Kit shook her head and winced as the movement made her head ache even more. "No, Winston, that was *not* sarcasm. I promised myself that the man I fell for, would be average looking but sexy, smart and funny, and a man who knows how to open doors, send flowers and write poetry that makes my toes curl. You just happen to be gorgeous, *not* average, which I'm doing my best to deal with. You're definitely smart and funny. You open doors *and* bring me flowers and your words might be coated with gaming lingo, but it's still poetry to me," she said, with a warm smile.

Hunter's face lightened and he grinned. "Kit, I hate to warn you, but I feel I probably should. I'm not going to be an easy boyfriend. I'm going to be pushy and territorial. I'm going to smother you at times and drive you crazy. I'm going to love you the only way I know how to. Wholeheartedly."

Kit bit her lip as she studied him. She'd only ever dated men who stingily gave her pieces and corners of their hearts. She'd never once been given a whole, beating, beautiful heart before. She wouldn't take it for granted.

"I think I can handle it. And I should probably warn you. You're the first man I've ever trusted enough to love. I've never been able to love a man before. This is a first for me too, and I have no idea how I'll be as your girlfriend. I might be moody, or annoying. I'll definitely be painting you every chance I get. It could get rough."

Hunter stared at her for a moment and shook his head. "Then it's a deal. You and me. Together. Loving each other as best as we can. Imperfectly, but honestly," he said, and held out his hand.

Kit sighed happily and shook his hand, agreeing to the terms. "It's a deal."

Chapter Twelve

DEAL BREAKER

The next day was Sunday, and she was grateful. She needed a day of rest. She got ready for church and texted Hunter the address and time he should be there, and then walked down for breakfast. Jane had made hash browns and eggs. *Yay*.

Kit smiled gratefully and sat down next to Layla. "This looks incredible. Thanks, Jane," she said, and took the plate being handed to her.

Jane smiled and glanced at Layla. "It's my little peace offering. I'm hoping that Layla will forgive me for leaving you on your own yesterday, if I feed her the best breakfast in the world," she said smiling brightly at Layla.

Layla grumbled but said a quick prayer and began eating. Kit and Jane exchanged worried looks before Layla looked up at Jane and sighed. "Okay, you're forgiven and this does taste amazing. But, *dang it,* Jane. Kit shouldn't have even been working at all, and you take off *with your boyfriend?* I come into the ‚kitchen and there's Rob, telling her in his own little way, how trashy she is *again,* and she's collapsed on the floor. I about lost it, Jane. I can't . . . I *can't* handle Kit getting hurt. Or you. I just can't. I won't let it happen, ever again," she said jerkily, shaking her head and looking away from her sisters.

Kit frowned and put her fork down as she scooted her stool over next to her sister's so she could put her arm around Layla's shoulders. "Layla, I was okay yesterday. I was tired and I got lightheaded, and yeah, Rob was being a jerk as usual, but no one was hurting me. And it's actually my fault Jane left. Garrett looked like he was rubbing it in that he was with Jane and I didn't want Tate to shoot him. I'm really okay. Layla, *what's the matter*? Ever since I was attacked, you're on edge and angry and upset. Please, tell me what's going on?"

Layla started to breathe hard and she leaned over the counter and rested her head in her hands, almost as if she were hiding her face from her sisters. Kit looked at Jane in alarm, but Jane was staring at Layla with concern.

"Layla? Did something happen to Kit when you two were little girls? Did you see our dad or one of his friends do something to her?" Jane asked softly, coming around the island to stand on Layla's other side.

Layla acted like she hadn't heard Jane but when she finally raised her head, she stared straight ahead. Her eyes were red and large and there was pain.

"*How did you know that?* Mom knew of course, but I've never told anyone else," she whispered, not blinking.

Kit's eyes went wide and she felt her heart speed up. "Layla, *tell me*. What happened?" she prompted.

Layla licked her lips and swallowed. "You were so little, Kit. You didn't know. You picked up a bag Dad had left on the counter, and you dumped it out. It was white powder and you thought it was sugar. I was putting the dishes away and I didn't think anything of it. I thought it was sugar too. You kept touching your finger to your lips and making funny faces though. When dad came into the kitchen and saw what you were doing, he hit you so hard, you went flying off the chair and hit the ground so hard your head bounced. I started screaming and mom came running into the room. She saw you lying on the ground bleeding, and Dad was cursing and yelling as he tried to get all the powder back in the bag. And I was just standing there, *doing nothing*, as you lay in a heap. I remember mom yelled at him and told him to leave. She told him to never come back. And then she put us in the car and drove you to the hospital. Which actually turned out to be a good thing, because you had a lot of cocaine in your system and you could have died. The policemen came after that and then the social workers came. They were so nice and they talked to me. But ever since that day, I can't handle it if someone hurts my sisters. When that guy attacked you, Kit and I started hitting him, it was like I was *finally* able to protect you. But instead of making it better, it just keeps bringing back all the bad memories," she said quietly, wiping her eyes as a stray tear slipped down.

Kit leaned her head against Layla's and kept her arms tight around her sister's shoulders as Jane wrapped herself around Layla's other side. They stood like that for a long time before Jane kissed Layla's cheek and stood up.

"Well, that explains your drive to protect all children and your career in social work. And for the record, no offense, Kit, but, Layla, you're the best sister anyone could ever, *ever* have. And I love you. And I'm sorry I wasn't there to protect Kit for you," she said, wiping her own tears away.

Layla laughed and hugged Jane's waist with one arm. "Thanks, Jane and *I'm* the one who's sorry. I came down so hard on you, but I was really just upset at myself."

Kit pushed Layla's soft blond hair over her shoulder and stared at the one person in her life, who she knew for a fact, would jump in front of a semi for her and felt a great wave of gratitude.

"You know, I don't remember any of that, Layla. *Nothing*. Not the hospital, the cops or the social workers. Nothing," she said, creasing her forehead.

Layla smiled sadly up at her and shook her head. "Good. I've remembered it all for you. I'll take that memory gladly. You've suffered enough."

Kit swallowed and lowered her head. "Crap, that did it," she sniffed, and wiped her own tears.

Layla and Jane laughed and they all hugged each other one more time before finishing breakfast and heading to church. Kit's mouth opened in surprise as they reached the church and saw Michael and Stella standing on the sidewalk, waiting for Layla, along with Hunter and Garrett.

"Garrett goes to church?" Kit asked wonderingly, looking at Jane in surprise.

Jane looked back at Kit just as surprised. "He mentioned getting together today, but I said, no, because I wanted to go to church. He must have asked Michael about the when and where. *Holy cow*," she said, not sounding very pleased about it.

Kit and Layla exchanged worried glances, but got out of the car, walking to the men in their life.

Kit had to grin as she looked Hunter up and down. He was dressed as fine as a Giorgio Armani model, and looking just as good with his short hair and freshly shaved face.

"*Wow*," she said, feeling her heart jump in her chest. He was going to turn heads today.

Hunter smiled bashfully and shrugged. "I have to step up my game if I'm going to be seen with you. You look so beautiful, Kit," he said, and leaned down to kiss her on her cheek before offering her his arm.

Kit smiled brightly up into his eyes and took his arm, realizing that everyone from Layla, Michael and Stella to Garrett and Jane were just standing there staring at them. Kit blushed as Michael winked at her and Layla smiled so big it looked like she was Miss Washington. Garrett smiled politely, but Jane looked sad. Hunter pulled her toward the church, so she didn't have a chance to ask her why, but she promised herself she would later.

Church was interesting. As expected, every single woman from fifty to thirteen, made it a point to introduce themselves to Hunter. Hunter's naturally reserved personality was stretched by all the flirting and she had to pull him aside to give him a break.

"Forget Tony. I should have just bought a good suit and started going to church. I swear, I've *never* had that effect on women before," Hunter said, blushing slightly.

Kit laughed softly and straightened his tie. "I hate to break it to you, but you're eye candy, Hunter. And when they find out you're financially stable and own your own home, there'll be no rest for you," she promised.

Hunter leaned down and nuzzled her cheek. "Was that what won you over? My house?" he asked, with a raised eyebrow.

Kit shook her head and slipped her arms around his waist. "No. It was just you. You were kind to me. You were so nice and sweet. You found my painting and hung it in your home. You worried if I made it home safely. And you came when I was hurt. You won me all by yourself," she said.

Hunter's eyes turned a brilliant blue as he looked around the hallway, as if he wanted to kiss her, but couldn't because of all the eyes. She laughed and shook her finger at him. "This is the Lord's house. You can't kiss me in church."

Hunter sighed. "Darn. Well, then I'll tell you when I fell for you. It was that first night when you were teaching me to do the Floss move. I felt as if the sun had broken open inside my chest and all this warmth was streaming out of my heart, aiming for you like a tractor beam."

Kit grinned at the sci-fi reference, and gave in and kissed him quickly on the cheek. "Winston Hunter, you are the man of my dreams," she said, and then turned and saw Rob standing close by, watching them with a fierce frown on his face.

"Hey, Rob," Hunter said coolly, standing up straight and keeping his arm securely around her waist.

Rob nodded his head and turned to Kit. "Man of your dreams, huh? Seems to me, that I overheard a conversation a couple months ago, where you had a dream about kissing *me*. What happened to *that* dream?" Rob taunted.

Kit rolled her eyes and moved to walk around Rob, ignoring him. Rob reached out and grabbed her wrist, stopping her. "Not so fast. I think your boyfriend should know that you promised to go out with me. *You owe me.* You've been charging me fifteen percent more for bread and you haven't paid up. I have a reunion up in Seattle this Tuesday. I want you to go with me as my date," he said, his eyes hard as glass.

Kit glanced around for Layla, wishing she could just hand this one off, but being a strong woman meant fighting your own battles. She opened her mouth to tell Rob not in his wildest dreams, when Hunter stopped her.

"Sure, Rob. We're exclusive, but this is just a business dinner, so I don't mind. But after Tuesday night, I'd appreciate it if you would back off. Kit's made it clear *many* times, that she's not interested in going out with you romantically. I hope this will be the end of it," Hunter said, staring Rob in the eyes.

Rob looked surprised and blinked a few times before nodding his head slowly. "Fine. If Kit still doesn't want anything to do with me after Tuesday night, I'll back off."

Kit watched, her mouth open, as Rob walked away whistling cheerfully. She turned slowly and stared up at Hunter as if he'd grown horns. "You just agreed, *without asking me how I felt*, to my going on a date with Rob. You told me that you wanted us to be exclusive and now *you're* the one throwing me to the wolf. *Have you lost your mind?*" she demanded, feeling angry and confused.

Hunter frowned, looking after Rob, and took her hand and led her outside into the parking lot. He took her to his car, a bright, silver Tesla, and opened the door for her.

"We'll talk about it on the way to lunch," he said, looking at her cautiously.

Kit stared grimly at him but got in, pulling her skirt over her knees as he shut the door for her. As they drove toward his home, she was determined to wait him out. He was waiting for her to jump into a tirade, but she wasn't going to give him the satisfaction.

After five more minutes of excruciating silence, Hunter finally cleared his throat and began talking. "Rob was a professional athlete. For someone, *anyone,* to make it to that level of a sport, they naturally have to have a lot of competitiveness. I think I mentioned to you already, that I was positive Rob was making this into some kind of game. Not intentionally though. He's determined to win you from me. Prove who the better man is sort of thing. The only way to get him to stop, is to give you to him. So I did," he said, looking over at her quickly to gauge her reaction.

Kit continued to stare stonily ahead, as if she hadn't heard him.

Hunter sighed loudly and reached for her hand. Kit crossed her arms instead. Hunter's hand fell on her knee and he left it there.

"It was the only way to stop him, Kit. But I couldn't have given him his chance with you unless I was positive there was no way in the world he could ever take you from me. When he realizes Tuesday night that there's no possible way you would ever have feelings for him, he'll back off gracefully. If he doesn't get his chance with you, he'll just keep hassling you," Hunter said quietly.

Kit looked out the side window and leaned her head against the seat as a slight headache started to pound.

"Your head's hurting, isn't it?" Hunter asked, and pulled the car over to the side of the road. He opened the glove compartment and took out a bottle of Ibuprofen and took out two pills for her. "Here, take this. It will help."

Kit took the pills from Hunter and the bottle of water he kept in the middle compartment and swallowed gratefully. Afterward, she turned and looked at him sadly.

"You should have asked me first, Hunter. I'm not a prize to be won by either of you. You don't get to make those kinds of decisions for me."

Hunter winced and looked away. "And this is where I mess up. I think I warned you I would be a rotten boyfriend," he said, looking up at her with a boyish smile.

Kit glared at him and looked away. "I won't put up with that macho, sexist behavior, Hunter. Not even from the man I love."

Hunter looked regretful and grabbed both her hands in his. "I'm sorry, Kit. Forgive me, but can't you see what I'm trying to say?"

Kit shrugged and pulled on her hands, but he was holding on too tight. "You might have a point, but if you ever make a date for me with another man again, I'll let Layla loose on you, and I am *not* kidding," she said, frowning darkly at him.

Hunter's eyes went wide and he nodded. "That's actually a pretty good threat. And I promise I will never set you up with another man again. Especially since the idea of you being with another man makes me physically ill," he said, his jaw clenched and his eyes dark.

Kit looked down at their hands twined together and she shook her head. "I hate this."

Hunter smiled and started the car. "Exactly. And that's why you're going," he said, and then drove her to his house.

Kit lay on the chaise lounge on Hunter's deck, while he grilled shrimp kabobs with pineapple, and red and green peppers. The salad was from a bag and the bread wasn't hers, but he had honestly tried, *really hard,* and she was impressed.

"For dessert, I was thinking of taking you over to my mom's for pie. But we can stay here and relax if you're not up to it," he said casually, as they took their plates into the kitchen.

Kit raised an eyebrow at him and he blushed. *Caught.*

"Sure, Hunter, but maybe not too long of a visit. I want to get to bed early tonight. I have a full day tomorrow," she said lightly.

Hunter grinned and kissed her happily. "You are the best. Let's hurry though. She was expecting us a half an hour ago."

Kit shook her head and decided to be a good sport about it and let it go as they drove over the bridge back into Tacoma. He drove her to a small, exclusive gated community and punched a code into a large iron gate before driving through.

"Now, you'll love my mom, but my dad isn't like me very much. He's actually more like. . . *Rob*," he said quietly, with no emotion in his voice.

Kit looked at him sharply and reached over to grab his hand. He glanced over and caught her gaze and smiled sadly. "We're not close."

Kit squeezed his hand as he pulled into a long winding driveway that led to a very modern and obviously expensive home. "Wow, what does your dad do for a living?" she asked, in awe at the three stories of stucco and wood.

Hunter got out of the car and walked around, opening the door for her. "My dad sells insurance. I bought them this house when I sold my first game. Kind of my way of telling my dad, *see, I can be a success*, just a different kind of success. It didn't help," he said, with a shrug of his shoulders and a tight smile.

Kit bit her lip and kissed his cheek as they walked up the long paved walkway to the front door. "You *are* a success, Hunter. You're a good man. That's the only success that matters," she said quietly, as the front door opened to reveal what looked like Ken and Barbie, the Baby boomer boxed set.

"You must be Kit!" squealed, the stylish, trim blond woman who rushed down the stairs to throw her arms around Kit's neck, squeezing her tightly and hurting her still sore head.

Hunter winced and pulled at his mom's arms. "Mom, Kit was hurt, remember? Her head is really tender, you have to be gentle," he said, pulling Kit back into his arms.

Hunter's mom looked aghast and blushed in embarrassment. "Oh, honey, I'm so sorry."

Kit smiled and touched the side of her head softly with her fingers. "It's okay, Mrs. Hunter."

The woman shook her head and put her hands on her hips. "Call me Julie. Win told us about that man attacking you at your bakery. I just can't imagine. I think if that happened to me, I would have died of fright. Jack, come on down and meet

Winston's girlfriend. Stop standing there like a statue," she said, with a nervous laugh.

Kit smiled politely as the tall, well-dressed man walked slowly down the steps toward them. Like Hunter, he had blue eyes, but where Hunter's eyes could turn from light and sweet, to dark and intense, this man's eyes were just distant, almost cold.

"Hi there, Kit. Nice to meet you," he said, and held out his hand to shake hers.

Kit smiled and shook his hand and felt a sizzle of something swim through her veins. *Challenge maybe?* She would win over Hunter's father for him, if it killed her.

"Thanks for having us over today, Jack. I've been so curious to meet you both. When I first tasted your peach pie, Julie, I was determined to beg you to come work for us. And Jack, after falling in love with Hunter, I wanted to meet the man responsible for raising the most loving, good and intelligent man, I've ever met," she said, and couldn't help glancing back at Hunter, who was smiling at her suspiciously with a raised eyebrow.

Jack cleared his throat and smiled a little more genuinely. "Winston is his own man and always has been. I don't know if I've been much of an influence on him at all, to be honest," he said, sounding a little annoyed about it. "I was always trying to take him to football games, and he was always wanting to go to comic book stores or museums," he said, with a derisive laugh.

Kit wrapped her arms around Hunter's waist, and leaned her head against his chest as he leaned down and kissed the top of her head. "Don't be so modest, Jack. A father is the biggest influence a man can have. You might have different interests and hobbies, but it's what's inside that counts. Hunter is an honorable man. He must have gotten that from you. I envy Hunter, since I grew up without a father. I'm thinking I might make him share you," she said, with a charming smile.

Jack's cheeks turned red and he smiled shyly at Kit. "I wouldn't mind. I didn't have much time to be a father to Win when he was younger, and I've always regretted it. It would be nice to think I could make up for it somehow," he admitted, glancing at Hunter hesitantly.

Kit felt Hunter's stiff muscles and knew this was hard for him. She hugged him tighter and looked up and saw Hunter looking surprised. "I'd like that," he said quietly, and smiled back at his dad.

Kit felt her heart expand and she walked out of Hunter's arms and put her arm through Julie's. "Where is this pie, Julie? I swear if it's as good as the other one, I might kidnap you and force you to work in our bakery," she said, walking up the steps with Hunter's mom, while Hunter and Jack walked much more slowly behind them.

Julie chattered on about picking her own fruit and pulled her into the kitchen. It was state of the art, but made to look like an old fashioned 1950's kitchen. The appliances were a bright sky blue and the counters were a modern white marble. Kit turned around in a circle and felt envious.

"I love this, Julie. Who wouldn't want to make pies in a kitchen like this?" she said, smiling at all the old fashioned touches and antiques.

Julie laughed and went to the fridge to grab a carton of whipping cream. "Winston insisted that I have the kitchen of my dreams. *That boy.* He was so determined to spoil me, I couldn't stop him," she said, with obvious love in her voice.

Kit leaned on the counter and smiled encouragingly. "Tell me all about Winston."

Julie glowed as she prattled on about Hunter from the time he was born until first grade. She finished adding the cream to the pie and then frowned. "I'll have to tell you the rest later. Let's take the pie in. Follow me," she said and picked up two plates of pie leaving Kit to get the other two.

Kit followed Julie down a hallway and into a large family room with a two story stone fireplace. It was the focal point of the room. And hanging over the fireplace, *was one of her paintings.*

Kit gasped and almost dropped the plates, as she stared in

shock at one of the first paintings she'd ever sold. It was a painting she'd done of a city scene out her window in Seattle. She felt her throat close up and she closed her eyes as strong emotions overtook her. Gratitude. Relief. *Love.*

She concentrated on breathing slowly in and out, as someone took the plates from her and then pulled her into a warm, strong embrace.

"I think I first fell in love with your art. Then I fell in love with you," Hunter whispered into her ear.

Kit nodded her head and swallowed, before opening her eyes and pulling back to look into Hunter's tender, searching gaze.

"How long has that painting hung there?" she asked, licking her lips and staring at her painting again.

Hunter turned and looked at the painting with a faint smile. "About two years. I found it at an art auction and bought it. At first I didn't even realize the same artist that had painted *Choices* had painted this one. You signed this one K. Kendall and the one I have, is signed Katrina Kendall. No one could tell me what the title is. What is it?" he asked, kissing her temple.

Kit closed her eyes and leaned her head against his solid shoulder as her heart felt like bursting. "I called it, *Rebirth,*" Kit said, and then turned in Hunter's arms and put her hands on both sides of his face, not even caring if his parents were in the room or not, and pulled his face down to hers and kissed him.

Hunter tightened his arms around her and when she finally pulled back, kept his forehead on hers. "I was always meant to find you. I was always meant to love you," he said softly, for her ears only.

Jack cleared his throat loudly. "When you two are um, *done,* why don't you join us on the back terrace," he said, and disappeared out the patio doors.

Kit grinned at Hunter's reddening cheeks and kissed him again. "Tell me I'm not the first girl you've brought home," she teased.

Hunter looked away and took a deep breath. "Yeah, actually

you are. My parents thought I was gay for a while. Instead, I just had the world's worst luck with women."

Kit looked at the gorgeous man in front of her, and shook her head in bemusement. *What woman wouldn't jump at the chance to be with Hunter?*

"Well, your luck has just changed, Winston, because no one is ever going to love you, the way *I'm* going to love you," she said, loving the way his eyes brightened and crinkled at the corners. He leaned down to kiss her, but she pulled back, frowning all of a sudden.

"*What?*" Hunter asked, kissing her neck instead.

"I'm just not buying it. I know you've been working out and dressing differently and whatever, but I'm sorry. I saw the way women reacted to you at church. You'd be hot in jeans and a t-shirt and glasses. You can't tell me women didn't throw themselves at you," she said, looking at him with narrowed eyes.

Hunter blushed again and shrugged. "Well, actually there were a lot of girls who, um, made it clear they were attracted to me, and uh, *you know*. But the type of girls that were attracted to me, weren't the uh, type of girls *I* was attracted to," he said, sounding very uncomfortable.

Kit's eyes widened and she grinned. "Oh, gotcha. You had a thing for the cheerleaders, huh?"

Hunter looked away and bit his lip. Kit laughed and tickled his ribs, making him jump and laugh. "All those poor little honor roll girls, who were probably pining away for you. You should be ashamed of yourself, Hunter," she said, leaning up to kiss his chin playfully.

Hunter's eyes gleamed down at her penetratingly. "I can't even imagine what I would have done if I'd met *you* in high school, and you ignored me. I probably would have made a fool of myself over you."

Kit smiled happily. "I would have loved it. And you never know, I always had a thing for guys in glasses with large IQ's. You probably wouldn't have liked me though. I wasn't a cheerleader, I was a softball player."

Hunter laughed. "It wouldn't matter what you did in school. But I'm glad we met now. I can handle you now. And you can handle me," he said softly, running his hands down her hair softly. "And my parents too, it turns out," he said dryly.

Kit sighed happily. "They'll never know what hit them," she murmured, staring at the large comfortable couch in front of the fireplace, tempted to just sit on the couch and cuddle and look at her painting.

Hunter read her mind and pulled her toward the doors. "Later. Come on, our pie is waiting," he said sternly, and pushed her through the doors.

She spent the next hour listening to more stories of Hunter, while he sat quietly in embarrassment. Jack stayed quiet too, but when Julie brought out the photo albums, he was the one who pointed out his favorites. Kit kept glancing at Hunter and noticed he looked embarrassed, but happy too. Hunter soon got tired of memory lane and turned the tables on her, announcing that the artist who had painted the picture over their fireplace, was sitting right in front of them. Julie and Jack were both so stunned and thrilled that she had to spend the next half hour describing the artistic process and then explain *why* she wasn't painting full-time anymore.

Hunter smiled at Kit as he massaged the back of her neck lightly. "She's painting again, but it's just part time. She says she wants to use *me* for a model," he said, and then laughed as his mother waved her hand in front of her face, fighting back her emotions. Jack looked pleased at the idea too. Kit stared at Hunter silently for a moment with a small smile on her face as he stared back at her, his eye twinkling and soft.

Later, driving back to the bakery holding hands, Kit turned off the radio. "I liked your parents. They love you, you know," she said, twisting her body, so she could sit sideways and study Hunter's profile.

He glanced at her quickly and grinned. "Not half as much as they like you. You, Kit Kendall, are a dangerous charmer. Who could ever withstand you?" he asked, and kissed her knuckles making her sigh.

"You'd be surprised," she said dryly. "I envy you, your parents. I lost my mother to a car accident, and I lost my father to drugs. Maybe you *should* share with me," she said, running her fingers through his hair.

Hunter looked over at her and smiled crookedly. "I was waiting for you to propose. I'm so relieved. I thought I'd have to wait a few more months, and then get down on one knee. I like your feminist approach to everything. This makes everything so much easier. I'm free next month," he said, with a gleam in his eyes as he watched her carefully for her reaction.

Kit's mouth fell open, before it snapped shut. She looked away and shook her head. "*Interesting*," she said softly.

Hunter pulled the car over to the side of the road and turned off the engine as he grabbed her hands in his, staring at her so intensely she had had to look down.

"What do you mean by, *interesting*?" he asked.

Kit smiled and pursed her lips. "I didn't know you were thinking in that direction. That's all," she said, almost shyly.

Hunter breathed out slowly and put one arm over her shoulders, bringing her closer. "I won't alarm you and tell you how long I've been thinking in that direction. But does that shock you? Does my saying that, make you want to run away, or, not take my calls or um, see me anymore?" he asked, sounding uncertain.

Kit tilted her head and studied the man she loved. He was adorable. And he was all hers.

"No," she said softly, leaning over a few inches to kiss him on his cheek. "It doesn't make me want to run," she said, and kissed him on his other cheek. "I don't scare that easy."

Hunter's eyes brightened and his mouth opened as he stared at her with hope battling his insecurities. "*Then* . . ."

Kit put a finger over his mouth and shook her head. "Then that means exactly what you think it means," she said, and kissed him, putting her hand behind his neck pulling him closer.

Later, when she walked through the door to her bedroom, she walked straight to her closet and went to the large white dress, hanging amongst her skirts and jackets and sundresses. She pulled it out and walked out into her bedroom to stand in front of her full length mirror. She stared at her face and saw something she didn't know she'd ever see. A woman on the verge of getting her prayers answered.

Chapter Thirteen

MONDAYS

Monday morning turned out like a lot of Monday mornings. *Bad.* Kit woke up late and was scolded by Layla and teased by Jane. Her first batch of bread didn't turn out. And she had bad hair. It was fluffy on one side and flat on the other. Monday was being flat out out cruel.

As she rushed to do another batch of bread, Layla and Jane opened the store and were busy with customers. They hadn't had a bad review in a while, so hopefully people would forget and come back. She switched her playlist to Camila Cabello, and sang along, trying to get in a better mood.

When her bread was done, she walked in the store with a tray of sourdough and stopped as she saw Garrett kissing Jane, and Layla looking on with a frown. The bell rang over the door and she and Layla looked to see who it was.

Alex Foster.

Kit frowned and Layla glared automatically. But Alex ignored them as he walked slowly over to Jane looking horrified. Garrett finished kissing Jane, and pulled back ,grinning happily.

"Now, that's how to start a Monday," he said, with a laugh.

Alex turned bright red in the face and his hands clenched at his sides. "What is going on here? Jane? *Who is this?*" Alex demanded, with his fists on his hips.

Garrett turned to look at Alex with a frown facing down the much shorter man. Kit looked at Alex and saw what Garrett must be seeing. A man in his forties, with a slight paunch, trying too hard to look young.

"I'm Garrett, Jane's boyfriend. Who are *you?*" Garrett asked, in a cold, but polite voice.

"I'm Alex Foster, a business associate of the Kendall sisters. *And,* a special friend of Jane's. I don't know when you two started seeing each other, but it seems like this has all happened rather quickly. Jane, I'd like to talk to you. *Privately*," Alex said, looking on edge and upset.

Jane's eyes were huge as she shook her head. "No, Alex. *No.* We're *not* special friends or *any* kind of friend. If you have anything to say, you can say it here in front of everyone," she said, with dignity.

Garrett looked at Jane's upset face and then turned and stared at Alex as he crossed his arms over his chest, making his already massive muscles look twice as big.

Alex ignored Garrett and moved around him to face Jane. "You know you and I have always had a special connection. From the first day I met you, Jane, I knew that you and I were attracted to each other. I know I've been gone for a little while, but seriously Jane. Get rid of this loser and let's go to lunch. There is so much I want to talk to you about. I want you to know how I really feel about you," he said reaching out and taking her hand in his.

Garrett's eyes turned black as he bared his teeth and Jane pulled her hand quickly out of Alex's grasp. Layla took out her cell phone and walked over to the corner of the store and dialed a number, putting the phone to her ear and talking quickly.

Kit swallowed and walked forward, hoping she could diffuse the situation.

"Mr. Foster, Jane really likes Garrett. He's a great guy. He's a veteran and now he runs his landscaping company. He's a wonderful man and has done so much to serve our country. I think maybe you should let go of whatever feelings you think you might have for Jane, and find someone else. She's *not* interested," she said, as bluntly, but as kindly as she could, as she nervously glanced at Garrett, who was staring at Alex as if he wanted to hurt him.

Alex grunted and rolled his eyes. "Well, I pay taxes and I helped pay for the military. *Big deal*. I can take care of you, Jane. I can promise you that *this* guy can't give you the lifestyle I can. I bet he can barely afford his rent," he said, with a laugh.

Jane's mouth fell open, just as the bell rang and Tate Matafeo in uniform walked in, looking alert.

Garrett looked over at Tate with a frown. "Oh, *great*, another one."

Tate raised an eyebrow, ignoring Garrett as he looked over at Layla. "Everything okay here?"

Layla walked forward and put her arm around Jane's waist. "Alex has been trying to convince Jane to dump Garrett, and go out with him. I think Alex was a little shocked to come back from his trip, and find that Jane has a boyfriend," she said, looking at Alex with a frown.

Tate sighed and rubbed his forehead. Kit smiled, knowing he was having a Monday just as bad as hers.

"Alex, Jane is involved with this man. It would be a good idea to leave the bakery now, until you can come to grips with it," he said, in an authoritative way, that made even Garrett stand up straighter, and look at him with a creased forehead.

Alex sniffed and shook his head. "There's no possible way Jane could be attracted to *The Rock,* over there. Jane is a woman of distinguished tastes. She's a woman of refinement. She needs a man like *me*. Someone intelligent, well off and someone who can spoil her. What do you two even do for fun? *Work out?*" he asked, with sneer.

Kit shook her head in awe at the stupidity. Jane grimaced and bit her lip. Tate raised his hand in a peaceful gesture, just as Garrett reared back his arm and let his fist fly into the side of Alex's face, sending him flying across the shiny, tiled floor where he lay in a lump. Not moving.

Everything erupted after that. Jane screamed as Layla rushed toward Alex, and Kit went to Jane. Tate walked purposefully toward Garrett shaking his head.

"You shouldn't have done that, Garrett. I know the man's an idiot, but now I have to arrest you. Seriously? Hitting the guy right in front of a cop?" he asked, with a slight smile on his face, as he took out his handcuffs.

Garrett was breathing heavy now, and his hands were bunched at his sides as he stared at the cuffs in Tate's hands. His face was tense and his eyes were wild. Tate frowned as he stared at Garrett and shook his head.

"Hey, now, calm down, Garrett. We'll take you down to the station and I'm sure Jane will bail you out. I'm going to read you your rights now. You'll probably get off with community service," he said, in a calm soothing voice.

Garrett swallowed hard and shook his head as if he were in pain. "*Don't touch me. If you touch me, I swear I'll take you out,*" he said, in a rough voice that didn't even sound like his.

Kit grabbed Jane's arm and dragged her back away from Tate and Garrett. Layla stayed where she was by Alex. He had been knocked out and looked like a limp rag doll. Layla stared hard at Garrett and then looked at Jane and Kit.

"Get her out of here," Layla said to Kit.

Jane shook her head jerkily, staring back and forth between Tate and Garrett. She shook off Kit's hand and moved cautiously toward her boyfriend.

"*Garrett?* Listen to Tate. Just let him put the cuffs on. I'll come down with you to the station and we'll get you out. It's okay, Garrett. *It's okay,*" she said soothingly.

Garrett acted as if he hadn't even heard her. Tate was staring at Garrett's eyes with a frown and he took his radio out of his back pocket. "I need backup assistance," he said into the radio, and slipped it back into his pocket.

"Jane, back away. *Now*," Tate ordered, his voice hard and deadly.

Jane stared at Garrett, stricken and helpless, but she obeyed Tate and moved slowly back from him.

"Garrett, you're a good guy. Anyone would take offense at what Alex was saying. No one blames you, but the law is the law. This is just a simple altercation. I promise you'll be out before you know it," Tate said softly, reaching for his cuffs again.

Garrett's breathing turned even more erratic, and his face looked strained and red as he stared at Tate unseeing.

"I'm not going to jail," he said, in a husky voice and then launched himself at Tate, pounding his fist into the right side of Tate's face.

Tate took the hit but didn't fall, just shook his head and moved backward, ready now for the attack. "*Get Jane back!*" he yelled angrily at Kit, who was still pulling on her sister's arm.

Garrett jumped for Tate again, grabbing him around his waist and bringing him down to the ground, in a brutal take down. Tate was ready now though, and flipped Garrett onto his back and let his own fist fly into Garrett's face, so hard, that he should have been knocked out. Garrett shook it off and started pummeling Tate in the ribs. Tate blocked most of the punches, trying to get in a position to restrain Garrett.

Garrett roared in anger as Tate put him in a headlock and then used his body to twist him around so that he was now on his stomach. He kneeled on Garrett's back, ignoring the blood running from the side of his mouth, as Garrett twisted and roared, trying to get free.

Jane stood against the wall, with tears running down her face. Layla left Alex's side and moved to stand in front of her sisters. "Tate, what can I do to help?" she asked, staring at Garrett sadly.

Tate didn't look up as he answered her. "Just keep Jane back.

Garrett has lost it. If he gets free, he's going to come after me again," he said calmly.

Layla nodded, but looked ill as she walked over to Jane and Kit, and put her arm around Jane's shoulders protectively. Within minutes, the backup Tate had requested showed up and assisted him as he read Garrett his rights. Tate left to go outside with the other policemen, but came back in just minutes later with the paramedics. In a few moments, Alex was on a stretcher and out the door.

Kit stared at Tate's bruised and bloodied mouth and winced. "Can I get you a wet cloth, Tate?" she asked and he nodded.

Jane walked slowly over to Tate and touched his face gently, before she began sobbing. Tate looked at her stonily for a moment, before his face gentled, and he put his arms around her, hugging her and rubbing her back.

He looked over Jane's head at Layla and cleared his throat. "I'm going to need you all to come down to the station to make statements. Will you be able to close up shop for an hour or so?"

Layla nodded her head quickly, and walked over to pat Tate on the back. "Tate, I'm so grateful you came when you did. I don't know what would have happened if you hadn't showed up."

Tate kept his arms around Jane, soothing her as she continued to cry into his chest, as Kit reached him and began dabbing at his face. He grinned suddenly and looked at Kit and Layla. "I guess this is what it feels like to have sisters," he said, and then glanced at Jane. His arms tightened automatically and Kit smiled to herself. She was positive Tate didn't feel brotherly towards Jane.

"Well, I was thinking it would be a fair fight between you two, but you were able to take him down easily. I'm kind of impressed," Kit said lightly, wondering if he would need a couple stitches in his lip.

Tate laughed and looped his arms easily around Jane's waist as she started to calm down. "I grew up playing Rugby with all of my Samoan cousins. There aren't too many people who can take me down," he said with a shrug before leaning back from Jane and tipping her face up.

Jane looked up into Tate's eyes and his face went gentle again. "You're a little shaken up. Why don't you take a half an hour to calm down, and then come down to the station? I'll look out for your boyfriend," he said, pulling away as he said the word, realizing belatedly that he shouldn't be holding someone else's girl.

Jane looked crestfallen as she was forced to step back from him. Layla put a supportive arm around her shoulders and nodded. "We'll be there. Thanks again, Tate. It's nice to know we can always count on you. If we ever did have a brother, you'd be the one I'd pick," she said, with a warm smile.

Tate smiled back and nodded before disappearing out the door without another word.

Jane watched the spot where he'd been standing just moments before and her shoulders sagged in defeat. Kit smoothed her younger sister's hair down and stared at Jane's tortured face, wanting more than anything to help her.

"Jane? Are you okay? I guess seeing your boyfriend fight another man must be traumatic," she said lamely, glancing at Layla for help.

Layla looked at her and shrugged as Jane laughed cynically. "You mean, it was traumatic for me to see my boyfriend fight the man I'm *actually* in love with? Yeah, that wasn't fun," she said lightly, but with so much pain in her voice that it made Kit groan.

Layla turned the sign to CLOSE and pulled Jane over to one of their tables by the window and forced her to sit down. "Honey, tell me," she said softly, sitting down and pointing Kit to the other seat.

Kit sat down next to her sisters and grabbed Jane's hand in hers. "You're in love with Tate? Like all the way, heaven and earth, body and soul in love with him?" she asked.

Layla smiled at Kit and tilted her head. "Wow, you are in love with Hunter. You never understood before."

Kit blushed and shrugged. "No one can understand until they've felt it before."

Jane licked her lips and looked out the window silently for a moment. "I feel that for Tate. Like, when he comes into the bakery, my whole body comes alive. I can see clearer, I can hear better, my heart pounds and I have to fight myself from running to him and jumping in his arms. And when I run into him at the store or the movie theater and he's with another girl, I feel like I could die. I see him with his arm around another woman and I know that it's wrong. His arms should be around *me*."

Kit frowned and looked away from her sister's tormented face. "Is that why you started dating Garrett? Because you saw Tate with another woman?"

Jane laughed, a tortured pain filled sound that made Layla and Kit wince. "Not just one woman. He's never with the same woman twice. He'll date everyone but me. I put my heart on the line and threw my pride away and asked him out. I told him I wanted to go out with him and he said, no, I was too young, and too different from him. And that was the end of it. I keep telling my heart to stop loving him, but it won't listen. I think about him *all* the time. At night, in the morning, when I'm baking. He's constantly with me. *I can't get rid of him*," she said, sounding desperate.

Layla sighed and pushed Jane's hair out of her face tenderly. "Jane, from what I just saw, Tate has just as many powerful feelings for you, as you have for him. The way he held you just now, was so tender and sweet and . . . *loving*. That's the only word I can think of that fits. I don't know what's going on inside his head, that he doesn't think he can date you, but his heart has a mind of its own too. Something's going on between you two. We just need to figure it out."

Kit smiled slightly. "Good plan. But in the meantime, what are we going to do about Garrett?"

Jane ran her hands through her hair and leaned her head on her chin. "I'm going to bail him out. But I'm going to insist that he gets counseling in return. He's talked to me about some of the things that he went through in Iraq and he's not over it. He says he's always angry. For no reason, he's just always angry. He can't sleep well either. Some of his memories are always with him. He needs help."

Kit nodded. "So maybe this is a good thing that happened. It's crappy that he has to get arrested to get the help he needs, but on the plus side, he knocked out Alex."

Layla laughed and sat back, leaning her head back as she stared at the ceiling. "Talk about needing counseling. It's like he has this fantasy relationship with you going on inside his head. He really thinks you belong to him. I think we should bring that up with Tate. Maybe, bring up the fact that he's basically been stalking you. I mean, a little out of shape, wimpy guy like that, antagonizing a Marine? He has to be insane."

Jane shivered. "Hopefully, this will be a good wakeup call for both of them."

Kit stared off into space as her sisters chatted about local therapists. Alex wasn't the one to attack her in the store. He was a different size and shape than her attacker had been. And if it wasn't him, then that left only two options. A random thief *or* their father. She looked down at her white clenched hands and willed herself to relax.

She was betting it was her father.

Chapter Fourteen

REUNION

Hunter lay on her bed, looking relaxed as he watched her get ready for her date with Rob. With his hands behind his head and his knee up and a half smile on his face, you'd think he was fine. *Unless you looked at his eyes.* They looked lethal. Kit leaned over her bathroom counter with one arm as she applied a second coat of mascara. She looked at herself and smiled. She'd never looked better.

She was wearing a dress she'd borrowed from Layla. It was black over silver and had a scoop neck, sweetheart outline, with a knitted overlay, mesh hem and a flowy skirt that came to above her knees. She fluffed her hair around her head and finished off with a light coat of gloss on her lips.

She looked one more time in the mirror and then walked toward the man she loved slowly, swinging her hips for effect. "Well, how do I look, handsome?" she asked, walking to the edge of the bed and sitting down, next to his long legs.

Hunter stared at her for a moment and shook his head. "I was an idiot. Don't go," he said quietly.

Kit tilted her head to the side and smiled slightly. She could sense how tense he was and felt a little satisfaction at it. Served him right for sending her off on a date with Rob without asking her first.

"Problem?" she asked lightly, as she followed the line of the muscle on his arm down to his shoulder.

Hunter pulled his arms down from behind his head and sat up, grasping her waist with his hands. "You look breathtaking, what man wouldn't do anything to have you?" he said, his face twisting in what looked like pain.

Kit frowned and raised her hand to his face. "Good thing the choice is up to me then, huh?"

Hunter stared at her with his eyes now dark and intense. "Where's he taking you again?" he asked.

Kit shrugged and fluffed her skirts out around her legs. "Some baseball reunion party up in Seattle. All of his old buddies are getting together or something. What are you going to do tonight, while I'm dancing and partying?" she asked, right before she was suddenly on her back with Hunter leaning over her.

Kit gasped in surprise and raised her hands to Hunter's shoulders. "*Hunter!*"

Hunter stared down into her eyes, their noses almost touching. "You're torturing me on purpose, aren't you? Even the night of the party, when I first met you, you never looked like this. You're punishing me for agreeing to this date. *Admit it*," he said quietly, his eyebrows together.

Kit licked her lips and stared up into Hunter's face, studying the planes and contours of the face of the man she treasured, but definitely *was* punishing.

"And what if I am? Don't you deserve it? I should be going out with you tonight, dancing. I should be kissing *you* under the stars. Instead, I'll have another man's arms around me. *I'm furious with you*," she said softly, smoothing his eyebrows with the tip of her fingers.

Hunter closed his eyes and lowered his head for a moment, making a growling sound in his throat. And then he was kissing her, but not like he'd ever kissed her before. There was too much heat and passion. But before she could wrap her arms around his neck, he was gone. Walking quickly out the door and running down the stairs.

Kit slowly sat up and touched her lips with her fingers as her heart beat wildly in her chest. She smiled and stood up, walking back to the bathroom to fix her lipstick. *Winston Hunter had just learned his lesson.*

A half hour later, Rob came to the door, wearing slacks and a dress shirt opened at the throat. He looked tan, gorgeous and very pleased with himself. Jane opened the door for him as she walked over to the counter to grab her clutch.

"I've never seen a more gorgeous creature than you," Rob said, as he watched her walk toward him.

Kit smiled coldly at him, now wishing desperately she hadn't gone all out. She should have changed after Hunter left and put her hair up in a ponytail or something. Rob was now thinking she'd gone all out for him. She felt a sick sinking feeling in her stomach and looked at Jane for help.

Jane was frowning as she stared back but raised her hands helplessly. They were stuck. She couldn't back out. Because of Hunter. Kit felt a little anger toward Hunter spark inside like a Fourth of July firecracker. She could do this.

"Thanks Rob. You look nice yourself. Ready to go?" she asked, looking over her shoulder as she heard footsteps.

Layla walked into the store, ignoring Rob as usual and came to stand by Jane. "Kit, you look so pretty," she said, with a sad shake of her head and a questioning lift of her eyebrow.

Kit shrugged and slipped her clutch under her arm. "Yeah, it's amazing the lengths I'll go, to get a fifteen percent hike," she said dryly, watching both of her sisters wince in tandem.

Rob cleared his throat and opened the door for her. "We need to get on the road, Kit. We're going to be driving in rush hour traffic."

Kit took in another deep breath, straightened her shoulders and walked past Rob out the door and down the steps to his black sports car. He opened the door for her and she smiled her thanks.

During the hour drive to Seattle, they talked about business and customers. Rob was trying to live up to his side of the bargain as he told her about a few bad reviews he'd received when he'd first opened up his restaurant. He explained how he countered the bad press by sponsoring t-shirts for local 5k-runs and donating food to local schools. And of course, sponsoring a Little League baseball team.

She found herself relaxing and could tell he was honestly trying to give her good advice. Kit made up her mind to try and enjoy the night. It was just a few hours of her life and then she'd be back in Fircrest, baking and dating the man who owned her heart.

When they arrived at the restaurant, the valet opened her door and assisted her out. Rob joined her and escorted her inside with a possessive hand on her waist. Kit frowned and tried to move away, but Rob tightened his hold, leaning down to whisper in her ear.

"You're mine tonight, remember that. Your only job is to look good and look like you belong to me. I want every man here to be jealous, because I have the most beautiful woman in the room," he said, with a wolfish smile.

Kit shuddered and looked away. Rob would only ever see her as arm candy. *An object.* He would never bother to look past her exterior to her soul. She ached for Hunter, but found herself nodding to Rob. "Fine. I'm yours for a few hours, but watch your hands. It's all just for show. Don't forget that."

Rob paused, making her stop as he looked down into her face. "Oh, this isn't for show, Kit. *This is real.* After tonight, you're going to see the difference between being with me and being with a nerd. I'm the only man for you, Kit. You know it. *I* know it. You're punishing me for messing things up with you. I can respect that. But let's stop playing games. You *are* mine," he whispered, and then swooped down, capturing her mouth in a kiss that was too intimate for public.

Kit ripped her mouth away and pushed him hard in the chest. She glared up at him and wiped her mouth with her hand. "You *little* . . ." she said, but was interrupted by loud laughter coming from right behind her.

"Rob! You showed. And what do we have here?" came a purring voice, that made her want to run to the bathroom and wash her hands.

Rob cleared his throat, his face turning red as Kit turned to face a large, red haired man with a thick goatee and an earring in his ear. The leer in his eye was unmistakable. She was in dangerous territory. Rob seemed to sense that as well and put a possessive arm around her shoulders, bringing her in close to his side.

"Hey, Rusty. Long time, *brotha*," Rob said, smiling proudly.

Rusty ignored Rob as he continued to stare at Kit. "Introduce me to my new girlfriend, Rob," he said, with a shark like smile.

Kit put a plastic smile on her face, feeling more like a Barbie doll than she ever had in her life.

"This is Kit Kendall. She bakes the bread for my restaurant," Rob said, somehow making her feel diminished.

Rusty ran his hands over his goatee and looked even more interested. "She cooks?" he asked, as if she couldn't speak for herself.

Rob nodded proudly. "You can say that again. I am one lucky man," he said, smiling at her.

Kit ignored Rob as she kept her eyes on Rusty. Like a jungle predator, if she made a run for it, this man looked like he'd run her down.

"Rob, I hate to break this to you. buddy, but I'm going to have to steal your woman away from you," he said, with a big grin. "A gorgeous woman who can cook? Kit, how do you feel about weekends in the Caribbean and diamonds?" he asked, reaching out and grabbing her hand, kissing her knuckles in a romantic gesture, that made her want to gag.

"I feel fine about it, Rusty. How do you feel about the Me Too movement?" she asked, turning the tables on him.

Rusty looked mystified for a second and then laughed. "I look forward to being kept on my toes. Save me a few dances, Kit. I've gotta run and say hi to Dennis. But *don't* go anywhere. I'll find you," he said, with narrowed eyes before striding away.

Kit turned and looked at Rob with a cold stare. Rob shrugged and grinned. "Rusty is so jealous of me he's dying. This is great. Come on, I want to introduce you to everybody. When everyone sees you and hears about how well my restaurant is doing, no one will ever feel bad for me ever again," he said, with a hard look, as he grabbed her hand and pulled her into the crowds.

Kit's cheeks hurt after smiling for an hour straight and being dragged from one group of ball players and their girlfriends to another. She was relieved when they began to be seated for dinner, since the four inch heels she was wearing were killing her feet.

The dinner was nice but geared toward men. A lot of meat selections, a few vegetables and four potato dishes. The dessert carts were unreal though and Kit took a pen out of her clutch and began writing down the different dessert descriptions and taking pictures on her phone, so she could show Layla and Jane.

Tonight might not be a total waste of time after all. She was determined to get back to the kitchens, and see if she could wheedle a few recipes from the chef. She ordered everything they offered, in spite of the raised eyebrows of their waiter. She started with the Spiced Brownie with Ancho Chile, and then tried a bite of the Ginger & Cinnamon Chocolate Tart with Hazelnut Brittle & Banana. But she *adored* the Vanilla Bean Cupcake with Lemon Curd & Blood Orange Marshmallow and knew that Jane had to have the recipe. But when she tried the Steamed Malaysian Coconut Cake with Basil Buttercream &

Candied Pine Nuts, she closed her eyes, picturing all of Layla's wedding guest's gasps of pleasure, when they devoured the wedding cake. There would be nothing left over for their first anniversary.

Kit grinned and licked her lips. *She had to get those recipes.* She opened her eyes and blinked in surprise as Rob and a few other men were staring at her. Rob leaned over and whispered in her ear. "Maybe you should give me a taste of what you're eating?" he whispered, in a sexy voice that had her rearing back and putting a hand on his chest.

"You can have the rest of mine. If you'll excuse me, I need to run to the ladies room," she said, and stood up, smoothing her dress down.

She didn't need to glance back. She knew every eye was on her and grimaced. She took her phone out of her purse and glanced at the time. It was only 9:30. *Ugh!* She had at least another hour of purgatory. They hadn't even started dancing yet.

She glanced at her phone and saw she had a text message from Hunter. She looked up and pushed through the door to the ladies room and sat down on the long cushy chaise, kicking up her tired feet to the side as she leaned back to read her text.

He kissed you. I saw the pictures.

Kit frowned and leaned her head back. *What in the world?* How could Hunter have seen Rob kiss her? He had to have had her followed, or he had planted a wire on her somehow. She looked all over her dress for some small computer type recording device but didn't see anything. He must have sent a spy. She glared at her phone and texted back.

Following me, Hunter?

Kit waited for his response as she tapped her finger on her phone. She didn't have to wait long.

Ever since you were attacked, I've had you followed. If I couldn't be there to protect you, I wanted someone around. Why did you let him kiss you?

Kit's frown eased and she smiled slightly. *Hmm*, that made sense. She might just forgive him.

According to Rob, I belong to him for the night. Punching him in the nose in front of all of his baseball buddies, might not look too good.

She wondered how Hunter would take that.

I'm going to kill Rob.

Kit rolled her eyes and kicked off her heels to massage her arch.

Why? This is all your doing, Hunter. I'll probably have to kiss him good night too, on top of fighting off all of his hormonal ex-teammates. Thanks again.

Kit knew she was being snotty, but couldn't seem to stop herself.

But what was worse than being kissed by someone you didn't want to be kissed by? And now she'd have to go dance with Rusty and all his buddies. She sighed and wondered if she could plead a headache and call Jane or Layla to come pick her up.

Her phone vibrated again and she glanced down at the screen. Hunter again.

Your bodyguard is inside the restaurant, keeping an eye on you. Say the word and he'll drive you home. Kit. Please. Say the word.

Kit leaned her head back against the wall, closing her eyes, so tempted to do just that. But if she didn't see the night through, Rob would never leave her alone. She slipped her phone in her clutch and stood up, groaning at the pain in her feet, as she opened the door and headed back into the crowd.

She danced for the next hour, being passed from one set of arms to the next. She watched as Rob danced with other women, flirting and laughing, but mostly reliving his glory days with all of his ex-teammates. He looked so happy, he was almost hyper. She felt a stirring of pity for him, knowing that tomorrow, he would be back in Fircrest, running his restaurant. Rob had lived a life that most men could only dream of, and being torn from that by an injury had been hard to take.

Two strong, hair covered arms slipped around her, and pulled her tight up against a steel-like chest. "There you are, gorgeous. I've been looking for you. Take off, Dave. It's my turn," Rusty said, turning her in his arms.

Kit swallowed nervously and looked for Rob, but he was busy talking in a circle of men and was completely ignorant of her peril.

"Hi, Rusty. Having a good time?" she asked, wrinkling her nose as she smelled the alcohol on his breath.

Rusty nodded. "I am now. Let's dance," he said, and pulled her into the middle of the dance floor, wrapping his arms so tightly around her, she felt claustrophobic. If she screamed in this crowd, no one would notice. But logically, what would Rusty do in public? She was probably safe here in the middle of the crowd.

"Let's spend the weekend together, Kit. I've got a house on the beach and a King size bed. Rob won't mind," he said, in a husky voice, as he stared down into her eyes.

Kit felt her heart speed up nervously, but she'd been born to handle men like this. She could handle Rusty. *Maybe.*

"If only I'd met you first, Rusty. But my heart belongs to Rob. I could never leave him, although it is tempting," she said, with a friendly smile. *Yeah right.*

Rusty looked down at her with a frown. "Really? You're seriously turning me down for Rob? He runs a restaurant. I make six figures a year and I have one of the best batting averages on the team. Honey, I thought you were smart," he said, with narrowed eyes.

Kit bit her lip and looked away. Rob was still laughing and slapping some guy on the back. Totally on her own. *Great.*

"Well, that's true love for you, Rusty. It makes you do stupid things. Now, be honest. I can't believe you're single. Look at you. You're gorgeous, you're rich and you have a great batting average. You *have* to have a girlfriend," she said, trying to pacify him.

Rusty grinned. "I have a few ladies on the side. But I'd get rid of everyone for you," he said, almost sounding sincere for a moment.

Kit smiled brightly and looked around for any excuse to get out of Rusty's arms. She was being pulled tighter and tighter against his chest. Pretty soon, she'd be a pancake.

"You know what, Rusty, I think I need to take a break from dancing. My feet are killing me," she said, being completely honest.

Rusty frowned and looked down at her four inch heels and grinned. "Good. I was just going to suggest we get you off your feet anyways. My car is just outside. Let's take a ride and I'll show you my house," he said, leaning down to whisper in her ear, and then taking a detour to her neck on the way up again.

Kit frowned. *Enough was enough.* She pushed out of Rusty's arms and held up her hands, wishing she had borrowed Layla's baton. "Good night, Rusty. The answer is, *no*," she said bluntly, with no smile and no pretense, as she turned and walked quickly away.

Rusty hurried to her side and grabbed her arm, stopping her. "Not so fast," he said, in a hard voice.

"Problem here?" asked a tall, black man, wearing a silk black t-shirt and black jeans.

Kit looked at him in relief and nodded quickly. This guy had to be Hunter's bodyguard. "Actually, *yes*," she said hurriedly, as Rusty pushed her aside and stood in front of the man.

"There's no problem, buddy. Take off. We're just having a friendly conversation," he said, clenching his hands at his side.

Rob walked up and looked at her and the men and rolled his eyes. "Kit, the effect you have on men is ridiculous. You have *two* men fighting over you, and *I'm* your date," he said, with a frown.

Kit's mouth dropped open and she ignored him. "This man has a hard time taking no for an answer," she said, to the black man, who looked at her grimly and nodded.

"Time to call it a night?" he asked, with a small smile.

Kit nodded in relief. "Yes, please. Will you take me home?"

The man nodded his head and held out his hand for her. "All part of the package deal," he said, with a frown at Rusty and Rob.

Rusty glared at the man and pushed him back with his hand, sending the guy back two steps. "She's not going home with anyone, but me," he swore, pushing his sleeves up.

Rob's eyebrows rose and he stared in surprise at his friend. "Rusty! Dude, Kit is *my* date. Why would she be going home with *you*? I'll be taking her home tonight."

Rusty glanced at him and looked confused. "Rob, I told you I was taking her from you. It's no big deal, right? Kit's way too hot for you, dude," he said with a smile, and a shake of his head.

Rob's face became expressionless for a moment, before he snarled and sent a left hook at Rusty's nose, making horrible contact and sending Rusty flying back toward Kit. The body-guard grabbed her quickly and led her swiftly toward her table where her clutch was.

"Grab your purse and let's go," he said, looking back over his shoulder as screams erupted and tables and chairs went flying, as Rob and Rusty starting beating each other up in a brutal, no holds bar way.

Kit grabbed her clutch, took off her heels and ran after the man and out the door into the night. He gave the valet his ticket and stood still in the night as he watched her gravely. Kit felt a moment of nervousness and decided she'd better make sure she wasn't going from the fire in to the frying pan.

"What's your name?" she asked, in a small voice.

The man smiled at her. "My name is Jabari Kondo, at your service. I've worked for Hunter for almost three years now. You are safe with me," he said, his dark brown eyes, kind in the moonlight.

Kit relaxed and nodded her head tiredly. *Thank heavens for Hunter and his foresight.* Although, now that she thought of it, she would have never been in this mess if it weren't for him. Jabari helped her into his sleek, silver sedan and they sped off into the night. Jabari didn't seem interested in conversation, so she leaned her head tiredly against the headrest and closed her eyes.

She must have fallen asleep, because she woke up when the car came to a stop. She blinked tiredly and smiled at Jabari. "Thanks again for saving me. I wasn't sure how I was going to get away from that guy."

Jabari smiled and nodded his head. "You were never in danger. I was watching you the whole time, Miss Kendall. Have a good night," he said, and she slipped out of the car, wobbling on her heels.

She turned around in confusion and realized he hadn't taken her home, he'd taken her to Hunter's house. "*Wait!*" she yelled, after the disappearing car, and began to run down the gravel drive, holding her hand up and waving it back and forth wildly.

"Kit, I'll take you home. I told Jabari to bring you here."

Kit turned slowly and looked at Hunter, walking toward her in the moonlight. The sound of the crashing waves coming from the beach was soothing after the loud pop music that had been cracking her skull for hours. She frowned at Hunter, knowing she was too tired and too angry, for anything productive to come from a conversation with him right now.

"I'd like to go home now," she said stonily, and crossed her arms over her chest as she watched him come to her.

Hunter stared at her, with his hands deep in his front pockets and frowned back at her. "Worn out from partying with Rob and his buddies all night, huh?"

Kit blinked in surprise and realized that Jabari hadn't called Hunter and told him what happened. He'd probably expected her to fill Hunter in.

"Yeah, Hunter. That's right. I'm tired from having the time of my life with my boyfriend, Rob. Wish you could have been there. Rob has some really decent dance moves. He could have taught you a few things," she said coldly.

Hunter glared at her, his eyes looking silver in the dark. "Watch it, Kit. I've had about all I can stand tonight. Hearing about the long and passionate kiss you shared with Rob wasn't enough?"

Kit looked down at her feet, closer to tears than she thought, and concentrated on breathing in and out. "Take me home, *right now*," she said tightly, and turned away from Hunter.

She heard the crunch of gravel and moments later the sound of his car coming to her side. "Get in," Hunter said, in a voice laced with anger and impatience.

Kit opened the door and slid in, pulling her seatbelt tight over her chest. She turned away from Hunter and stared out the window.

"Kit," Hunter said, his voice more calm now. "We need to talk this out. We're both angry and upset right now. But tomorrow I'd like to take you to dinner and we can work through this," he said, as he came to a stop in front of the bakery.

Kit unbuckled her strap and got out of the car. She turned around and leaned down to see Hunter's face. "What right do you have to be angry at *me*? I was just doing what *you* told me to do," she said, and slammed the car door hard and walked up the steps. She opened her clutch and took her keys out as she heard Hunter open his car door and get out. Her eyes turned to slits and she moved quickly through the door, slamming it so hard in Hunter's face that the glass shook. She locked the door with a firm twist of her wrist, as Hunter stared angrily at her through the door.

"You're being childish," he said clearly, and loudly enough so she could hear.

Kit's mouth fell open and she felt steam come out of her ears. "Go away, Hunter. Leave. Just. Go," she said loudly, and then walked over to the wall and turned the lights off and turned on the security system. She walked through the doorway without looking back at Hunter and then tiredly walked up the stairs to her room. Date or no date, she still had to get up at 4 the next morning, and she could just imagine how fun that would be, working for hours on her aching feet, with hardly any sleep.

She turned the light on to her room and stripped off her dress, laying it over the back of a chair. She collapsed on her bed, not bothering to take off her makeup or brush her teeth. She immediately fell asleep and dreamed of running along the beach, her long red hair streaming behind her. And in pursuit, were Rob and Rusty. She ran faster, leaving them in her dust.

Chapter Fifteen

THE CURB

Kit woke up as expected, exhausted, bleary eyed and in a horrible mood. She took a quick shower and put her still damp hair up in a bun. She decided to go without makeup and grabbed a pair of crocs she'd been given by an old roommate as a gag gift. She sighed as she moved slowly down the stairs to the kitchen, yawning so wide her jaw cracked.

Layla and Jane were turning on the lights and grabbing ingredients as she slapped the paper she'd written everything down on the night before.

Layla and Jane stared at her in shock as she yawned again and slowly tied the apron around her waist. "Best desserts I've ever had in my life," she said, pointing haphazardly with a finger at the paper as she grabbed her bowls and utensils.

"How did it go last night?" Layla asked, walking over to stand in front of her.

Kit shrugged and stretched her tired back out. "Oh, it was great. You should have been there. Rob went on and on about how I *belonged* to him for the night, and then proved it by kissing me. Without my consent. Needed a napkin after that one. *Then,* he threw me to the wild animals, so he could yuck it up with all of his old buddies."

Jane walked over and touched her shoulder timidly. "*Wild animals*? What do you mean?"

Kit blinked at her sister blearily and yawned again. "By wild animal, I mean a 6' 5" red head, by the name of Rusty, who happened to have too much to drink. He was determined to *acquire* me for his collection of women. Hunter sent his body-guard, Jabari, after me and he had to save me. Rob realized at the last second that his caveman friend was about to drag me off, so he decides to be the big man. As I was being whisked away by Jabari, tables and chairs were flying all over the place. I would not be surprised if Rob is in a body cast right at this very moment. *Not that I care*," she said venomously.

Layla's mouth tilted up in a smile as she stared at Kit. "Only you could go on a date, and end up causing a blood bath. You should have been a 1950's movie actress. Your charisma and beauty are wasted on our little bakery, here in Fircrest," she said, laughing softly as she turned and grabbed an apron.

Jane grinned at her and put her apron on too. "I'm not even surprised. Of course, what do you expect from someone voted, *most beautiful*, in high school? I think I would have been surprised if a riot *hadn't* happened."

Kit glared and muttered to herself. "I was honestly scared there for a moment. You have no idea what this guy was like. It was like, he took one look at me, and thought I was dessert. It was scary," she insisted.

Layla looked at her doubtfully. "Kit, you've been handling guys like that since the day you turned twelve. You sure you were in over your head? Or are you just mad, that you were there in the first place?"

Kit shrugged and rolled her eyes. "I should have never had to go out with Rob! It was miserable. I used to crave dancing and the night life, but last night, it just made me want to run for the exit."

Jane sighed. "Well, I'll feel bad for you, Kit. I know what it's like to be in one place, trying to have fun, all the while, you wish you were somewhere else with *someone else*," she said, her voice trailing off as she stared at her hands.

Kit blinked in surprise and then looked at Layla with a raised eyebrow. Layla nodded her head and moved in.

"You never told me how it went yesterday, after bailing Garrett out. *Is he okay?* Are *you* ok?" Layla asked, as she took a carton of eggs out of the fridge.

Jane sighed and massaged her temples. "It was weird. He was so silent. He wouldn't even talk to me. It was like he'd been turned to stone. And at the station, Tate was so formal, like he didn't even know me. And he kept calling Garrett ,my boyfriend. Like, *your boyfriend* will have to appear on this date in court. And, *your boyfriend* this and *your boyfriend* that. I felt like shooting Tate after the tenth time," she said grimly.

Kit measured her ingredients as she stared at her sister with a frown. "Sounds like you might not want a boyfriend right now. Maybe you and Garrett should cool it for a while?"

Jane shook her head and opened her laptop bringing up a new cupcake recipe. "I can't just abandon him now when he needs me, Kit. What kind of friend would I be?"

Layla nodded slowly. "Exactly. You're Garrett's *friend*. Maybe you shouldn't continue being someone's girlfriend, if you're really just friends."

Jane frowned and slipped off her stool to open the fridge and grab a pound of butter. "What does it matter? Tate will never see me as anything but a stupid little girl. At least Garrett looks at me like I'm a mature woman."

Kit bit her lip and shook her head. "There has to be more to a relationship than that, Jane," she said quietly.

Layla nodded her head in agreement, but didn't make any further comment on Jane's love life. She picked up Kit's paper, with all the new recipes on them and smiled slowly. "Kit, these sound amazing. I want to try making them."

Kit smiled dreamily remembering all the little bites she'd taken of all the desserts. "They were so good, Layla. If there hadn't been a brawl, I was going to sneak back to the kitchen and try and get the recipes. But I was whisked away before I had a chance," she said, with a pout.

Layla bit her lip and tapped her chin with the paper. "I want those recipes. I'll have Michael take me to this restaurant on Friday. He's taking me up to look at a few more bridal boutiques. I can't believe I only have a couple weeks left until the wedding, and I *still* don't have a dress. Michael says he's going to pick it out for me," she said.

Kit grinned at her older sister and sighed. After a night like the one she'd had, seeing her sister's soft expression and dreamy eyes gave her hope in mankind.

"Why can't there be two more Michaels. One for me, and one for Jane," she said musingly, as she measured her water for her bread.

Layla and Jane frowned identically at her. Jane was the first to speak though. "I love Michael, but I wouldn't want to be *married* to him. I want Tate," she said morosely, and walked back into the pantry.

Layla tilted her head and studied Kit in a way that always made her squirm. "What's wrong? Are you mad at Hunter?"

Kit started to say no, but then changed her mind. "No. I'm *furious* at Hunter. He's the one who made me go on the stupid date. Then, his bodyguard tells him that Rob kissed me, and he's all mad about it. Like it's *my* fault. Can you believe his nerve?" she asked, spitting mad all of a sudden.

Layla's eyes went wide and she grinned. "Oh, Kit, *he's jealous.* Come on. He's trying so hard to be mature and let Rob have his date, so you guys can move on, and then when he finds out Rob kissed you, it drives him crazy. He's just your typical, red blooded American man. Very territorial and *very* much in love with you."

Kit turned her mixer on and turned to face Layla with a frown. "Again. His fault. His fault. His fault. I tell the man, I love him. I tell him, I want to be with him. And what does he do? *Hey, Rob? Date my girlfriend. Here she is. Have at her,*" she said sarcastically, pushing a stray lock of hair out of her eyes.

Layla shook her head and laughed. "This is going to be good," she said to herself, and went back to work.

Kit ignored her and while the bread was being mixed she pulled up her next order for a cake. It was for a fiftieth wedding anniversary and was very simple. Three tiers. White frosting with lattice work. It wasn't exciting and she wouldn't have to get creative with it, but she'd still rather decorate a cake *any* day ,over making brownies or macaroons.

When it was time to open up the shop, Layla put a hand on her shoulder, stopping her. "Why don't you take a nap? I can handle the morning and you can take the afternoon shift. You're a little worse for the wear," she said, with a half-smile, and then went through the door.

Jane laughed and passed by her with a tray of cupcakes in her arms. "She's right. You look like you've been up all night partying. Dark circles. No makeup. Straggly bun. And *crocs*. Scary," she said, and disappeared too.

Kit looked down at her crocs and then headed for the stairs. Her sisters were right. She was not herself. She took a two hour nap, fixed her hair and makeup and then ate a quick sandwich. She felt so much better, she smiled as she walked through the door to the shop. The first face she saw though, *was Anne Downing's.*

Not good.

"Hi, Anne," she said sunnily, and walked around the counter as two people stood impatiently behind her. "What can I get you?" she asked the older gentleman, who wanted a dozen cupcakes for his grandson's birthday.

She boxed up the man's order and took his payment, as Anne stood to the side, visibly seething. Layla looked uptight and angry, but she wouldn't lose it in front of customers. She was a professional. Jane pulled out six cream puffs for the middle aged woman, with short blond hair, and wished her a good day. The bell sounded over the door, leaving all four women staring at each other. Two of them, with angry frowns on their faces.

"Who do you think you are, coming to our place of business and yelling at us?" Layla hissed, as she moved around the counter to stand in front of Anne.

Anne was a strong willed woman, and wasn't used to *anyone* standing up to her. After a moment's shock, she straightened her shoulders and pointed at Kit. "*Your* sister just left my son to get pounded on, while she took off with *another* man. He was sticking up for her, and what does she do? Leaves him to find his own way to the hospital. Did you know he has a broken nose? And two black eyes. *Two!*" she shouted, moving to go around Layla.

Layla moved with her, not letting her get even an inch closer to Kit. "*Your* son, left Kit on her own, so that she was hit on by a drunk baseball player. Kit had to rely on the assistance of another man to help her. Rob *finally* noticed Kit needed help, and came to see what was going on. The other man was kind enough to take her home and make sure she was safe. Unlike *your son,* who was too busy living it up, and remembering the good old days to protect my sister from his predatory friends," she said acidly, with her hands on her hips.

Anne's eyes glittered angrily as she pointed a finger in Layla's face. "Your sister wouldn't have so much trouble with men, if she didn't dress the way she dresses, and look the way she looks. This is all *her* fault. Robby was just trying to be nice to her."

Kit gasped at the insult, and moved around the counter to stand next to Layla. "You're saying, *I* brought all this on myself? Because I put on makeup and wore a pretty dress?" she demanded, feeling stunned.

Layla surprised her and laughed. "Anne, she borrowed *my* dress to wear last night, and I can assure you, it was very modest. Kit can't help that she's beautiful. But you know what? Your son *could* help being a self-centered jerk. Now, I'm willing to still do business with you and your son. I'll even go back to the original price for the bread. But on one condition. Rob *never* bothers Kit again. I don't want him to talk to her about anything personal *ever again*. He can never ask her out again. *Ever*. No phone calls. No texts. No stopping by the bakery for a donut. No, *nothing*," she said, looking back at Kit for her approval.

Kit nodded her head quickly in the affirmative. *She was so done with Rob*. She wanted nothing more than to forget him.

Anne looked stumped for a minute, and shook her head. "Wait a minute. Rob said he wants to date Kit. He said, they were going to be together now."

Jane moved to stand next to Layla. "Rob tells you that he wants to date Kit, and the first thing you do is run over here *to yell at her?*"

Anne shrugged. "My boy got hurt. *She* was to blame. Of course, I come over here to set her straight. That's what mothers do."

Layla sighed loudly and massaged her temples. "Again, none of this was Kit's fault. Place the blame where it belongs. *With your son*. Now, let me make this crystal clear for you Mrs. Downing. It's not happening. It's *never* going to happen. Not now. *Not ever*."

Kit winced at Anne's shocked expression. "Layla's right. I don't want to see Rob socially. *Ever again*. I think the only reason he would want to date me, is because he thinks I look good on his arm. I would just be a tool to make all of his ex-teammates jealous. He doesn't even know me, Anne. All he ever sees when he looks at me, is what's on the outside. I need a man who can see the real me. He's not that man," she said softly.

Anne looked down at her feet and frowned. And then she sighed. "Well, this is not what I expected," she said tiredly, looking older all of a sudden. "Robby is not going to be happy about this. No, he is not," she muttered to herself.

Layla crossed her arms over her chest and frowned at the feisty older woman. "What did you expect to happen, Anne? Honestly?"

Anne paused with her hand on the doorknob and looked sad. "Well, I expected that Kit would be so concerned over Rob, that she'd rush over to make sure he was okay. I expected her to fall in love with my boy. I was sort of expecting a few grandbabies if you want to be honest. Goodbye, girls and . . . *sorry*," she said, and then was gone.

Kit frowned after Anne, hoping she would get her grandkids someday. "Hopefully, there won't be anymore drama today," she said, walking over to stare out the window.

Layla sighed and took off her apron. "I've gotta run over and pick up Stella from her art camp. Michael's signing went over. I'll be back with Stella in about fifteen minutes," she promised, and hurried out the door.

Kit went back to the counter as Jane grabbed one of her own cupcakes and sat down in a chair and peeled the paper back, licking the lemon curd frosting off the top first.

Kit leaned on the counter and smiled at her sister. "Drowning your sorrows with sugar, Jane?"

Jane nodded and took a big bite. "What other choice do I have, Kit? I mean, what would *you* do, if you were me? Say, you were madly in love with the most gorgeous man, and he didn't like you back. And say, at the same time, you're dating an emotionally wounded man, who is awesome in so many ways, but who just isn't the man of your dreams for some reason," she said sadly.

Kit leaned her chin on her hands while she thought about it. "Well, for starters, I'd break up with Garrett. It's not fair to him and it's not fair to you. Passing time with someone, just because they're there, just ends up hurting people in the end. Trust me, I know. And then, I'd put aside Tate and everyone else and just focus on yourself. If Tate isn't ready, he isn't ready, and nothing you can do can change that. He has to make that decision for himself. You can never force someone to love you."

Jane frowned and wiped some crumbs off her mouth with a

napkin. "Focusing on *myself?* That sounds kind of selfish," she said doubtfully.

Kit shook her head. "Not in the slightest. While you're waiting for your one true love, focus on improving yourself. Pick something physical, mental, emotional or spiritual to change and improve. And then do it. You've always wanted to learn to surf. Buy a wetsuit and sign up for classes. And you've always wanted to learn how to knit. Instead of moping around after Tate, show him that you're your own woman. Show him that you have many interests and talents. And of course, *date.* Have fun. Just don't turn into someone's *girlfriend,* because you're feeling insecure and vulnerable right now."

Jane chewed her bite slowly and turned to look out the window. "I'm not you, Kit. I'm not exciting and wild and beautiful. He'll never see me that way."

Kit frowned and shook her head. "Of course, you're not *me.* You're Jane Kendall and that's the only person you need to be. And if that's not good enough for Tate Matafeo, then you'll meet someone someday who will think you're God's greatest creation."

Jane sighed and stood up. "Garrett acts and talks like I'm the greatest already. It just makes me feel uncomfortable, to be honest."

Kit pursed her lips and stood up. "Just give it time. Let go of the idea of having Tate right now and put him and your love life on the back burner. Just focus on other things and know that everything will happen when it's supposed to."

Jane smiled sadly and nodded. "Good advice, Kit. I think I might even take it."

Kit laughed and threw her towel at Jane as the bell rang. *This time it was Hunter.* Kit took in a deep breath and straightened her shoulders, not smiling. She was still mad at him and from his expression, he was still mad at her too.

"Hi, Jane. Do you mind if I take Kit in the back room to talk for just a few minutes?" he asked, still looking at Kit.

Jane nodded her head quickly and motioned with her arm. "She's all yours," she said, with a wink at Kit.

Kit followed Hunter to the back kitchen and sat down on one of the stools while Hunter paced in front of the sink back and forth. She watched him for a while curiously, and then gave up.

"What, Hunter? What did you want to talk to me about?" she prodded.

Hunter paused and ran his hands through his spiky wild hair, making him look like a member of an English boy band. She noticed he wasn't dressed impeccably today. Tony must have been given the day off. He was wearing army green cargo shorts and an old T-shirt with a picture of Einstein on it. He looked rattled and gorgeous, all at the same time.

"Kit, I just don't think this is going to work between us," he said, coming to a stop in front of her, and putting his hands on his hips, as he looked down at his feet.

Kit's mouth fell open in shock. *Oh, no he didn't.*

"And the reason?" she asked calmly, as he pinched the bridge of his nose between his fingers.

Hunter finally looked up at her and winced, as if the sight of her was too much for him. "Because, I'm not cut out for a relationship like this. I'm turning into a crazy man, Kit. I'm jealous. I'm insane and I hate it. Just knowing that Rob kissed you last night, rips my heart out. Jabari showed me the pictures, Kit. I can tell you enjoyed it. How can I be with you, knowing that you enjoyed Rob's kiss? It would eat me up the rest of my life. I don't think I slept at all last night. I haven't been able to eat. The fact is, I'm falling apart. I'm supposed to be getting ready for a huge convention in Seattle this weekend, and I can't even think about anything but you. Kit, I can't do this anymore. You're too much for me. I should have known it the first minute I set eyes on you, but I wanted you too much."

Kit looked down at her hands, her heart beating fast and her breathing erratic. She was being dumped. Not that that hadn't happened before, but it had never happened when she'd been in love with the guy. "Don't, Hunter. *Don't do this*," she whispered.

Hunter's face twisted and he turned away, leaning on his hands over the counter. "I have to, Kit. You should be with someone dynamic and outgoing. Someone capable of having a deep emotional relationship with you. I'm just not on your level. I've failed, Kit. You're a hundred levels beyond me, and always will be. I have to press the restart."

Kit stood up and walked over to Hunter, touching his back with her hands. He flinched at the contact and looked away. "*Don't*," he said, in a gravelly voice.

Kit ignored him and rubbed his back soothingly. "You're scared, Hunter. *Don't be.* The only relationship I've ever had with a man that was deep and emotional, has been with *you*. *I love you*," she whispered, kissing his shoulder.

Hunter shook his head silently so she went on. "I'm sure the picture Jabari took of Rob kissing me was upsetting. But the fact is, I *didn't* like it. I hated it. I pushed him away, Hunter. He should have taken a picture of *that*. The only man I ever want to kiss me, is you," she said, and leaned her head against his back, as she wrapped her arms around his waist.

Hunter made a groaning sound and pulled away from her and headed toward the door. "I can't. It's for the best Kit. It's been . . . it's been amazing. But I'm just not cut out for amazing," he said, sounding anguished. She watched as he pushed through the door and left without another word. She winced as she heard the bell over the door, and sat down on the stool numbly.

Now she knew what they meant by being kicked to the curb.

Chapter Sixteen

PLANS

Kit helped the last customer, as Stella sat at the table by the window, and colored a picture. Layla walked over and flipped the sign to CLOSED and turned to survey her sisters.

"I've never seen two more depressed women in my life. Why don't we go to the movies or out to dinner. A girl's night out?" she asked, walking toward Jane and Kit with a hopeful smile on her face.

Kit shrugged and walked over to lift out a tray of leftover, old fashioned donuts. "I'm still tired from last night. You two go on without me," she said, with a smile.

Layla narrowed her eyes at her sister but turned to look at Jane. "And you? You're not going to ditch me for a book are you?"

Jane smiled brightly. "I would never dump you for a book. Jane Austen's Pride and Prejudice miniseries? *Yes*. I absolutely will ditch you for that," she said, walking around to wipe the glass cases down.

Layla frowned and walked over to Stella. "And how about you? Are you going to ditch me?" she asked with a grin.

Stella looked at her happily. "Grandma invited me over for a slumber party. But you can come too."

Layla laughed and stood up. "Fine. I'll hang out with my fiancé then. See if I care."

Kit swallowed and grabbed the broom. *It must be nice to have a fiancé. To have someone you always wanted to be with. Someone who loved you, no matter what. Someone who wasn't scared to love you back.* She felt a hand on her back and straightened up. Layla.

"You're muttering to yourself. What's going on? *Sit,*" she ordered, and pointed to the table were Stella was sitting.

Kit sighed and walked over, collapsing in the chair and crossing her legs. "Hunter broke up with me this afternoon. He said I was too much to handle and that he was turning into a crazy person and he couldn't take it anymore. He thinks I enjoyed my date with Rob. Jabari took pictures of the kiss Rob gave me and I guess Hunter's an expert on analyzing pictures, because he swears I enjoyed it. So that's it. I kind of begged him not to walk away, but he just ran out. He left me," she said, looking down at her hands. Again. Left by a man who was *supposed* to love her. *Story of her life.*

Layla and Jane grabbed chairs and came to sit next to her. "Oh, honey, I'm so sorry," Layla said, and touched her shoulder.

Jane gave her a crooked smile. "Want to sign up for surfing lessons with me?"

Kit laughed a little and wiped a tear off her cheek. "Oh, sure. What else is there to do? You know, the other day, when Hunter and I were talking about the future, I came home and got my wedding dress out. I could *see* it. I could really see myself married to him," she said, closing her eyes, as a wave of pain crashed through her.

Layla winced and shook her head. "Well, I can't blame Hunter, Kit. You scare most of the male population. I bet he comes back. That man is in love with you. I would swear it on your bread recipe."

Kit smiled and shook her head. "He is. He freely admits it. He just can't *handle* it. Too much emotion. Too much stress. So, here I am. *Dumped.*"

Layla covered Stella's ears for a moment as she spoke. "When Michael dumped me, I thought I would die ,it hurt so much. But things worked out. They'll work out for you too," she said, and let go of Stella's ears.

Stella looked at her curiously and then went back to coloring.

Jane tilted her head up and looked thoughtful. "You know the thing I've always liked about you, Kit? You always go after what you want. You never sit back and wait for life to happen. You're always out there on the edges, pushing the limits. Do you *really* love Hunter? Like, you love him so much, you can see yourself married, having his children, growing old with him, kind of love."

Kit blinked away new tears. "*Yes*," she breathed out. "It's him. I know it."

Jane shook her head with a small smile. "Then *get him*. Give him a few days to suffer without your overpowering presence, and he'll be so miserable, that when he sees you again, he'll fall at your feet."

Layla snorted. "Jane, sweetie. You know so much about business, but you're not the most experienced when it comes to men. That would be Kit. But Kit has no idea how to deal with a man she's honestly in love with. That would be *my* expertise," she said cockily, making Kit grin and Jane push Layla in the shoulder.

Layla laughed and pushed Jane back playfully. "No, I'm serious. If you want to get Hunter back, you're going to have to win his heart. He won yours, didn't he? He found your paintings and he was there when you needed him to be. How can you win his heart? What does he love? I mean, besides you, what is his passion?"

Kit looked at her like she was dumb. "Video games. Obviously. But I can't make a game. I can't even play one. I don't know anything about it," she admitted, feeling bad now that she hadn't learned more about Hunter's life.

Jane tapped her chin. "Didn't you say he has a huge convention this weekend? Maybe you could do something cool there, and prove that you're the only woman for him."

Kit pursed her lips and thought about it. Maybe. *Just maybe.*

A polite knock on the front door had everyone turning around. Layla jumped up to open the door, thinking it was Michael. It wasn't. *It was Tate.*

Jane blushed a little and looked away as Kit stood up smiling. "Hey there, Tate. We're closed, but we have a few chocolate muffins if you're interested. Half off, just for you," she said, walking around the counter.

Tate smiled but shook his head. "Not right now, Kit, but thanks. I'm actually here on official business."

That got everyone's attention and the women surrounded him instantly.

"Did they find the attacker?" Layla demanded, already looking angry.

Jane reached out and touched his arm. "Is he in jail?"

Kit looked at him, feeling slightly sick and bit her lip. "Who, Tate? *Who is it?*" she asked.

Tate ignored Layla and Jane and stared at Kit with sad eyes. "Kit, they picked up your father over in Lakewood. He was panhandling and he wasn't doing too good. He has some serious injuries to his face and head, that match the description of what Layla did to the attacker, and what I saw on the tapes. He's being brought in tomorrow for questioning. Right now, he's in the hospital. He's been walking around with a broken collar bone and a fractured jaw, and a broken nose."

Layla's mouth fell open and she turned white. Jane covered her mouth in horror, and Kit felt like throwing up. *What a nightmare.*

"He hurt you again. I swore he'd never touch you again, *but he did*," Layla murmured to herself, turning around to find a chair to sit in.

Tate looked at Layla with a knowing grimace, and then turned and looked at Kit with compassion. "He hasn't

176   SHANNON GUYMON

confessed to the attack yet. And you never know. Innocent until proven guilty. He could have gotten beat up in a bar fight. I'll be questioning him tomorrow and I'll let you know what happens. I just wanted to let you know, so you can prepare yourselves."

Jane nodded and touched his arm again. "Thanks, Tate. Thanks for looking out for us. You really are almost as good as having a big brother around," she said, with a grateful smile.

Tate frowned at that and looked away. "Um, well thanks. You should also know that Alex Foster has gotten his lawyer involved, and he's going after your boyfriend pretty hard. It's no longer a simple assault and battery. Alex is wanting us to press charges for attempted murder," he said, with a sneer.

Kit's eyes went wide in shock. "Can he do that?"

Tate shook his head in disgust. "He can try, but since I was an eyewitness, it's not going to fly. I talked to Garrett today and he's got a good lawyer. He'll be fine. Alex is just blowing smoke as usual. Not to change the subject, Kit, but I've changed my mind. I could really use a chocolate muffin," he said, trying to look pathetic.

Kit grinned and walked around the counter and put two muffins in a bag and handed them over. Tate handed her a couple bills and moved to leave.

"Bye, ladies. Call me if you need anything," he said with a wave, and then left.

Jane stared after him and sighed. "What if I need *you?*" she asked the air.

Layla and Kit groaned in unison. "Jane, please. I just ate." Layla complained.

Kit shook her head. "Jane, sweetie. Focus. Your new love in life is surfing. Say it with me. S–U–R–F–I–N-G," she said, and laughed when Jane stuck her tongue out.

"Well, look how gorgeous he is. Did you see him? I mean, did you even really look at him? He's the most beautiful man I've ever seen, or ever will," she said, pouting.

Layla paused after locking the door and shook her head. "I've seen one better," she said, with a cocky smile.

Jane rolled her eyes. "Yeah, yeah, Michael. Whatever. Michael is *not* half-Samoan. Sorry, not a contender."

Kit laughed and gathered the receipts for the day. "I know of one man, so gorgeous, he hurts my eyes sometimes. He passes Tate *way* up," she said, thinking of Hunter in his Einstein t-shirt.

Jane grinned and shook her head. "Oh, my heck, my sisters are blind. I'm making eye appointments for both of you, first thing tomorrow," she said, and walked over to dump the garbage can.

Kit smiled as she joined in the teasing, but inside she was reeling. Her dad had been the man who had snuck in their business, their home and attacked her. She shivered and closed her eyes. She might not have remembered being hurt by her dad as a little girl, but she remembered every detail in crystal clear, surround sound, 3-D, color vision, of her attack last week.

Her father had hurt her.

Layla's arms wrapped around her and Kit hugged her back hard. "It's okay, Kitten. I know it hurts, but it's okay. Like I told you before, that man who attacked us, is not even really our father. He's just a sad shell of the man, we used to know. It was his addiction that attacked you. His addiction controls his whole life."

Jane leaned her head against Kit's shoulder. "I'm going down to the station tomorrow. *By myself.* And I'm going to offer him rehab. We talked about helping him before, but he disappeared. Thanks to Jail, we know exactly where he is. We'll help him, Kit."

Layla frowned but nodded. "It's up to him, though. He'll probably say no, so don't get your hopes up. But you never know. People sometimes surprise me," she said softly, and then kissed Kit's cheek before getting back to work.

A half an hour later, Michael showed up and whisked his daughter and Layla away. Jane was true to her word and holed up in her room with a six hour miniseries of Pride and Prejudice, so she was on her own.

That left her with one thing to do. Devise a plan to get her man back.

Easy.

Chapter Seventeen

CLARITY

Hunter took his kayak out on the water and tried to clear his mind. After leaving Kit that morning, he'd been in a heavy dark, fog. He needed some clarity and the water was the one sure place he could find it.

He rowed around Vashon Island, pumping his arms so hard and fast he skimmed through the water like an Olympian. He paused when he couldn't catch his breath anymore and floated in the water. He had gone around the entire island and was now back in front of his house. His sanctuary. He'd designed the entire house himself and he loved it. For the last year though, he'd known something was missing. A family.

He'd met Kit and even in that first week, he had begun to picture Kit walking down the stairs to greet him. Coming out of the kitchen with something she'd just baked. Painting on the back deck. Walking with him on the beach. And for a glorious, short time, he'd believed it could happen.

Hunter closed his eyes and wiped the sweat off his forehead as he slowly guided the kayak to his dock. He should have known a girl like Kit couldn't be happy with a man like him. Seeing the pictures and hearing all about Kit's night with Rob had been pure torture. And at the end of it, when Kit had stood there looking at him so coldly, he should have realized. It was never going to work.

Hunter lifted out of the kayak and jumped onto the deck. He leaned over and picked his kayak out of the water and carried it on his shoulder to the shed, he kept his equipment in. He secured everything and locked the door, before walking back to his house. He felt tired, not just physically, but emotionally. He was so wrung out and empty, he wasn't even sure how he was standing up straight.

He walked up the steps to his house, but detoured and walked around to the deck. He leaned his forearms on the railing and stared out at the water, wondering why he hadn't been able to find clarity. Images of Kit that morning, looking tired and unhappy ran through his mind. The way she'd asked him to reconsider. When she'd held him and kissed his shoulder.

He clenched his fists and let his head fall forward. She was better off without him. Rob was more suited to her and she was more suited to Rob's lifestyle. They were both outgoing, beautiful people. *Unlike him.*

Hunter turned and walked inside and shut the door. He walked through his empty house and headed up the stairs to his room. He turned on the shower and stepped under the jets of steaming, hot water and knew some of the water on his face wasn't coming from the showerhead.

Chapter Eighteen

CON

The next day, Kit shaped her loaves as she explained to her sisters what *The Emerald City Comic Con,* was. "It's like a huge convention for geeks and nerds, but not really. The comic cons are so popular now, everyone goes. People dress up as characters from their favorite movies and comic books and video games. Hunter will be there this weekend, since he's a keynote speaker. Everyone's going crazy about this new game he designed. It's going to be really cool."

Jane laughed as she poured all the ingredients for frosting into the large mixer. "*You?* At a nerd convention? I won't believe it until I see it," she said, dumping three pounds of powdered sugar into the mixer.

Layla grinned as she melted chocolate in a double boiler. "Don't be so judgmental, Jane. Whoever thought Kit would end up falling for Hunter? Maybe underneath all that beauty and pizzazz, is a little nerdy girl, waiting to break out?"

Kit laughed off the teasing. "Hunter is the most gorgeous, nerdy, beautiful, genius I've ever met. How could I resist? So, in order to get my guy back, I'm going to this thing. I ordered my tickets last night online. They're almost sold out too. I was lucky. And I got an extra ticket. Jane? *You're coming with me,*" she stated, and turned around to get a bottle of water out of the fridge, scared of what Jane would say.

Silence

Kit slowly turned around and saw that Jane was concentrating on her cupcakes. Layla was looking at Jane with a frown and Kit sighed in relief. *Phew.*

"There are a few things, Jane, that you should be aware of. You have to dress up as a superhero or something. But so will I ,so you won't have to be embarrassed or anything. And there's a masquerade dance on Saturday night, right after Hunter finishes his speech. It'll be fun," she said, laughing nervously.

Jane raised an eyebrow and stared at her. "Fun? Are you sure, because it sounds a little lame."

Kit smiled brightly. "Remember, you have to push yourself mentally, emotionally, physically and spiritually. Consider this homework. After going to the comic con with me, your horizons will be spread wide open."

Jane began frosting her cupcakes and motioned with her spatula. "In what way?"

Layla laughed at Kit, and began slowly folding cream into the melted chocolate.

Kit bit her lip. "Well, as soon as Garrett finds out you went to a comic con, he'll probably never call you again."

Jane grimaced and shifted on her seat. "Garrett came by last night, and we talked outside on the front porch. I told him that I thought it would be better if we were just friends right now, and he got pretty upset and thinks it is because he attacked Alex. He's not too happy with me."

Kit winced and placed the bottom tier of the anniversary cake, center on the stand. "Are you okay, Jane? Feeling remorse?"

Jane frowned and moved to the next cupcake. "Not really. How sad is that? I kind of feel more relieved than anything else. But I feel so bad for Garrett. He attacked Alex because he was being overprotective of me. And now, he might go to jail," she said, looking sick about it.

Layla walked over and laid a hand on her shoulder. "Garrett lost it. He shouldn't have. No need to feel guilty, Jane. Just be his friend. That's what he needs the most right now anyways."

Kit nodded and began putting the white fondant through the press. "See, going to the comic con is perfect. It will help you get your mind off of things and give you a little distance and perspective. Plus, we're going to have a seriously good time."

Layla snorted. "Wait. So you go to the convention. Then what? How is that going to win back Hunter's heart?"

Kit pursed her lips and concentrated on her fondant. "I haven't gotten that far yet. I'm sure I'm going to be inspired any moment."

Jane looked at her thoughtfully and sat up. "He loves your art, Kit. He'd probably own all of your paintings if he could track them down. Why don't you paint him something amazing and present it to him at the Masquerade?"

Kit looked up and blinked in surprise. It was so simple, why hadn't she thought of it? "Jane, you're a stinking genius. I love you. But I only have a day. I'm not sure I can paint something amazing enough to do the job in one day."

Layla grinned and ran a hand down her red ponytail as she walked by. "Honey, if there's anyone who could, it's you. While you're working this morning, you can plan it all out in your mind. Maybe you should paint a picture of Hunter himself? If you ask me, he has a hard time seeing himself for who he really is. Help him see the man *you* see," she said, and walked back to her chocolate.

Kit watched Layla pour in a few drops of orange oil and nodded her head slowly. "If I had to have two sisters, you were the two to have. Both of you. Geniuses. I love you guys!" she yelled and then danced around the kitchen, kissing Layla on the cheek first and then Jane.

"This calls for a little, Whatever it Takes, by Imagine Dragons, anyone?" she said, grinning as she began dancing around the kitchen.

She would have heard someone come in the kitchen, if she hadn't been jumping up and down, singing at the top of her lungs.

"*Kit!*"

Kit stopped singing and opened her eyes. Jane pointed behind her and she slowly turned around to see Rob staring at her a little wistfully.

Kit pushed her hair behind her ears and smoothed her apron down as she walked over to Rob as if he hadn't seen her dancing and singing, as if she were on the VMA music awards.

"Rob. What a nice surprise. What can we do for you?" she asked, as she stared at his black eyes and purple and green swollen nose.

Rob shoved his hands in his pockets and motioned behind him. "I was wondering if you could spare me a few moments."

Kit glanced at her fondant and her rising bread and knew that she probably could. She groaned inwardly, but smiled and nodded. "Sure, Rob."

Rob walked back out the door that led to the back of the house, holding the door open for her. Kit motioned him over to a bench, by a grouping of bright orange lilies and sat down.

Rob sat down next to her and then reached over and grabbed her hand. "Kit, I just wanted to apologize for last night. It was my one chance to show you that you and I really work well together, and then like a jerk, I go off and spend the whole evening bragging and talking about baseball. I knew Rusty was a player. I'm sorry if he made you feel uncomfortable. He called and wanted me to tell you that he's sorry too. Dating jocks can be hazardous," he said, with a little laugh, and a smile at her.

Kit smiled back and shrugged. "Well, I'm *not* dating a jock, so I'm good. Look, Rob, forget the price hike, forget everything. Let's just go back to the way we were before all this mess started, okay? I'll make the bread for you. You get good reviews. End of story. Okay?"

Rob shook his head with a frown. "You mean, go back to me

staring at you, every time you deliver the bread, just waiting for you to turn and look at me? Or, go back to the way it used to be, when all I thought about was asking you out? Kit, *I can't*. I've had a thing for you since day one. We both know it. I've just been an idiot. I didn't know what I wanted. I thought I wanted or at least that I *needed* boring. Stable. I can't do boring. I need you, Kit. Please, let's just forget about this past month, and start over."

Kit sighed and looked away from Rob. "I'm in love with another man, Rob. Three months ago, when we moved to town, of course I wanted to go out with you. You're handsome and successful and charismatic. But then I met Hunter. I'm in love with Hunter. That's not going to change," she said softly, not wanting to be cruel.

Rob's eyes opened in surprise and he looked down at his feet for a moment. "Oh, well, okay. Michael told me you two broke up. He said that Hunter called things off," he said, studying her face.

Kit winced and tried to smile. "He did. But he's just scared. His bodyguard that he sent to watch out for me, the night of our date, took a picture of you kissing me. Hunter seems to think that I participated in the kiss and that I enjoyed it. He's upset right now. But we're getting back together. He just doesn't know it yet," she said grimly.

Rob looked away guiltily. "Oh. Wow, Kit, I'm sorry. I mean, I guess I really did think that you were just punishing me for my bad delivery that night at Michael's party. This whole time, I kind of thought you were using Hunter to make me jealous. I never realized that you really cared for him."

Kit stared at Rob and then shook her head. "You thought it was all an act for *your* benefit?" *Just when she thought Rob couldn't get any more narcissistic.*

Rob blushed and nodded. "Sorry. Look, let me make it up to you. I'll call Hunter and tell him about the kiss. I'll make things right for you."

Kit stood up and shrugged. "Knock yourself out, Rob. But I've got this," she said, and walked back into the kitchen without looking back. She was a strong, independent woman. If she wanted to get her guy back, she could dang well do it on her own.

Chapter Nineteen

SECOND CHANCES

Kit and Layla waited outside the police station, while Jane went in by herself. Layla folded her arms over her chest, as she leaned up against the red brick wall next to Kit.

"It's better this way, Kit. I'm the one that hurt him when he attacked you and you're the one he hurt. Jane is the one daughter that he doesn't even know. He's more likely to accept the help from her. If we were in there with him, everything would be clouded with guilt and anger."

Kit nodded and looked up as a stray breeze picked up a lock of red hair and sent it flying. "I just feel bad for her. She's going in there all by herself. I don't know if I'd be able to do that."

Layla winced and put her arm around her sister's shoulders. "Of course, you couldn't go in there by yourself. You probably relive the attack every day. No one's judging you. And besides, Jane's tough. That girl has steel. She can handle this, I promise. Besides, she won't be alone. She'll have Tate right there with her."

Kit grinned and relaxed. "True. She probably volunteered just to be next to him."

Layla snorted and shook her head. "That was terrible, Katrina Kendall."

Kit laughed and rubbed her arms. "So, what happens if he says yes? What if he takes this chance we're giving him and he goes through rehab and gets clean. He wants his share of the bakery. Are we going to give it to him?"

Layla ran her hand through her long silky blond hair and looked up at the sky. "Yes. *Maybe.* I don't know. No. I know our grandmother didn't leave it to him because she knew he was on drugs and that he'd just sell it and use the money for more drugs and more ruin. If he's clean though and he wants to start over, he'll need money to do that. He's our father Kit. Regardless of what he's done, he's a human being. We'd help anyone if we could right? I mean, helping him get clean and on his feet again, doesn't mean that we have to have a relationship with him."

Kit nodded her head in agreement but she still felt a little sick to her stomach. The thought of having her father in her life made her feel queasy and scared. Layla reached over and grabbed her hand. "There's no pressure, Kit. We're still figuring it all out. But just remember, he's been controlled by his addiction practically his whole life. We're not sure who is underneath it all, once the addiction is gone."

Kit closed her eyes to the wind. "What if what's left is bad and violent and cruel?"

Layla hugged her sister. "Then we just go on the way we've been going. We're happy here in Fircrest, Kit. None of that is going to change."

Kit smiled and nodded. "Okay. I believe you," she said quietly.

A black sports car drove up to the police station and Michael got out, walking toward them with a worried frown on his face.

"Baby, what are you doing here? I thought we agreed that you'd wait back at the bakery with Kit?" he said, pulling Layla into his arms and kissing her temple.

Layla hugged him back and looked up. "We had to be here for Jane. I wanted her to know that we were just outside waiting for her."

Michael grimaced and then surprised Kit by giving her a quick hug too. Kit smiled and hugged him back. Brothers were nice.

"I don't like you girls standing here outside a police station, looking sad and thinking sad thoughts. Why don't we go across the street and get a yogurt? We'll be able to see Jane as soon as she comes out. And we'll have a yogurt waiting for her in case she needs a treat," Michael said, with a half-smile.

Layla and Kit agreed quickly and ran across the street. Ten minutes later, they were ensconced at an outdoor table eating their yogurt. Layla had picked a swirl of peanut butter and chocolate with Reese's Peanut Butter cup chunks sprinkled on top and then covered with hot marshmallow cream. Kit had picked a chocolate hazelnut and a caramel yogurt covered with Heath bar chunks. Michael, who didn't have a sweet tooth, got a tiny cup of pineapple and coconut, but ended up letting Kit and Layla eat it all.

As they waited for Jane, they talked about the wedding arrangements. Since Layla no longer had a mom and this was Michael's second wedding they were planning everything on a small scale. Small wedding party. Just family and close friends and a small reception down at the Point Defiance Gardens. Layla had handed everything over to Michael's mom and she was taking care of all the details. Except one. The wedding dress.

Michael looked at Layla with a small smile. "Sweetie, you know I love you and that I don't care if you show up in jeans and a t-shirt. But right now, that's all you have. The wedding is only a week away and you don't have a dress. When I took you shopping on Monday, you looked at a hundred dresses. We're running out of places to look," Michael said, sounding worried.

Layla smiled brightly but her eyes looked tense. "I know, Michael. I just haven't found the right one. I insist on looking like your dream come true, on our wedding day," she said, biting her lip.

Michael laughed and leaned over to kiss her quickly. "You're *already* my dream come true. The dress won't change that. It's just something to wear, Layla. Don't make the dress into some big symbol that it's not. You standing by my side agreeing to love me forever and be my wife is what's important."

Layla sighed and smiled sweetly back at Michael. "You're right. I'm being silly, huh?"

Kit cleared her throat. "The girl I was doing a wedding cake consult with this afternoon, was telling me she found her dress at a new boutique in Lakewood. It's called the Princess Palace. I know, stupid name, but the dresses are amazing. Fit for a princess."

Michael laughed and kissed Layla's hand. "We're there. As soon as we know Jane is okay, I'm taking you there."

Layla nodded but looked worried. "Okay, this is it. I've been everywhere even online. So if I don't find my dress tonight, I'm borrowing yours, Kit."

Kit gasped in real horror and shook her head. "Oh, no, ma'am, you are not. That's *my* dress, and Hunter will see *me* in it. Either at his funeral or at our wedding."

Layla burst out laughing and Michael looked at her speculatively. "Kit, Hunter and I talked this morning. You guys aren't together anymore. He told me that he wouldn't even be coming to the wedding because it's just too painful for him to see you."

Kit's face went soft. "*Did you hear that?* It's too painful for him to see me. *The idiot.* No, Michael, don't worry about it. I'm getting him back this weekend," she said, and took another bite of her sinfully good yogurt.

Michael grinned and sat back in his chair. "Oh, really? That's a surprise considering Hunter's going to be a little busy this weekend."

Kit shrugged. "I've got this covered. Hunter will be at your wedding *and* he's coming as my date. So make sure you have a big dance floor, because we're going to dance like no one's ever danced before," she said.

Michael and Layla laughed but then everyone went quiet as

Jane walked out of the police station. Her face looked pale and her shoulders were stiff. Michael ran across the street and ushered Jane over to their table. Kit hurried and got Jane a cheesecake and apricot yogurt with fresh fruit on top. She put it in front of her sister and put the big red spoon in her hand.

"*Eat*," she ordered.

Jane took a bite and shivered. After a few more moments and a few more bites, Jane's face had more color and her shoulders weren't so tense.

Layla reached out a hand. "Tell us what happened."

Jane told them all about the small room and seeing her father looking bruised and broken and furious. "It's like he hates us. He broke into the bakery trying to get into the till. He figured if we wouldn't give him his share, he'd just take it. And then when you surprised him, he just went a little crazy. He was high at the time, of course, so he wasn't thinking clearly, but he says he didn't mean to hurt you Kit."

Layla frowned and looked away. "He never *means* to hurt her, but he always does."

Michael put a comforting arm around Layla's shoulders as he smiled at Jane. "Did you offer him rehab, Jane?"

Jane nodded and took another bite. "He says if we don't press charges and if we'll pay for everything, he'll do it."

Kit bit her lip and looked at Layla. Layla looked back at her and they nodded their heads at the same time. "Let's do it then."

Michael leaned forward and looked at the three sisters separately. "I hate to be the one to point this out, but he could just be agreeing to the rehab so you'll drop the charges. He can't get drugs if he's in jail. He'll probably take off as soon as he's free. Will you be able to handle that?"

Jane shook her head at Michael and flipped her long rich brown hair over her shoulder. "Tate has already thought of that. He says the judge will most likely drop the charges *after* rehab is finished. He'll be taken straight from jail to a rehab center in two days. There's a great one in Seattle, Tate was telling me about.

It's spendy though. We'll probably have to take out a loan to cover it," she said quietly.

Kit winced and Layla looked pained. "I figured as much," Layla said, as Michael massaged her neck. "Okay, enough of this. Jane, you need to find a costume for tomorrow. Kit you need to be painting your little heart out and I'm off to find my wedding dress with my handsome prince. I'll see you two later," she said, and stood up.

Michael pulled on Layla's hand and she looked at him curiously. Michael winced and blew out a breath as Layla sat back down. "Michael? What's the matter?"

Michael ran a hand through his hair and leaned forward. "There was another reason Hunter called me this morning. He found out who wrote all of those bad reviews."

Kit's mouth fell open and she leaned forward. "*Hunter found him?*"

Michael grimaced. "Actually, it's a *her*. And yes. I guess he stayed up all last night hacking into yelp. Your bad reviews all originated from one email. An email belonging to Anne Downing," he said somberly, as he glanced at all three sisters.

Layla's eyebrows shot up in shock. Jane's eyes narrowed to slits, and Kit just sighed tiredly.

"I'm not surprised. We all saw her yesterday. That woman would do *anything* for her son. She's not the type to sit by silently, while Rob gets a fifteen percent price hike for being a jerk."

Michael winced and nodded. "I can't even tell you how many times I've been over to Anne's house for dinner. She treats me like a son. So I feel a little strange being in the middle of all this. But I have to point out, that she's been maliciously slandering your business, and it's affected you financially. You could sue her for slander at the very least," he said, looking slightly ill.

Kit immediately shook her head. "No, Michael. *No*. This has to stop. I don't want to involve the courts. We've been at the police station enough this month to last a lifetime. I would be fine if you acted on our behalf and told her that we are aware that she is the one who wrote the reviews and that we would appreciate some good reviews from her to make restitution."

Layla smiled at Kit and nodded her head. "I'd be good with that."

Jane frowned and looked away stonily. "I suddenly feel like throwing a very large, very moist cupcake at Anne."

Kit laughed and shook her head. "We need to make a New Year's Resolution to figure out a more productive way of dealing with conflict."

Layla sighed theatrically. "But it's so emotionally soothing to see that soft explosion of chocolate."

Michael cleared his throat and stared at Layla with concern. "Um, okay then. I'll have a chat with Anne and Rob and let them know that we're all good. No more bad reviews and no more price hikes?"

Layla shrugged and looked at Kit and Jane with a grin. "If our supplier's prices go up, Michael, we'll have no choice. You know how it is. But we can promise not to raise the prices every time Rob irritates us."

Jane snorted and pushed her empty cup away. "I feel a huge price hike coming on. I can't believe Anne is just going to get away with it. We lost so much money because of her."

Michael leaned forward and patted Jane's shoulders. "About as much as Rob lost with the price hike?"

Jane rolled her eyes. "Not even close, Michael. But I'm willing to let it go. However, Anne is toast if she says even one more derogatory word about Belinda's Bakery."

Kit and Layla nodded in agreement. Michael smiled in relief and nodded his head as he stood up, reaching down for Layla's hand. "You Kendall sisters are a force to be reckoned with," he said, with feeling.

Layla grinned and leaned up and kissed him sweetly on the cheek. "Just don't forget it."

Kit and Jane watched Layla and Michael walk off hand in hand and they both had wistful expressions on their faces.

"I better get my turn," Jane muttered, as Tate walked out of the police department with his partner and got into a police car, driving out of the parking lot quickly.

Kit sighed and scraped the bottom of her cup for the last bite of yogurt. "Well, I know I will. Which is why I've gotta get going. I'll be staying up late painting a beautiful portrait of my true love."

Jane smiled and stood up. "I really hope this works, Kit."

Kit threw her cup in the garbage. "As if there was any chance it couldn't."

Jane looked at her doubtfully but didn't say anything. Kit smiled all the way back to the bakery, but inside she was a little messy. A little worried, a little depressed, a little hopeful and a little frantic. But in the end, hope won out.

Chapter Twenty

THE EMERALD CITY

Kit stared at Jane and shook her head in disgust. "I thought I explained what this was, Jane? I said superheroes and stuff like that. What were you thinking?" she demanded.

Jane put her chin in the air and crossed her arms over her chest. "Well, I wasn't going to go out and buy a costume. Money's a little short now that I spent all my cash on my *never to be worn* wedding dress. Oh, and our father's rehab, so excuse me if I don't measure up to your high nerd standards," she said, narrowing her eyes and looking Kit up and down. "Look at you! You look ridiculous. *Your hair!*" she said, laughing.

Kit sniffed and looked away. "I'm a star princess and it's better than going as a cheerleader. You're going to get thrown out," she muttered, turning away and grabbing her painting.

Jane looked over her shoulder and grinned. "Hey, I didn't think you could do it, but you did. Hunter looks *amaaaazing*," she said appreciatively.

Kit smiled at the portrait and nodded. "That's Hunter. *Amazing.* We better get going. I don't want to miss his speech."

The sisters drove up to Seattle and after handing their tickets to a man with a purple Mohawk and long black beard they walked into the large conference center. There were booths and posters everywhere. The people walking past them were laughing and talking animatedly. Some of them gave Jane weird looks, but they were left alone.

Kit looked down at the map the guy had given her and pointed to the largest auditorium. "Right here. It starts in fifteen minutes. I called the director over the convention this morning and he says that if I get the painting to him before the speech, he'll present it to Hunter at the end."

Jane winked at a man dressed up as Boba Fett from Star Wars as he walked by. Kit rolled her eyes. "I swear every time you put on your cheerleader uniform, you turn into a monster."

Jane laughed and waved at a group of ninjas. "Then I'm in the perfect place. I'm surrounded by monsters."

Kit grinned and pushed past a group of people dressed up in Steam Punk fashion. They entered the auditorium and Kit told Jane to grab them two seats before they were all taken, while she hurried down to the stage area. She was looking for a guy named Stan Rollins. She had absolutely no idea what he looked like.

She held her painting protectively against her chest as she scanned the men and women milling around the front of the stage. She reached out and grabbed a guy walking by with a mic. "Hey, do you know where Stan is?" she asked.

The guy was wearing a comic con hat and wearing a t-shirt with Spock on it. "Yeah, he's right there," he said, pointing to a man who looked to be in his fifties, who was sporting a beard and glasses. He looked a little like Peter Jackson, but she was probably just thinking that because a man dressed as a hobbit just bumped into her.

"Stan! Stan, it's me, Kit Kendall. I have the painting here for Winston Hunter," she said, striding up to him.

Stan looked her up and down and grinned. "Wow, you look amazing," he said, and then glanced at the painting. His eyebrows went up and he looked at her intensely for a moment. "Wait, *you* painted this?"

Kit frowned. "Of course, I did," she said, looking at the

portrait she'd painted of Hunter. He was leaning against the railing on his back porch and he was grinning as he stared out at the water. The wind was playing with his hair. He looked happy, fit and confident. He looked beautiful.

Stan looked at her doubtfully. "Okay, let me get this straight. You say you're Hunter's biggest fan, and you've played every computer game he's ever designed."

Kit cleared her throat and tried to look innocent.

Stan shook his head as he stared at her. "Have you *ever* played a computer game in your life? You look like you should be walking a runway."

Kit nodded her head firmly. "I painted this for Hunter to show my deepest regards for all the many hours of joy he's brought into my life. Please present it to him. *Please*," she begged.

Stan sighed and hefted the painting in his arms. "Fine. It looks fantastic. He'll love it," he said, and walked off without another word. She watched as he stopped and talked to a camera guy before heading behind stage.

Kit headed back to find Jane and found her sitting next to a guy dressed up as a zombie. Kit laughed and sat down, swishing her robes out of the way. Jane was having the time of her life.

The lights flickered and Stan stood at the podium, lifting his arms up to get everyone's attention. "Okay, everyone. This is the moment you've all been waiting for. Winston Hunter, the man who brought you, *Werewolf Hunter* and *Metro Crisis* is here to tell us about his newest game, *Necron's Nemesis.*

Kit had to cover her ears from the roar of the crowds. "These people are insane," she said in Jane's ear. Jane just nodded and screamed along with the crowd.

And then Hunter was on the stage. Kit put her hand over her heart and leaned forward to see him better. She was twelve rows back, so it didn't help much. He looked so wonderful. So tall, and his hair was extra spiky today, she noticed.

Hunter waved to the crowd and even went so far as to bow to

everyone before he went back to the mic. Kit looked at the full auditorium and for the first time realized that the man she loved was a superstar. *Holy crap.*

"I know you're expecting me to tell you everything about my newest game. Right?" he asked the crowd.

The crowd went wild in answer. Hunter grinned and held up his hand for silence. "I'd love to, but I can't. I'm going to do something better, I'm going to *show* you," he said, and stepped back as a large screen lowered behind him.

"Everyone, welcome to Necron's Nemesis," he said.

Kit watched for the next ten minutes, what looked like a movie trailer. The graphics were so real, it was like she was watching a movie. There were a lot of explosions and weapons, but the characters were incredible and complex.

Jane grabbed Kit's arm hard and pointed to the screen. "That's you!" she shouted, making all the people around them turn and stare angrily.

Kit stared in shock as the main girl ran through a post-apocalyptic world, carrying some large and heavy looking machine gun. *It was her.* The same face shape, the same eyes and the same hair.

"Holy crap, holy crap," she said, for the millionth time, shaking her head in awe that the man she loved was capable of creating something so incredible. So mind blowing.

"He's going to laugh at my painting," she whispered to Jane. "Here I thought *I* was an artist, and he's been the world famous artist this whole time," she said with a frown.

How could she know so little about him, she wondered sadly. The lights came back on and Hunter clapped with everyone else. When he came back to the mic, he was smiling at everyone's reaction to the game.

"And because you came tonight, everyone in this room will get a code that gives you ten dollars off the game."

Kit and Jane both put their hands over their ears as the

screaming became so loud that she was sure she was getting ear damage.

Just then, Stan came on stage with her painting in his hands, and she sat up straight, holding Jane's hand so hard, Jane had to kick her in the leg to get her to let go.

"In gratitude for all you've done, Hunter, one of your biggest fans wanted me to give this to you tonight," he said, lifting the painting up high so the crowd could see it first. A bunch of *oohs* and *aaahs* erupted, along with whistling and clapping.

Kit bit her lip so hard she thought she tasted blood. Stan slowly lowered the painting and handed it to Hunter. She watched breathlessly as he stared at the painting with a smile on his face and then his mouth dropped open as he stared at the painting intensely in silence.

Stan laughed and slapped him on the back. "Now, see there everyone? The man can't even speak, he's so grateful. Any last words, Hunter?"

Hunter took a breath and then scanned the dark auditorium before stepping back up to the podium. "Kit, come here. *Now.* I know you're here, Kit. You're in this room. I can feel it," he said, in a voice that would make Tate Matafeo jealous, it was so commanding.

Kit slowly rose from her seat, and walked down the carpeted aisle to the steps going up to the stage. She walked even slower up each step, as if the robes she was wearing were cement instead of cheap polyester.

She stared at Hunter as he held her painting in one hand. He looked at her, his eyes so brilliant blue she could cry. His face looked tense and he didn't exactly look happy. She swallowed nervously as she came to stand in front of him.

"Stan, hold this for a second. *Be careful with it,*" he said, and handed her painting to Stan, who was grinning his head off, just thinking of all the hits on youtube he was going to get.

"Kit," he said brokenly, and then grabbed her in his arms, holding her so tightly her buns quivered.

Kit held him back just as tightly and leaned up to whisper in his ear. "Have I mentioned that I love you," she said with tears in her voice.

Hunter leaned back to look down into her eyes and a grin overtook his face, starting with his eyes crinkling at the sides. "Oh, Kit. You dressed up as Princess Leia for me."

Kit laughed and touched her buns on the side of her head. "You said you had a thing for her."

Hunter frowned and shook his head. "No. Actually, you're the only woman I have a thing for. Kit, I'm so sorry. You're right. I was scared. But standing here right now, in front of all my friends," he said, and kneeled down on one knee in front of her.

Kit gasped and grabbed her throat. *No way.*

"Katrina Kendall, will you do me the greatest honor and biggest service you can ever do mankind, and be my bride?"

Kit grinned as the crowd exploded in cheers. She leaned down and lifted him up from his knee and put both of her hands on either side of his face. "Don't kneel before me, Hunter. I'm not above you. We're equals in this relationship. You and me, Hunter, side by side. I love you so much. Yes, *yes*, I will be your bride," she shouted, as Hunter picked her up in his arms, holding her tightly. At last, after Hunter had his emotions under control, he leaned down and kissed her.

Kit wrapped her arms around his neck as she gave into the kiss and felt all of the emotions swimming through Hunter's heart. So much happiness, relief and joy that she couldn't help the tears streaming down her cheeks.

Hunter pulled back and reached back to grab his painting. "Thanks, Stan. Look, I've gotta go. It's been fun," Hunter said, and pulled Kit off the stage.

Hunter pulled her through crowds of people, all reaching their hands out to touch him or talk to him. He waved them all off with a smile, as he relentlessly pulled her toward the exit.

"*Wait!* Kit, Hunter! Wait!"

Kit yanked on Hunter's hand and turned around to see Jane

running toward them in her cheerleader costume. She laughed as people turned around to stare at her sister.

Jane reached them and threw her arms around Kit's neck, hugging her tightly as she grinned happily. "Congratulations. You said you were going to win him back, but I had serious doubts," she said, finally letting go.

She then turned to Hunter, who was blushing slightly and looking a little nervous. Jane walked to Hunter and nodded her head. "Welcome to the family, Hunter," she said, and then hugged Hunter hard too.

Hunter laughed and hugged her back. "Thanks, Jane. I appreciate that."

Jane sighed happily as she looked back and forth between Kit and Hunter. "I saw it with my own two eyes, but I still can't believe it. My big sister getting engaged in front of every nerd in Washington. You always have to do things on a big scale, don't you, Kit?" she said, her eyes twinkling.

Kit rolled her eyes as Hunter put his arm around her shoulders. "Go big or go home, right? And as you can see, I got my honey back. Look and learn Jane," she said, grinning up at Hunter.

Hunter raised an eyebrow and she knew they'd be having a chat later about her plans to win him back.

"Jane, I'm going to take off with Kit now. Are you okay getting home on your own?" he asked.

Jane frowned. "Hold on, there's a masquerade dance coming up. You two can't miss that. *I* can't miss that!"

Kit laughed as she realized Jane was deadly serious. "Here are my car keys. Stay and have fun if you want."

Jane glared at them but snatched Kit's car keys in her hand. "Fine, but you two are going to miss out. Seriously, this is the most fun I've had in months."

Hunter grinned at Jane and shook his head. "I think I might be a bad influence on your family."

Kit grabbed him and led him away from the crowded hallway

as she waved goodbye to her sister. "We were long overdue for some good, old fashioned, nerd fun. I bet next year we get the whole family to come," she said, as Hunter opened the door for her and led her out into the sun.

Kit was a little disappointed that they hadn't stayed for the masquerade, but Hunter, being too depressed over their breakup, hadn't bothered to dress up and he would have been mauled by everyone.

"Kit, I hope you don't mind missing out, but I just want to go home and be with you," he said. "And besides, you know every dwarf and wizard will be asking you to dance. I want you all to myself tonight."

Kit buckled her seat belt and smiled gently at her fiancé. "I've been yours all along, Hunter."

Hunter pulled out of the parking spot and headed out of the parking garage and out into the fading sunlight. "I'm starting to realize that. But, Kit, you can't blame me. I mean, what's a girl like *you* doing with a guy like *me*?" he asked, still sounding confused but grateful too.

Kit shook her head with a frown. "Don't you mean, what's a guy like *you*, doing with a girl like *me*? Hunter, I saw it. You're a rock star to those people. *And your graphics*. I was stunned. I never realized how intensely talented you are. I'm still in shock. Hunter, you are amazing. I'm the luckiest girl alive, to be with you," she said, grabbing his hand in hers.

Hunter blushed and looked away. "Do you really mean that?" he asked quietly.

Kit pointed to the painting in the backseat. "I stayed up all night painting that for you, because I wanted you to know who you really are. You're beautiful," she said simply.

Hunter cleared his throat and looked away. "Thank you for my portrait. I'm going to hang it right next to yours at my house. Right where I belong. At your side."

Kit sighed happily and looked down at her ring finger, imagining the ring that would be there soon.

Hunter looked over at her and just stared at her for a moment. "You're going to be my wife."

Kit nodded happily, feeling bubbles of joy burst inside. "Yes I am."

Hunter laughed and pushed his car faster on the freeway. "I'm the *luckiest* man in the world."

Kit grinned and shook her head as she watched Hunter's finely sculpted profile. "You're going to be my husband," she said wonderingly, making Hunter look at her with a lifted brow and a grin. "I'm the luckiest woman in the world."

Kit scooted over and leaned her head against his shoulder as they held hands and talked all the way back home. Kit pulled her buns out to Hunter's disappointment, but she made him home-made fettuccine Alfredo, so he forgave her.

And as they sat on his back deck, holding hands and talking, they dreamed together of their future. When Hunter pulled her onto his lap and kissed her, Kit knew, absolutely, at long last, that she was getting her prayer answered.

EPILOGUE

Kit moved to the music as she danced to Earth Wind and Fire's song, *September*. Right next to her, dancing his heart out, was her fiancé, Hunter. People started making a circle around them and she grinned as Hunter laughed as he tripped and almost fell. She took his hands in hers as they continued to dance.

"Stop stealing the spotlight, Kit. This is *my* day," Layla said, dancing next to her.

Kit grinned and turned to look at her sister in her wedding dress. Layla had *finally* chosen a beautifully classic dress, very similar to the one worn by Megan Markle. The Princess Palace hadn't been kidding when they promised to dress you like a princess. Michael looked impressive too, and was wearing a very sharp black tuxedo. She'd never realized two people could smile so much.

"Forgive me. Please take the spotlight," she said, grabbing Hunter's hand and stepping back into the shadows.

Layla laughed and she and Michael began doing the *Floss* move together.

Hunter leaned down and whispered in her ear. "Hey, I know this one."

Kit leaned up and kissed Hunter lightly before he stood

behind her and wrapped his arms around her. They swayed to the music as Layla and Michael danced to the shouts and cheers of the crowd. Stella ran out to the dance floor in her bright pink dress, determined not to be left out. Kit glanced around looking for Jane and found her in a corner, talking to Michael's mom and dad. Kit frowned, wishing Jane would join the dancing.

Kit watched the crowd and saw all of their new friends from Fircrest. There was something magical about Belinda's Bakery. For some reason, they were finding their lives, their loves and the happiness, they'd always craved. Layla was a completely different woman than the one who had arrived months before. Before, she'd been so traumatized and injured she'd felt like she'd been dying inside. Now? Nothing but happiness and life. A *good* life.

Kit turned in Hunter's arms and wrapped her arms around his neck.

"Let's elope."

Coming Soon - Book 3 in the Love and Dessert Trilogy, *My Sweet Heart*

Sneak Peek at Chapter 1 of My Sweet Heart

Chapter Twenty-One

HOW TO FALL OUT OF LOVE

Jane waved goodbye to Layla and Michael as they drove away in Michael's car. She grinned as the strings of cans made a horrendous sound on the pavement. She might have overdone it on the whipped cream and toilet paper, but it was her big sister's wedding. How could she hold back?

"I swear, Jane if you destroy Hunter's car at our wedding, I'm going to get revenge."

Jane glanced over her shoulder at her other sister, Kit and stuck out her tongue. "You're no fun, now that you're engaged. Hunter won't mind. I was planning on decorating his car with cinnamon buns to remind him of your Princess Leia hair, the day he proposed."

Kit grinned and shrugged. "That's kind of cute. I'll consider it."

Jane rolled her eyes and turned around to survey the last of the wedding guests making their way to the parking lot. "She did it. She really went and got married on us. Now what?"

Kit put her arm around her little sister's shoulders as they walked back toward the crowd. "As Hunter always says, we move on to the next level. There's no going back, Jane. And I don't want to," she said softly, staring at her fiancé as he walked toward her with a half-smile on his face.

Jane sighed as she watched Kit move seamlessly into Hunter's arms. Hunter dipped Kit low over his arm and kissed her, before picking her up in his arms, making her sister laugh like a sixteen year old. She smiled as they walked away in their own world, and realized how alone she was. Layla was gone now. Married and on her way to a two week honeymoon. Kit was engaged and would be married in two months. And her? She was all by herself.

Jane let out a small sigh and plastered on a stiff smile. She needed to go say her goodbyes to everyone before heading back home. She found Michael's mom and dad and gave them both brief hugs and then leaned down to say goodbye to Stella, her new niece.

Stella looked a little left out too. Jane grinned, knowing exactly how she felt. "How would you like to come by the bakery for a couple hours on Monday? Since your mom is gone on her honeymoon, we're going to be shorthanded," she said, watching the little girl's face turn from pouty to excited. They weren't really going to be short handed, since Hunter's mom had agreed to come in and bake pies for them for two weeks, but everyone needed to feel needed.

Stella clapped her hands and jumped up and down. "Can I wear an apron and a hat like last time?" she asked, her little face beaming.

Jane laughed and reached down to run a hand down Stella's soft pale brown hair. "You better believe it," she said and grinned at her niece.

She said goodbye to a few more friends and acquaintances and then headed for the parking lot.

"Jane! Wait up."

Jane inwardly cringed and turned around, recognizing the voice immediately. Garrett, her ex-boyfriend. She watched him walk towards her and she smiled politely. He was so gorgeous and tall and strong and good. She didn't know what was wrong with her that she couldn't fall for him.

"Hey, Garrett. Did you enjoy the reception?" she asked, as he fell in step with her.

Garrett put an arm around her shoulders as they walked and Jane bit her lip as she fought the urge to step out and away from him.

"Yeah, it was great. Michael's like a brother to me. Seeing him happy at last with your sister does my heart good. What about you? Having fun?" he asked, looking down at her curiously. "I didn't see you dancing."

Jane looked up and smiled quickly. "Are you kidding? I loved every moment! Layla was so beautiful. I know they're going to be happy. And now they're on their way to Paris. Can you believe it?" she said, with a soft smile on her face.

Garrett smiled and tightened his grip on her, pulling her closer. "I can believe it. A man in love will do anything for the right woman."

Jane winced and paused to get her keys out of her purse. She needed to change the subject. *Fast.*

"So, how's everything going with Alex Foster? I heard he dropped the charges against you. How did that happen?" she asked, her smile turning into a worried frown.

Garrett let his arm drop as she moved to open her car door. "I think he just realized what an idiot he was being. That, and my lawyer is a shark. Plus, I don't think Alex wants any more bad press. His reputation has been a little battered since his wife left him. If the press found out why I punched him, it could hurt business."

Jane bit her lip and nodded. "Well, I'm glad you don't have to deal with that anymore. Now you can just go back to your normal life and not have to worry about trials and lawyers. It must be a relief to have that over," she said, leaning up against the side of her car.

Garrett moved in closer and nodded, his slightly wavy brown

hair turning gold under the soft fairy lights strung throughout the parking lot. His eyes turned dark and intense as he reached over and grabbed her hand in his.

"It is over. I know that seeing me hit that idiot upset you. I know you hate violence and you broke up with me because you were horrified at what I'd done. But it's over now, Jane. I'm getting help and I see a therapist every week. You don't have to worry about me ever losing it again. I want you back. I want us to be together," he said softly, moving in closer.

Jane's eyes went big and she looked away. *Oh, crud.*

"*Garrett* . . ." she started, but was stopped when Garrett swooped in and began kissing her.

She put her hands on his shoulders and gently pushed him away. Garrett stepped back with a frown, his eyes hurt and confused.

"I didn't break up with you because you hit Alex, Garrett. I broke up with you because things started going too fast between us, and I realized that I didn't have the same feelings for you, that you had for me. You're so amazing. You're the most gorgeous, incredible man I've ever dated, to be honest. But I didn't want to lead you on. I'm sorry," she said softly, hating that she was hurting him. *Again.*

Garrett stared at her silently for a moment and stepped back, giving her space. His eyes turned shuttered and hard and he looked away stonily. "It's not you, *it's me,* is what you're saying? Seriously, Jane? That's such crap. You're not even willing to give you and me a chance?" he asked, staring at her with a shake of his head, and then he stopped and stared at her in surprise.

"*There's someone else, isn't there?* You dumped me because you have feelings for someone else? I'm right, aren't I?" he demanded, staring at her angrily.

Jane sighed and looked away, feeling even worse now and very vulnerable. "Garrett, I didn't realize how strong my feelings were, until I began dating you, and realized that no matter how amazing you were, I couldn't fall in love with you, because I already was . . . *in love*, I mean," she whispered.

Garrett sighed and ran his hands through his hair. "Well, that sucks. Because when I look at you, I see the girl of my dreams," he said, his voice laced with pain. "Call me sometime if you ever get over this guy," he said, and then turned and walked away from her without another word and without looking back.

Jane watched him disappear into the shadows and knew she was crying. Garrett was beautiful, strong and amazing. And she was letting him walk away because she was in love with a man who had made it *abundantly* clear, that he wasn't interested in her.

She was an idiot.

Jane drove home and changed into a pair of sweats and an old WSU t-shirt. She flopped on the couch and leaned her head back. *What now?* Kit had talked about new levels, but she was still stuck on level one, with no hope of ever seeing level two. No progression. No nothing. Jeez, that was depressing.

She heard a car pull up to the bakery and she walked over to Layla's room and looked out the window. It was Hunter dropping Kit off, but every time she moved toward the door, he pulled her back to talk or to hug her or kiss her, as if he couldn't bear to let her go. Jane leaned her forehead against the cool glass and closed her eyes. It was too painful to watch.

She sighed loudly and turned to walk back to the little family room. She was so hung up over Tate Matafeo, it was pathetic. If she could just stop loving him, then she could *maybe* be open to someone else. Someone who would love her back, the way Michael loved Layla, and the way that Hunter adored Kit. How stupid was it to love someone who didn't love you back?

She walked over to the counter and grabbed the laptop. She Googled, *How to Fall Out of Love*, and was surprised when there were a ton of articles on the subject. She clicked on the first one and grinned. *Perfect.* Ten easy steps. This she could do. She read the first item on the list, *Make a list of all the reasons it wasn't meant to be.*

Jane frowned and looked at the wall. There was only one reason. *Tate didn't want to be with her.* She winced and moved on to step number two. Step one was brutal.

See their faults. Huh. Did Tate have any? Jane tapped her fingers on her thigh and sighed. She couldn't think of any except he had a huge uncontrollable sweet tooth. The man was addicted to chocolate and there was no denying it. But then who wasn't?

Step three, *Think of what you want from a significant other, that you didn't get from this person.* Jane bit her lip. The list of what she didn't get from Tate. Easy. *Love.* She wanted him to love her so much, that he'd crawl on his hands and knees through a desert to get to her. Was that really asking so much?

Step four, *Ask yourself, if it was really true love you were feeling for this person.* Jane closed her eyes and concentrated. Could it just be lust? She blushed as she had to admit how attracted she was to Tate. He was tall, incredibly strong and had the most beautiful face she'd ever seen. He was half Samoan and so his skin was an amazing light brown color and the planes of his face made him look like some warrior out of a history book. *Yikes.* Maybe she was in lust. Or maybe it was just infatuation. But if it had just been lust or infatuation, then being with Garrett for even five minutes would have bulldozed through her feelings for Tate. But her heart hadn't budged. Nope, it was official. She was head over heels for the man. *Dang.*

Moving on. Step Five, *Remove as many traces of their presence from your life, as you can.* Jane pursed her mouth and knew that wasn't going to happen. She was part owner of a bakery he couldn't seem to stay away from. He came in at least once or twice a week. Unless she put out a sign that said, *No Police Officers Allowed on the Premises*, she was stuck seeing his gorgeous face. Okay, next step.

Step Six, *Distance yourself.* Jane glared at her computer screen. Whoever had written these steps, just didn't understand her life at all. She was stuck seeing the man for the rest of her life. She'd tried distancing herself from him by dating Garrett, and that had just ended up hurting a good man. *Ugh!*

Step Seven, *Practice thought stopping, a technique that helps you to become more mindful and in control of what you think (or don't want to think about, as the case may be).* Jane's eyes went wide in wonder. She could be the master of her thoughts. She could control what she thought about. She put her laptop down and hurried to their Junk door. She pulled it open and grabbed a rubber band and slipped it over her wrist. Every time she thought about Tate, she'd pull on the rubber band and let it go. She'd heard about this. Addicts used this exercise sometimes. Fine, she was addicted to Tate. She'd just get un-addicted.

Step Eight, *Do all the things you've ever wanted to do, that you wouldn't have done if you were still with this person.* Jane groaned and moved on. How lame was it that she was head over heels in love with a man and they'd never even been on one date.

Step Nine, *Mingle.* Jane sighed stared at the screen, urging it to say something else. She didn't want to mingle. She didn't want to get out and make new friends. She wanted to hang out with her sisters and wait for the moment when Tate walked through her door. *Pitiful.* And now her sisters were going off and getting married and she was going to be left on her own. Maybe she did need to get out and meet new people. Or, in other words, *get a life.* So rude!

Step Ten, *Understand that your feelings may never fade completely.* Jane stared at the screen angrily. *What?* She might have to feel like this the rest of her life? Aching, lonely and miserable? Oh, no. *She refused.* She narrowed her eyes at the list and then flicked her wrist with the rubber band for good measure. She was going to dang well get over Tate Matafeo, if it killed her.

She put the laptop down and stood up. She refused to Google if anyone had ever died of a broken heart. She didn't want to know.

ACKNOWLEDGMENTS

There are many people I'd like to thank who helped me along my way. I'd like to thank Jessica Guymon for her feedback and editing and also Christina Tarbet.

Biography

I live in the Rocky Mountains with my husband and children and love my home when it's not snowing. I'm the author of 37 books so far. I also write YA Paranormal Romance under my pen name, Katie Lee O'Guinn. I enjoy the outdoors, reading and being with my family. To find out the latest on my books, check out my blog. You can purchase all of my books at Amazon.com. I'm also a huge supporter of Operation Underground Railroad. Check out their website to learn more.

BOOKS BY SHANNON GUYMON
Fircrest Series

You Belong With - Me Book 1

I Belong With You - Book 2

My Sweetheart - Book 3

Come To Me - Book 4

Be Mine - Book 5

Tough Love - Book 6

Falling for Rayne - Book 7

Dreaming of Ivy - Book 8

A Passion for Cleo - Book 9

My One and Only - Book 10

Free Fallin' - Book 11

At Last - Book 12

Accidentally in Love - Book 13

The Belfast Series

Love and Karma

Printed in the USA
CPSIA information can be obtained
at www.ICGtesting.com
LVHW040307071124
795928LV00032B/642